Requiem For The Living

Mariam Dodd

DEDICATION

Chances are, you already know how these dedications go. You pick up a book, skim the first couple pages, and see that once more this book is dedicated to someone else.

Not this time.

I can't say your name. Not yet at least. The reasons I wrote this for you are secrets the world isn't ready to hold, and so, for now, I will keep keep you hidden beneath the blessing of anonymity."

It's ok, you already know this book is for you. You know why, or at least you will.

For what it's worth, you won't believe how proud I am of you.

To the candle children.

Whether you hold the candle, or the flames are lit for you,

You will forever shine like gold in my eyes.

OPENING

People say that you can never truly die until your name is spoken for the last time. That while your body may fail, the memories of your legacy will live on. They say that you can never be fully gone, so long as you have a story.

Det är vi som aldrig dör. *We are the ones who never die.*

The phrase is written on pamphlets, it's whispered on the backs of coins as they are passed from hand to hand. *We are the ones who never die.* Our country prides itself on that saying. We are the people of Durnon. We are the living men that poets make stories of.

It's meant to be a source of pride, I think. A point of patriotism. A sort of comfort for those who grieve. An excuse to push us on to bigger and better heights. It's why we tore down the mountains to forge iron. It's why we stripped the trees of their skin to make way for more paper. Det är vi som aldrig dör. So long as we can manage to exist in a story, even Death himself can be cheated.

There's a sort of hysteria that arises from this, of course. After all, the problem with living in a world built on fairytales is that, gradually, the people around you start to lose touch with reality. They forget that people still die, regardless of how famous they are. They forget that people are still human, that others should be valued for nothing more than the sake of being alive.

(1)

BEFORE – HELEN

Everyone remembers the first time they meet Death.

I was small the first time it happened, so small that I couldn't quite tell you how old I was, whether I was closer to five or six or perhaps even eight. I'd found my cat lying dead on the side of my driveway, flesh torn from its stomach from where some big hungry animal had taken a bite. Its fur was wet, and slightly matted. I tried hugging it, but the cat didn't move. I'd held the pieces of its fur in my hands and sobbed, shook the little ball of fluff in my arms and wondered why the animal wasn't purring the way it used to.

My mother had hugged me that night. Shot the coyote with an old shotgun and held me tightly as I broke down and started crying.

"This is merely the order of things." She had murmured, tucking my hair behind the edges of my ears. "The strong are forced to kill the weak in order that they might live. I am sorry that your pet was not strong enough. I will get you a new one, whenever you are ready. One with sharper claws and tougher skin. One that can keep not just itself alive but also you as well."

"But I don't want another cat!" I'd protested wailing. "I don't care if the new one's better. I just want to keep my old one." Mom had held me tighter then, stifled my sobs as she patted my back and when my sobs had turned to hiccups, she squeezed my hand. She hadn't had a response, I don't think. No way to tell me that I could have my cat back when it was already gone. I think out of everything, that silence is what stuck out to me the most.

That was the first time that I realized that death could be gentle. But it was hardly ever fair.

Even the small, soft things could vanish, with nothing but an empty shell left in their place.

It is a common fact that the people of Durnon do not bury their weak. They leave them to lie in ditches, copy their names down in stories and then move on. They claim that there is no point in mourning a body when the impacts of a person's life still ring out against the earth. Because according to them, a part of you still lives after your body falls. That so long as you were strong enough to make a difference, your legacy will never die. The weak will fall and be forgotten, but the strong will live on through their legacy.

They use this as a way to excuse their brutality. If you kill all the strong men around you, then eventually you will become the strongest. They use it as a way to excuse their callousness; why should they care for the corpses on the wayside when they were too weak to keep themselves alive in the first place?

I still buried my cat in spite of that.

I met a boy once when I was walking through the woods. He had eyes that shone with a mixture of sunshine and hellfire, and I watched in silence as he cradled corpses in his hands before laying them in the ground.

"What are you doing?" I'd asked, and he looked up at me carefully from where he kneeled. There was something strange, about how softly he carried the bodies. About how old his gaze seemed, on the face of a boy too young to be a man.

"I'm burying the bodies." He'd replied simply. "I'm giving them the peace that they deserve."

"But why would they deserve that?" I'd questioned. "Neither of us know anything about them. What makes them so worthy of such respect?" The boy had stood up then, ruffled my hair affectionately as he knelt down to look me in the eyes.

"Because they were alive." He'd answered then with a far off look in his eyes. "Because they existed, in this vast and messy thing that we call life. They felt anger, and joy, and sadness. They failed at some things and succeeded at others. They were alive, even if for a short time. And shouldn't that fact alone be something appreciated?" He'd smiled again, and in a tone so kind it made me want to cry murmured, "You are already enough, kiddo. The fact that you are standing here today automatically makes you something worth remembering."

I never quite forgot the gentleness in his voice. The way he made me imagine, even if only for a second, the possibility of being loved simply for being me.

I don't quite know what I believe about death. I don't know what happened to that boy with amber eyes, or my old cat I buried beneath a tangled rosebush. But I hope they get some type of peace in the afterlife. I hope that boy goes to a world lit up by the light of a thousand suns and that the bumblebees drink from sugar as sweet as the honey they made in life. I don't know how I feel about death, but I hope that it is something gentle. And kind. Something that wraps its arms around everyone, whether strong or frail, and welcomes them all with the same soft smile.

I'm thinking about death now, as I stare down at the broken rosebush. It's quiet. My hands are bleeding. The rain is falling, in sheets around the garden. No one is going to find me; I realize with a start. No one's going to come looking for me. Not with all the rain.

It's quiet here in the greenhouse. Rain bashes against the windows so loudly that after a while even that becomes its own sort of silence. My shoulders are shaking. My hands are twitching. I can't quite tell if it's from exhaustion or something else but in the end it leaves me shuddering, curled up with my head against the glass as I try to stop the tremors.

I light a candle. Strike a match and watch as it flares up, the light glowing as it bounces off the darkened glass. I turn on the radio, and as I sit there I close my eyes and tip my head back. I pretend that I am somewhere warm. And whole. And safe. I am sitting in a garden that I raised with my own hands. I am sitting in a world that I built from the ground up. Nothing can touch me here, not the rot not the noise not the dark not the cold. I am sitting in a home that I have created by myself. No one can touch me here.

"...*Teenage girls,*" the voice on the radio remarks *"will sometimes do this fascinating thing where they will dress up death in bows and ribbons. They will wrap a corpse in flowers and drape a shroud as soft as silk and they will turn a funeral into a wedding. They will make a romance out of a tragedy.*

It is unclear why exactly they choose to do this. Perhaps because they feel that suffering is ugly, and ugliness is something that they cannot accept. Especially if, as is a common occurrence with these girls, they find such suffering within themselves. Perhaps they feel that if they glorify their anguish, the pain will become worth something. Unfortunately, this ideation is but a delusion meant to...” The radio stops. I look up tiredly at the figure that stands before me, their bony fingers fiddling with the dial until some old pop song warbles from the speakers.

"Oh, Child," the figure's voice is soft from where they stand. Soft, and caring. Gentle. They wrap a blanket around my shoulders as they kneel down beside me. "What are you doing sitting here in the rain like this?" For a moment, I am silent. I can feel thorns scratching at the back of my throat, and I'm scared that if I open my mouth something big and ugly is going to claw its way out.

"Child what are you doing out here all alone?" The shadowy figure asks, and I raise my head to look them in the eyes.

"My name is Helen." I answer eventually, pulling myself up to my feet. It feels like an ending, as I stand there. A quiet setting of the sun, as I place my hands in his. "I've been looking for you." I tell the shadow man.

"Why?" The figure whispers, and now it is his time to be silent. Outside the sky storms, stars streaking past the windowpanes as they hurtle through the heavens, their light crashing into the earth as they desperately try to fly. Outside the sky storms, winds wail and thunder rages until the very lightning tries to tear itself in two. But here it is quiet. And warm. And safe. I tug the shadow man closer, wrap my hands around his fingers as I look up at him.

He's dangerous, in the stories. And yet never to the children. None of the Old Ones are ever cruel to the children.

"I wanted to tell you a story." I confess as the rain continues to pour, tears running down the sides of my face as I laugh. "*My* story."

"Helen, do you know who I am?" There's a trace of pity to his words, and it makes me want to scream. To snarl, to yell, to grind my teeth into jagged points and watch him startle as he stares at me. Don't you pity me, I want to tell him. Don't you dare be gentle. Love me, protect me, but don't you dare act sorry for me. I am not weak.

"Your name is Thanatos." I respond, and a part of me wants so desperately to scream. To spit and curse and *bite* at the sympathy that wraps itself around this man's shadow. But my teeth have been filed down, and my throat scrubbed raw. I am too tired to bite. "The god of gentle deaths." Maybe, maybe it's okay if I let this person be gentle with me. Maybe I'm tired of always being forced to be strong. It would be nice, I think, to be treated as something precious. Like the porcelain teacups my mother used to cradle in her hands. I just want someone to be gentle. Not because I'm fragile, but because they love me too much to risk the chance that I get hurt.

"Why do you want to tell me a story, Helen?" Thanatos murmurs from where he stands. "Surely there are other gods more suitable for a tale than I." Why are you really here? He seems to ask, and I feel my shoulders slump.

"I don't actually have a story. I just thought that if I did have one, I would seem interesting. And if I was interesting, I thought there might be a chance that you could want me." I admit quietly, the words tasting like ash as I scrape them off my tongue. "I want someone to love me. To see me as worth something. So that by the time I am gone, there will be someone left who cares." *Look at me*, a part of me whispers. *Look at this weak, fragile shell that makes up my body. Watch me. Stare inside at the way my heart pounds with sap instead of blood and let me bloom into a person who is capable of being loved.* "I'll do anything, I don't care what it costs."

Why do you think I'm here, a part of me whispers. *Why do you think I'm out here begging in a storm like this? Why do you think there is no one here with me besides this broken rosebush that keeps tearing at my hands?* "Do you think that you could be that person?" I beg, tears in my eyes. "I have no one else."

For a moment, Thanatos is silent. I watch him closely as he thinks. I try to push down the pleas that are rising at the back of my throat. Everything hinges on this being's answer. I have nothing else left.

"Give me your name." Death's words are decisive as he stares at me. "And I'll give you a new one. I'll give you a hundred names. A thousand. Proserpine, Persephone, Kore, I'll make you so blessed that the very stars would sing of my love for you. I will give you an understanding of the essence of life, from the vastness of space to the smallness of atoms. I will give you the power to grow your own garden, one born not merely from plants but from all of life itself. I will give you everything," Thanatos promises "so long as you give me your name and follow me when I call."

"Which name do you want?" Deep down inside, my thoughts are racing. There's a certain power that a god gains when they are able to possess a name. After all, a name is what people use to describe or remember someone's identity – when given away, a person abandons all sense of self in a show of complete submission. If placed in the wrong hands a person's identity could be warped so thoroughly that they would be unrecognizable to anyone that knew them before the loss.

Overall, each person in the land of Durnon is given three names: A legacy, a secret, and an oath. The first is the way that the world sees you, the echoes of an untold story embedded beneath your skin until you grow the strength to write it. If lost, no outsider will ever truly remember you. The second is your hidden name, a word picked after your birth that dictates how you and you alone view yourself. If taken, you will be lost for eternity within the edges of your mind. The last name is your surname, a title shared between you and those you consider to be your family. If stolen, you are forever separated from those you call home.

"Give me all of your names little one, from the first to the last." Thanatos states. "I will not steal them away, but instead examine them under a magnifying glass before tailoring my gift to match you as perfectly as possible. Give yourself to me with all of your mind, heart, and body, and then I will give you every part of myself in return. Give me your fealty, and I will offer you my protection."

"That's not fair." I protest, trying my hardest to wipe away frustrated tears. "A name is a lot; everyone I know says that you can't just give it away." I may be thirteen, but that doesn't mean I'm dumb. I know all the stories that poets write about foolish mortals that try to make deals with Death. I know that nothing good ever comes from signing a contract with some otherworldly spirit. It's important, after all, to always read the fine print. "I'm scared, Thanatos. And I'm so *tired* of being scared."

"I know, little one." Thanatos's words are soothing, his eyes gentle as he looks at me. "I know it's a lot. But how about this, Helen. You've read my stories right?" He smiles at my hesitant nod. "Then you know that it is impossible for my kind to lie." Hesitantly, I nod. Thanatos is right, it's practically impossible for him to lie. But the truth can still break

20

you. "Then I want you to understand I mean it when I say that so long as you are under my protection, nothing in this world or the next will be able to ever truly harm you." Thanatos insists. "I will keep you safe to the best of my ability. Because you are *treasured. Wanted.*"

I think I'm too much of a realist to trust Thanatos fully. There has to be a catch. There always is when you make a deal with Death. But that- that idea of being treasured. It's all I've ever wanted. Even if this is a trap (which I know it is, no one *ever* smiles that much when they look at me) at least someone wants me. It's just so *heartbreaking* that the only time I can get a love like that is from something that isn't human.

"Do you accept the contract?" Thanatos asks, and he holds out an old-fashioned scroll, the offer neatly printed out in the center of the parchment. My hands shake as he passes me the pen, but I make sure the ink comes out dark as I sign my name. *Helen Althea Cermak.*

"I do." I reply, and it sounds like a vow. The type that brides make, their vows doing nothing to muffle their voices as they place themselves before the altar. The type of vow that soldiers make, as they stare down at this weapon of murder they hold in their hands that now bears their name etched across its hilt.

"I do." I repeat once more, and lick at the words as they fall off my tongue. They sound like a promise. They feel like a prayer.

(2)

AFTER: NATALYA

I don't think any words can describe the feeling you get when you're squeezing a limp, tiny hand and realize that you have outlived your child. That you have to go to funeral homes and try to pick out a casket that should NEVER be that small.

I don't cry that much anymore, funnily enough. I used to in the beginning. Used to scream until my throat went raw, wailing and shrieking until I vomited into the kitchen sink. Nowadays, my sorrow has turned numb. Quiet. It lives in the small things: pop songs she used to sing that broadcast on the radio, chipping sunflowers that she'd painted on her bedroom walls, the way the sky shines the same as it did on the day she died.

People told me it would get easier. That time heals.

Time hasn't brought my daughter back.

Perhaps it would have been better if I'd found her earlier, if I could have realized that something was wrong. There must have been signs, how could there not be in this type of situation? I guess I was blind, was dumb and so desperate to think that things were going to be better that I ignored all the warnings until it was too late.

It didn't help that she chose to hide things. I could have helped her if she reached out, instead of hiding away in her room so often. I could have helped her if she'd came to me.

Then again, I suppose Helen always had a sort of stubborn streak. It was quieter than that of her brothers, simmering under the surface as she gritted her teeth and worked through problems on her own. I can't fault her for that, I suppose. After all, she got that stubbornness from me.

She'll never be stubborn again. Never tell me no. Never scream or slam the door in my face or walk off crying. It's funny, almost. How much you can miss a person when they're gone, even the ugly parts.

Sometimes, I find myself going into her room and staring at the faded flowers. She'd just turned fourteen you know; just started growing into her own opinions, her unique sense of style, her personal type of humor. She'd started calling me "mom" instead of "mommy".

I'd hated it if I'm honest. Her growing up. I'd wanted her to stay small, wanted her to stay mine. Maybe she realized that. Is that why she made that deal with Death? I keep wondering, late at night when I'm too tired to sleep. Is that why she left me?

It doesn't matter anymore I guess. Me being mad at her growing up. After all, it's not like she's going to grow ever again.

They had to drag me out of the funeral before they laid my daughter in the ground. They had to drag me out kicking and screaming, because maybe I drank a little bit more than I should, and maybe I cried a little bit more than I should, and maybe I *felt* a little bit more than I should for the girl lying in the big black casket. Maybe they were right. But how else is a mom supposed to react when their baby is being lowered into the dirt?

"Why should we mourn her?" The fools had whispered as they stared at my daughters corpse. "If anything we should be happy. We should be grateful. She died for us. We didn't ask for her to be our Messiah."

I've stopped spending as much time at home. I just can't…can't handle being there anymore. Not when the house is so haunted by her presence. When I sleep, I sleep on the couch in the front hall and try to avoid the little room that lies curled up in the back of the house. Try to ignore the way that the closed door creaks every time I go up the stairs, how the flowers painted on its wooden beams are slowly fading. I don't know what to do about the flowers. Don't know if it's better to paint over them or just let the colors chip off. I'm a grown woman, and I'm still breaking down sobbing over a couple of brightly painted flowers.

My dog keeps sitting in the corner and staring at Helen's room. He won't eat, even when I try to feed him his favorite meals. He won't sleep either. All he does is sit and stare at the closed door that leads to her room, like maybe if he looks hard enough he'll figure out where his girl has gone. He's too little to understand death, too small to comprehend that that really was his girl's body inside the big black casket.

At least *he* still waits for her.

"It's too large to fit her." My eldest protests, over and over again at random moments. I want to scream at him to shut up, that *I know that* and addressing the fact isn't going to make the truth any easier to handle. Instead I hold him. I hold him tightly while he sobs, his face scrunching up in frustration as he asks over and over where his Helen has gone. I don't know how to answer him. Don't know how to explain what he already knows: that she's not coming back.

My youngest son asked if we could give her a nightlight so that she wouldn't be alone in the dark.

You know, the funny thing is that people like to pretend that she was older, when they talk about the death of my daughter. They make statues of her all wrapped up in veils and call her "Persephone, the bride of Death. Queen of the Underworld." They forget that she was a child, that when she died they had to pad her coffin with cushions because she was too small to properly fit. That as I held her while she was gasping for breath she had a little stuffed animal curled up in her arms. Because maybe she wasn't a child. Maybe she was much too old to be going to sleep with childhood toys and hoping for happy endings. But she was too young to be properly called an adult either.

I'm rereading this as I sit here and a part of me is realizing that I'm not that good at telling stories. Or not this one, at least. I don't know how to use fancy prose or make the words flow all poetically. Hell, I can't even keep this all in the same tense. I keep drifting… in and out of past and present like a drunken sailor stumbling about a deck. I think that's because a part of me is still stuck in that moment when I learned that she was gone.

My baby's gone.

I don't even really know why I'm telling you this in the first place if I'm honest. I guess I'm just trying to explain why I did the things that I did.

Because one morning I got out of bed and realized that I am tired of dealing with the fading flowers and the too big casket and the constant, *constant* crying. I am tired of waking up each day grieving for a child that no one else seems to really mourn. So, I threw on my boots and grabbed my sturdiest walking stick.

Because I'm not a writer. I'm not a poet. I can't make stones cry out at my words like you so often hear described of Orpheus. But I am a mother. And part of being a mother means that you don't stop searching until you can bring your child back home.

(3)

BEFORE: HELEN

It's stopped raining when I get up in the morning. Yet the dampness still clings to the grass as I walk, still hovers in the air and trails goosebumps across my skin. Thanatos is gone by the time I leave in the morning. But I can still feel his gaze burning, the song from the radio humming as it runs grooves along the worn track. I place one foot in front of the other as I leave. Watch almost absentmindedly as the ground squelches from where the mud clings to my shoes. Quietly, I begin to run through the names as a lone bird calls. Kore. Proserpine. Persephone, Izanami, Aerecura, the words echo until they wrap around my limbs, until they bloom in my heart and my brain and my esophagus. There's no more rain, and yet the trees hang heavy with droplets. I walk towards home through towering gardens lit by the rising sun and feel my shadow writhe and twist behind me.

I sit at the table, and nobody realizes. They don't notice the way that my hands shake because of the twitching in my veins; they don't see the way my eyes shine with an almost manic light. Look at me, I want to tell them. Can't you tell the difference?

I start looking at books. Sneak out late at night to the library and study texts on biology. And alchemy. Anatomy, chemistry, physics, I go through page after page until the papers start tearing. Until the spines crack in my arms from how often I have cradled them.

It is ironic, perhaps, that as a child of such a nation as Durnon, I have never been quite skilled at fighting. That's not to say I'm bad, of course. I'm just good instead of great. Violence doesn't come to me as naturally as it does others, doesn't wrap around my shoulders like a contented housecat. And maybe that's alright. Maybe I don't have to prove something to be loved.

I look into healing instead. Start falling behind and dragging my feet at practice, take note of each bruise that blooms on the surface of my skin and every ache that strains from protesting muscles. Bruises, I learn, are much harder to heal than scrapes, funnily enough. It's harder to reverse patches of clotted blood than to simply mend split skin together.

I move slower, in practice. Stop dodging attacks and see how long it takes for me to grow everything back. In the span of a few weeks, I can completely regrow a patch of torn skin.

Thanatos is waiting when I arrive at the greenhouse. He picks the music while I light a couple of candles. It's some sort of old classical song. The type that's got no words, but the notes speak for themselves. He watches quietly as I rummage through the gardening tools for a hammer.

"I'm not quite sure how long the process of ossification works," I explain offhandedly, pointing down at my charts and diagrams as I slowly raise the hammer higher. "After all, this is more of a test run than anything. I'm trying to see how quickly I can repair the bone instead of just straight-up new growth. Hematoma is easy- I mean it's tedious, but it's easy. I'm more worried about all the calcium channels I'll be rapidly depleting." Death looks on with a small frown on his face.

"Why are you doing this?" He asks.

"Oh, it's just my left arm, I don't use it that much anyway." I shrug and adjust my grip on the hammer. "Only problem is that they usually take several months to heal, and that means heroes are left too injured for several months to properly work." A virtual death sentence for the people of Durnon. "Besides," I add with a frown, "I don't think I've been trying hard enough to control this gift."

"Why use it on yourself?" Death presses. "I mean, other healers practice on patients and wounded animals."

"I'm not nearly close enough to the level where I can help other people without hurting them more than they actually are." I counter. "And animals hardly have enough similarities to humans to make treating them practical. Even if they were, I don't like the fact that they couldn't tell me to stop if I was accidentally hurting them." I frown then. "I was not born for needless violence."

I drop the hammer. My arm crunches at the impact. I grit my teeth and reach inwards, sparks flaring behind the back of my eyelids as the flesh around my appendage swells up, bruises blooming as I snap the break in place. I fill in tissue gaps with marrow and weave the hardened bone together around a calcified matrix. Slowly, ever so slowly, my bone mends. Death offers me a slice of marzipan when I finish.

"Nice job." Thanatos compliments, and I take the candy with a shaky smile. The room is spinning, roses swelling up and shrinking from where they bloom in my peripheral vision.

It's interesting, really, seeing how Death's gift has merged to become my own. I've been researching his former followers in the past, but none of them have been so closely associated with growing things. I think the closest thing to healing that the previous patrons used was necromancy, but that was more of a form of reanimation than revival.

Maybe it's because my hidden name, Althea, means "healer". Maybe it's because I summoned Death in a greenhouse instead of the standard graveyard. I'm not quite sure how it happened, but I've been gifted with creation instead of the typical destruction associated with Thanatos.

I mess up a lot at first. I twist tendons and tear ligaments, and one time I lost mobility in my legs because I injured a nerve pathway in my spine. I harden joints until they are more likely to snap than bend and mangle the veins in my hands so badly that I cut off circulation and nearly lose my fingers.

A small, feral part of me wants to stop whenever I reach a certain point in practice. I'll hunch over on the floor in my bathroom and vomit until tears bleed out of the corners of my eyes. Some desperate, animalistic part of my brain snarls every time I try to train. It doesn't care about all of the reasons and justifications. It doesn't even really care about helping anyone if I'm honest. In the end, there is a part of me that is just simply tired of being hurt.

So I kill it. Systematically cut every single nerve pathway until I lose all traces of sensation and grow them back when I can confidently mend every stitch together. My pain tolerance grows in the meantime. I get back up every time something knocks me to the ground. I erase every weakness from my body. I eliminate any chance of imperfection.

I begin to crave the adrenaline rush that rises every time I face another injury. The dizzying sear of pain that swells up before inevitably fading into the burn of triumph. The subtle crunch that rings out whenever I snap and secure my bones. The satisfaction that comes with breaking something and building it back together, the way I can look down at my skin and not only see but *feel* all the tiny ways I have shaped and rebuilt the frameworks of my body.

By the time summer arrives, not a single part of my body is older than the course of three months. The knowledge makes my head spin, causes my shoulders to shiver and shake as I struggle between the urge to either laugh or cry. In the span of a season, I have rebuilt myself from the ground up. It is both a terrifying and thrilling realization. I run my fingers up and down my arms, pretending that my touch extends down to bone and muscle and tissue. I have been reborn, become a mother almost to this new version of myself. It is a dizzying, *addictive* feeling.

(4)

AFTER: NATALYA

When Helen was younger, I used to take her and her brothers to see the dandelions. I'd sit down with her in the middle of the grass and pick them, watch the way she'd stare at the way their fluffy tops bobbed in the wind.

"I don't get it." She'd said the first time I took her there. She'd crossed her arms, rolled her eyes, and tried to act *so grown up* that I had to look away so she wouldn't see my grin. Fourteen-year-olds are funny like that, you know. They like to think that they're so much older than they actually are.

"What's the point in sitting here and watching a bunch of weeds?"

"Why Helen," I'd protested, clutching my chest scandalized as I staggered back with a gasp. "These aren't just any regular old weeds. They're wishing weeds. Legend says that if you can knock all the seeds off when you blow on them, all your dreams will come true."

"…But they're weeds," Helen argued. "Nothing good ever comes from weeds. They're useless." I watched as her lip wobbled at the words. Carefully - ever so carefully - I reached out and tucked a dandelion behind her ear.

"Maybe you're right." I'd agreed calmly. Pretended to ignore how Helen's hands shook as she clutched the plant between her palms. "Maybe they are weeds. But that doesn't mean that they're any less special." I softened my voice then, watched as her breathing sped up when she started hyperventilating. I kept my smile gentle while my daughter broke down. "After all," I'd murmured, "they've always been my favorite flower. Always have. Always will."

"Always?" She asked then, voice shaky.

"Always." I'd repeated.

She painted dandelions on the edges of her bedroom door after that. Kept vases filled to the brim with them in her bedroom, used to make this big, wide smile every time she saw them growing in the yard. My flower child, I wanted to call her—my lovely, darling flower child. I never actually said that out loud. A part of me still hates myself for that.

Stories say that whenever a person goes looking for the entrance to the underworld, the god of journeys will make a trail by lighting a string of flames over a line of marching flowers. I think a part of me always knew that they would be dandelions.

It's quiet as I leave the house. I bring a backpack with me, inside of which I pack a thermos, gun, lighter, and collapsible tent. I tie the straps of an old camera onto the end hooks. I follow the flowers as they dance over meadows and brooks, past bloated, sundried corpses that lie rotting on the wayside.

Sometimes I think I see her, running up ahead of me. Green eyes and the darker hair she'd dyed to match flicker in the corners of my vision. I catch her from the corner of my gaze as she hides behind trees and dances in the twirling shadows. I hear her giggling from where she splashes in the nearby creek. I pull out my camera and take a picture every time I think I see her. She never shows up, of course. Not in the way that she used to before. But I can still see her face etched out in grooves along the faces of towering boulders and catch the edges of her footprints left behind in silver starshine, and a part of me likes to think that she's still there only… different.

I keep the photographs so that I can show her when she ends up coming home. Show her, I went out looking for you in the woods one day and saw this thing that made me think of you. I went out looking in the woods one day because I don't ever think I'm going to be able to stop searching for you, regardless of how much time has passed.

The woods grow darker until eventually I become unable to tell the difference between day and night. I grow lost, unable to tell which way I am headed except for the flaming flowers that constantly bloom in front of me. The darkness creeps in until I am forced to practically crawl through the underbrush, scrabbling around on my hands and knees as branches snatch and thorns tear. Somewhere in the distance, Helen laughs, laughs, laughs.

Eventually, I find myself standing in front of an old, cared-for greenhouse. Vines and moss blanket the walls on the outer panes and run up and down the sides of the indoor garden as they protectively shield it from view. Pooling in between the moss stretches creeping roses, and between the roses gather dancing, flickering dandelions. Gently—*ever so gently*—I go up to the door and tug on the doorknob. The hinges open without a fuss.

A candle wobbles from where it rests on a nearby wicker table. On the floor, a pile of pillows and quilts lie jumbled into a halfhearted children's fort. Flowers twirl up and down the walls as they reach out with curling stems. The colors glow cheerily as they blanket the inside of the little greenhouse. In the corner, a portable radio sputters, its voice crooning as it sings.

"...But I would walk five hundred miles, and I would walk five hundred more...

...Just to be the one who walked a thousand miles to fall at your door..."

Outside, the sky has slowly begun to storm. I look around the room, drink in raindrops and whispering roses and old, cracked radios that never stop singing. Somewhere, crouched behind the potted lilies and hanging ferns, a small smile flashes.

"Show me the way, please," I murmur silently. I look outside at where the water pours and drowns the dandelions. The trees curve around the path, their shadows thickening like molasses in the firelight. It's dark in the hollows between the trunks. It's quiet while here in the greenhouse tiny flames fizzle and pop.

A sharp crackle resounds through the air, and I glance at the old candle that sits beside the buzzing music. Sparks sizzle from where it has burst into flame. Frozen, I watch as the embers trail off the wick in golden currents and slowly start to hover in the air.

I snatch the candle. Take off running into the woods as the sky storms around me, rain pelting down in torrents as I cover the light with desperate, shaking hands. In the darkened hollows between the trunks, pale faces peek out as I rush past. Up ahead, the ground slopes as it turns into a mountain, the woods slanting from where the trees hang sideways. At the top of the hill a lone willow tree sits, branches flying in the wind as electricity arcs and sizzles past. In the shadows of the branches, a lone girl dances.

Unlike the flames of the previous flowers, the light from the candle doesn't fade out. I raise it higher as I sprint, wave it like a torch as I race through the darkened woods, branches snatching at my skin and roots clawing at my footsteps. The ground shivers and shakes every time I slam my feet into the earth.

"Helen!" I scream, lightning pouring out in continued flashes. Slipping in the mud, I claw myself up with bloodied fingernails. In the shadows between the tree trunks, ghosts continue to gather and watch impassively.

By the time I reach the tree my legs are shaking so hard that I find it almost difficult to stand. My clothes lie sopping as they're plastered to my skin from the pouring downpour. I double over gasping, chest heaving as I cough up water. I can't quite tell if it's rain or tears that are seeping down my face. A few feet away, the willow tree stands. Dandelions bloom in the gaps between the roots.

The girl is gone. I can still see the remnants of her shadow as it dances. My girl is gone. And a part of me wants to break down and scream over how useless everything feels when I'm left just chasing the remnants of a ghost. But I force myself to still and slow my breathing. I look around the murky woods, and then turn to face the candle instead. In the midst of the unending downpour, sparks float slowly towards the back of the tree. Nestled between the tree roots sits a hole, granite steps trailing down in circles as they spiral into a watery grotto. Even when submerged amidst the darkened pool, the candles continue to shine. I pause and square my shoulders. Inhale, and then exhale. Place one foot in front of another as I brace myself and take a step. And then a second. Gradually—*ever so gradually*—I begin to descend into the underworld.

BEFORE: HELEN

I start bringing a portable radio with me whenever I go on walks through the woods. Static crackles along with birdcalls while all around me the trees hum. I sit down against a pair of matted roots and tip my head back, place my hands in my lap and grow still like the little dolls that sit perched in the shells of vintage toy shops.

I like to listen to the woods breathe. Dig my hands into the dirt and pretend that I can feel the earth whirling around in orbit. It makes me feel small. And safe. And still. I don't have to prove myself in this vast and dizzying chaos of a thing we call existence. I can just breathe, sink my fingers into the soil beside nearby tree roots and drift.

Sometimes I wish I had roots like the trees do. I wish I had something to anchor myself to the ground with, something to grab onto tightly and hold, something I could call my own. I wish I could stay here, here in the forest with the birds and the trees and the sound of growing things. I wish I didn't have to go home each night.

I made a heart last night. Peeled open my chest and reached inside, watched the organ pulse in my hands from where I held it. I raised out my other hand and made sure to copy it, cells and tissue building over and over each other in layers until the thing resembled an artichoke or a flower about to bloom.

"… *You have to treat a woman like you treat an artichoke,"* a voice from the radio remarks suddenly, making me jump. *"You have to put in work to get to her heart."* I snicker and double over laughing, my giggles almost hysterical as they ring out in the surrounding stillness.

I start carrying seeds with me that settle along the edges of my pockets. I weave flowers into my hair, make them bloom and wither when I play with them in class. My shoes grow streaked with mud and grass stains.

Sometimes I wonder about how easy it would be to simply disappear, to fade away until I am nothing more than scattered stardust, or a whisp in the wind that ruffles roses as it rushes past. A part of me wonders if anyone would miss me.

"Your teacher called me today to have a concerning talk with him this morning." I still as Mother stares, my fingers tense from where I grip my silverware. Quietly, I set them down on either side of my plate.

A part of me is confused by when, exactly, I ended up here at dinner. Time has been moving sluggishly since I started leaving the house. I feel caught up in a dream, almost. One so realistic that it makes you question if you're actually awake or not.

"He said you've been skipping school. Said that he hasn't seen you in days, in fact." I look at her silently. "Are you going to say something?" She demands. I am silent. Still, like the porcelain dolls that sit perched on the shelves of old antique shops. I open my mouth, but the words refuse to come out.

"Say something." She snaps.

"I'm trying," I whisper.

"Trying isn't good enough!" Mother snaps, slamming her fork down as she stands up and starts pacing around the room. "Sometimes, Helen." Her voice is shaking as she leans in, "Sometimes I wonder if you even *want* to be my daughter. Because you go around acting like you belong to someone else, someone who doesn't give a damn if you live or not." She pauses, pinching the bridge of her nose.

"I'm sorry." She says at last. "I'm sorry, I'm trying to calm down, honest to God, Helen, I swear I'm trying. But there's just no way my child could be this much of a *failure*. Tell me, Helen, do you even try? Do you even try to be a good kid, or do you just roll over like a dog whenever something that requires a bit of effort presents itself?" She pauses suddenly, voice breaking.

"What am I going to do with you, Helen? I mean, honestly, I'm starting to run out of patience. Don't you want people to like you? Don't you want to matter?" She leans in closer until I can feel her breathing near my shoulder. "Because right now… you're just wasting everything I've worked so hard for."

I smile from where I sit. Leave my food untouched as I let my eyes glaze over, picture a garden in a forest where my greenhouse is waiting. My hands are fuzzy in the candlelight. I wiggle them numbly, watch as they move slowly, ever so slowly, like swimming in molasses.

Mom's yelling louder now, her face is all swollen and red like the pickled plums on my plate. But everything's okay because she's not yelling at me. She's yelling at Helen. And I don't know who I am if I'm not Helen, but everything feels all soft and fuzzy the way the radio is when it rains, the way the lighter is when it makes a flame, the way it always is when Mom yells.

I am sitting in a garden that I raised with my own hands. I am sitting in a world that I built from the ground up. Nothing can touch me here, not the rot, not the damp, not the noise, not the cold. No one can touch me here.

I go to sleep the next night and dream that I am standing on the shore of the river Styx. I wiggle my toes in a sand made of crushed starlight. Though the lights are warm, they never burn my feet. I sit down beside the water, listen as it murmurs while thousands upon thousands of dead rush past. Their robes flutter in the moonshine as if they were made from mothwings.

"You look like a train ran you over." Death's words are blank, emotionless. A statement instead of a question. And yet his eyes are worried, as he stares at me. Somewhere in the distance, a radio is crooning. "I thought you had gotten to the stage where you could heal your wounds."

"My mom made me pancakes for breakfast," I tell Thanatos. "She hugged me and ruffled my hair and said she was sorry for being so angry. We watched a movie, and afterward we went strawberry picking in the garden. She said she only wants what's best for me, you have to understand. She saw a lot of kids die growing up because they didn't work hard enough. She said she's just doing this to keep me safe, that I've got a lot of potential and she doesn't want me to waste it." Thanatos's expression is blank as a trickle of blood slides down my temple. "She told me she loves me."

"Why are you still allowing your wounds to lie open like this?" Thanatos asks, as if I haven't already answered the question. "You can heal your wounds now, can't you? So why do you allow them to stay?" I hesitate and try to explain.

"I think that Mom always acts a little nicer when she feels guilty," I answer finally. "She's a lot softer when she can see the bruises. Sometimes she forgets just how strongly she cares. And so when she sees the bruises, she becomes gentler. Handles me softly while she waits for the wounds to heal. She just wants to do what's best for me." I state defensively. "She loves me, I know she loves me, but sometimes she doesn't quite know how to love something without breaking it."

Thanatos is silent as he sits beside me. We watch the river flow in the meantime, watch the souls dance across the water, and Charon's boat bob up and down in the soundless wind.

"Helen, I'm going to ask you again. Why, of all the gods that dwell in the earth and sky, did you summon me?" Death's voice is quiet. Quiet in a fury so consuming that it is practically impossible to vocalize.

"Because I love you, Thanatos," I answer simply. "I love how gentle you are. I knew that if I looked for you, you would be kind." Shakily, I confess, "I thought that if I loved you, you might love me back."

"Oh, child, you don't really love me." Thanatos declares sadly. Pity and despair twist in his tone as he turns to look at me. "No, you don't really love death at all, do you? You just simply hate life."

I try to speak, then stop. Start again. Only no words come out. Eventually, I remain silent. Thanatos starts to laugh. An ugly, bitter laugh. Filled to the brim with mockery and rage. I watch as Thanatos laughs until he cries. Annoyed, I shoot him a glare instead. Cross my arms and burrow my feet into the softened sand. For a while, we sit there in silence. I on account of anger, and him on account of grief.

"Why do you call me Thanatos?" The god blurts out after a pause. "After all, I have millions of other names, each one greater than the last. Hades and Pluto, Letum and Osiris. Even the simple word *Death* would have sufficed. I don't think people have called me Thanatos for centuries."

"Thanatos means gentle death," I answer simply. Look down at the scrapes and cuts that line my arms. "It means peaceful as well, the type of passing that's as soft as falling asleep. I guess… I guess I wanted to see if you would remember being gentle if I called you by that name. Everyone in

Durnon calls you cruel, claims you're a selfish thief who steals the living away to join in his halls. I wanted to know that if you took me away, you would at least be gentle."

"Are you not curious?" Thanatos asks at last, turning his head, "How you ended up in a place like this?"

"I figured if it was something important, you would tell me eventually," I respond. Carefully, I begin to scoop up the stardust and watch it sift between my fingers. I watch out of the corners of my eyes as Death struggles to speak.

"You went too far last night." He announces at last. "With your training. You bled out on your bathroom tiles after you tried to slit and then resew your throat." I feel myself still as he pauses.

"Am I dead then?" I ask at last. The words feel strange as I say them. "Because I, I didn't mean to. I've just been taking it too easy, and I could always try harder because I was falling behind in school, and I have to get better because otherwise I'm going to let everyone down, and I'm not supposed to let everyone down because then they won't want to be around me, no one likes disappointments you know, and I could have sworn I could have handled it and…"

"No," Thanatos answers firmly. He keeps his gaze locked on the shapes floating on top of the water. He does not dare to meet my eyes. "I told you in the bargain after all, I get to choose when I bring you home. No sooner and no later."

"Oh," I mutter blankly. "Am I allowed to know when that might be?" Death is silent as he mulls over his words.

"Come with me." Death says at last; stars spill out in currents when he pulls me to my feet, "I want to show you something." He turns and I follow, legs shaky like a newborn deer as I try to keep up with his hurried strides. I follow him along beaches strewn with specks of time itself, where comets whirl and planets buzz like eager bumblebees when they whizz past.

He leads me to a giant door, its face as pale as marble with large weeping roses trailing up and down its sides. Carefully, Death unlocks it with a shiny silver key.

"Are you coming?" Thanatos asks gently, and I force my sore muscles to move faster as I chase after him.

The first thing I notice when I step through the door is the sunshine. I close my eyes instinctively as I wince at the harsh light, peek through trembling fingers as I gaze blearily out at where the sun sets into the sea, its vibrant golds and oranges distorted from where the water swallows them up. Even while dying, the sun is still so alive that it nearly hurts.

I look around once I tear my gaze from the falling light. Cobblestones crackle as they crunch beneath my footsteps. Towers of iron hang covered in vegetation, an abomination of a creation half nature, half man. A river runs its way through the city towards the sea, its contents clear as it flows past bloodstained beaches. A boy lies sprawled out beside my feet. His eyes weep with an amber that glows with the warmth of a thousand suns. Bloodred spider lilies have started to bloom around the edges of his broken throat. I watch as Death weeps, tears of ichor flowing down his hollowed face as the god mourns.

"I did not know that you could care so much for a mortal," I call out hesitantly. Thanatos stills.

"Of course I do." He responds. "I love all my children."

"Sometimes, I think I want to burn all you humans to the ground." Death's tone is blank, a sort of quiet fury that shudders as it tries to keep itself still. "The other gods don't really understand this, you know. After all, they don't really have to see the suffering that comes each time a person dies. No, they get to act all noble as they recline upon their little clouds and act as if mankind is nothing more than a horde of writhing ants. They don't see the atrocities that humanity has committed against each other. Can you imagine how it feels, Helen? To hold the sick, the old, and the injured? To cradle babies who have known nothing more than suffering their entire lives, who have been hurt so badly that all you can do is hug them gently and whisper that you are sorry?" His eyes are wild as he looks at me. "Can you imagine having your ears grow deaf from the constant screaming? Have you ever wondered what it would be like to cry so hard that you exhaust your tear ducts? To have the skin around your eyes crack and bleed because your body is physically unable to keep up with the force of your weeping?

This was my child." Death wails then. "This was my child, and he used to cry to me at night that he was scared to die alone. And what a foolish fear that was," Thanatos chuckles wetly. "For how could anyone die without Death beside them?

I used to despise the people of Durnon. I used to hate them with a burning passion, wanted to wipe them out with a plague or a pestilence, and just blot them off the face of the earth. Because they have chosen to leave the corpses of their vulnerable to rot along the roadside. They have chosen to desecrate the souls of those they deemed inferior, leaving their spirits to wait confused and alone as they move on without a second glance. Mortality is something that should be treasured, Helen. Because it teaches you to value the things you still have." I watch him in silence. Watch as this god breaks down over the grave of a child abandoned far too young. Dully, I stare down at the boy who lies in pieces around my feet. Did he have flowers bloom inside of him, too, I wonder? Did the flowers wrap around his bones until he wished for another name, too?

"You will be like an evergreen," Thanatos says at last. A hint of desperation tinges his words, making his movements more erratic as he guides me back to the river Styx. "Known throughout the land for its ability to bloom even in the coldest frosts. You will be a symbol of hope, kindness, and love. A way to teach the mortals how to truly love the balance between life and death. Not as a contest between the weak and strong, but an inevitable and gradual passing of seasons. You will show the others why they are wrong. Through peace, instead of violence."

"And then?" I ask quietly, and Thanatos nods to himself.

"And then you will join me in the spring." Thanatos gives no further indication of what that phrase might mean. Still, I wrap his hands around my own. Lean my head against his shoulder and watch as spirits dance along the river like a flutter of butterflies. I sit there with Death on the side of the river Styx, and in the safety of the night, allow myself to relax and finally breathe.

(6)

AFTER: NATALYA

Everything is quiet when I land on the side of an unfamiliar riverbank. I look out over the darkened water and burrow my feet deeper into the sand while I stop and stare at the empty shoreline. All around me flock the dead, their fluttering robes rustling like impatient birdwings as they wait for a way to cross.

Nervously, I open my bag and examine the contents inside. Ensure my gun is loaded as I root through the contents of my bag. Sand made from crushed stars sticks to the edges of my shoes as I shift in place. It settles over everything in a layer of fine powder, as sweet as sugar and dead men's wishes.

I don't think that I quite realized just what a world with nothing living inside it meant. The only light that illuminates the shore is the tattered dust of decaying stars. The water of the river is swollen with trash and bile and bloated bodies. The beach is barren. Nothing grows or breathes or laughs or screams, and there is nothing here on the bank of the river Styx. Nothing besides a dry, barren beach.

"You're not a psychopomp, are you?" I look up impatiently at the stranger's question. A figure is standing there, his face flickering with annoyance and confusion as he stares at me. His flesh hangs down in drooping folds, skin sagging over decaying muscles as it struggles to stretch over stark white bones. His eyeballs rattle in their sockets when he looks me up and down.

"I'm not a what now?" I ask reflexively, watching the being closely as all around him, corpses throw gold coins at his feet.

"Never mind. If you *were* a psychopomp, you would probably know." The decaying man sighs, smacking a bony hand against his forehead as he mutters under his breath. "Are you dead?" He calls out, annoyed.

"…Well, no," I respond at last, my hands sweating as my heart pounds. I stay rooted in place as the dead rush past, frantically throwing themselves against the edges of a darkened boat until they claw their way over the sides. The decaying man sighs once more and then fixes me with a glare.

"Alright." He announces at last, portions of fat and flesh dangling as he crosses his arms. "As the head ferryman of the river Styx and all other forms of transportation through the Underworld, I'm going to have to ask you to vacate the premises. You are clearly neither dead nor involved with transporting the dead, and as such, do not have the license to travel ahead through the following areas. Although I can understand that this may not be the response you were looking for, please know that we here in Hadestown hold no particular feelings of ill will and urge you to come again once you are no longer alive."

"I'm sorry, what's going on?" I stammer, confused. Time has been moving sluggishly since I first left my house. I feel caught up in a dream, almost. One so realistic that it makes you question if you're awake or not. "I mean, where am I?"

"Why, you're at the river Styx, of course." The figure drawls exasperatedly, jaw clicking as he grinds his teeth. "The entrance to the Underworld." He bends down to pick up all the fallen coins, back popping as several ribs pop out of place.

"But that's impossible," I protest, confused. A frantic soul slips, landing in the river with a splash. A faint sound of sizzling arises as the spirit screams. "After all, I'm not dead."

"No, not yet." The ferryman agrees. "But soon enough, probably. After all, you've been in that water for a while now. If the drowning doesn't get you, the cold will."

"Oh," I murmur dumbly. My hands are fuzzy in the moonlight. I wiggle them numbly, watch as they move ever so slowly, slowly like swimming in molasses. Lift them to touch my face, feel something cold and leathery where normally there should be skin. "I think I'm going into shock," I confess to the talking corpse. The words come out muffled, as if spoken underwater.

"That's alright." The corpse – Charon, if I can read his faded nametag correctly, assures. His voice his gentle now, sympathetic. He's got the same tone that the paramedics had when Helen was first hooked up to the IV drip. "Most mortals typically do when they land in this sort of situation. If it helps, you're still the same person as you were when you first entered the Underworld."

"Can I…. can I see my daughter then?" I ask, desperately trying to pull my thoughts together. "She's already dead."

"Of course." The corpse assures. "I've never understood why you mortals think it's so hard to see the dead again." The ferryman sighs, joints rattling as he shakes his head. "It's the easiest thing in the world, really; anyone alive can do it. You just have to come close enough to dying, and then you'll meet them in the afterlife." Quietly, the ferryman adds, "It's the coming back from that that's the hard part."

Coming back. I hadn't thought about that yet. Going back: to the empty house, and the shallow condolences, and the small, *sad* black coffin that should be far too tiny to fit a person. Going back to the dust gathering on the steering wheel and faded sunflowers that have started chipping off the walls.

"Could I bring Helen with me?" I ask hesitantly. "Home isn't home without the people I love beside me." Silence rings out in response. I blink my eyes, and then the ferryman is gone. With him, everyone else.

"Hey, come back here!" I shout, all panic and nerves, and what exactly did that guy mean? "You can't just leave me here! I need to see my daughter; I have to bring her back!" In the aftermath of the words, the only thing that rings out is silence. Frantically, I try to rack my brain.

"Do you want money?" I plead desperately, pulling coins out of my sack and throwing them onto the ground as my voice. "Because I can give you money. I can give you all my money. I'll give you anything, you can take *everything*. Please, just please let me have my baby back." I start to cry then, sobs rattling in the back of my throat as I struggle to breathe. The decaying man does not appear.

"No, no, no no *no* no no no." I chant, over and over until the words blend into a mindless shriek. I look out over the river, where the ferryboat has started to slowly drift past. A lone girl stands at the back of the ship. Her dress flutters as soft as moth wings as she stares off into the distance.

"HELEN!" I scream, giving up and sprinting along the edges of the shore as the boat sails past. The girl freezes and then turns her head. I stare into a pair of wide, stunned eyes. A pang shoots its way through my chest. My baby's there. My baby's there. And she's so, *so* close. But not close enough. My daughter leans over the railing of the ferry and starts shouting. But I can't hear her. Can't hear her over the sound of the pounding of my footsteps and the cracking of my heart.

"Helen, I'm coming, baby," I yell desperately, pushing my feet to run even faster while I sprint across the beach made of dying stars. Souls scatter at my touch like startled pigeons, and sand flies up in clouds each time my feet slam down into the sand. "Helen, it's Mommy, ok?" I'm trying to shove down the sobs that are rising at the back of my throat. "I've come to take you home."

The river Styx is known as the junkyard of the underworld. It's where the dead shed their bodies, all their heirlooms, all their burdens. This way, they can float freely on top of the ships. The river Styx is like a sludge, all tarred and sticky and filled to the brim with a sea of sinking bodies. The stench of decay reeks to the high heavens. I watch as piles of flesh are slowly swallowed up with a wet squelch. I look again at the girl who is leaning on the edge of the ship. There is no hesitation when I jump.

I throw myself into the water, limbs flailing frantically as I try to keep my head above the waves. All around me, decaying flesh rots, leftover eyes and tongues flopping limply as they roll about in the river. I look at the boat and struggle to swim faster. The liquid clings to the edges of my skin like a gelatinous membrane. It will not let me go.

"HELEN!" I scream, pockets of air bubbling from my throat. I'm struggling to keep my eyes above the surface of the river. Body after body slams into my side, causing me to stumble as the waves roar. I'm drowning. No matter how hard I try to swim, I can't stop myself from drowning.

By the time I reach the ferry, my vision has grown dark from lack of oxygen. I blink the spots out of my eyes as I claw my nails into the surface of the wooden beams. Up above me, the boat shudders and comes to a stop. The decayed man leans down and crawls like a spider over the side of the ship until he's hovering in front of my face.

"Your grief is pulling the boat down," Charon complains shortly. "There's a reason we don't allow the living to take the ferry. You should never have tried to join us on this ride." Wooden beams whine, and I watch through blurry vision as the planks start to sink. I lift myself higher and claw my fingers into the cracks until my nails tear off with bloodied pops. The skeleton is still talking, his voice calm while words continue pouring out of his mouth like water from a leaking sieve. And yet, I can't hear him when he speaks. Can't hear him over the sound of ringing in my ears. Can't hear him over the sound of the gasp, gasp gasping as the ship breaks beneath my hands from how tightly I grasp it.

"…You fool, you have to let go!" Charon finally shouts, panic and stabbing irritation poking out from his tone so sharp I flinch. "Let go and drown, you stupid mortal! And then you will be with your child again. Can't you see how much you're hurting her?" I look up then, at where a pair of bright green eyes silently watches. "Let your body sink beneath the waves, and then your soul can swim up and join us on the other side. Then the ship will be able to float, and you can see your daughter again."

I take in my daughter then. Stare at the way her tattered skin hangs off pearly bones and how her face stares back at me vacantly. That's not – well, I suppose it is my daughter actually. But my daughter shouldn't look like that.

Things weren't supposed to end like this.

My daughter was supposed to be *alive,* supposed to keep redecorating her room, complaining about school, and begging me for a pet cat. My daughter wouldn't want this. She'd wanted to *live.* She wouldn't be content with the pair of us dying. She would want me to *live* so that I could be alive with her. So that the two of us could experience all the joys of life that death can't offer.

I think again of the dust growing on the steering wheel and the faded sunflowers that are chipping off the bedroom walls. Being dead won't erase the damage. But being able to live again, to grow instead of rot, that could let me fix things.

"I can't do that." I rasp finally, eyes still locked on that small green gaze that stays staring down at me. "I can't let go, Charon. Not now. Not when I have only just started my journey. Not when there is still so much more that I need to see be done."

"What kind of things?" Charon sneers mockingly. The water continues rising until it climbs to the bottom of my chin. I keep my eyes fixed on the little girl who remains leaning over the railing. I make sure that she will be the last thing I see as my vision goes blurry.

"I want to see my daughter stand there on her graduation day," I answer, in quick, desperate breaths. "I want to see her standing there in a white dress and pick out her favorite flowers, not for a funeral but for her wedding. I want to throw a big party, bake a cake all piled high with gooey frosting, and tell her I think it's sweet that she turned sixteen. I want to see what it's like when she drives a car, whether she's cautious and reckless and yeah maybe it's a stupid thing to say but I'd like to see her drive a car, scream at her as we tear down highways and have her turn to me and say while rolling her eyes, *Mom I've been doing this for years now.*" My voice breaks, and water begins to pour into my mouth as I choke on my tears.

"I want… I want to see how tall she will be by the time she stops growing. I want to see my baby and hold her. I want to watch my child grow up. And I can't do that if we're both dead." I dig my fingers deeper into the sides of the wooden ship and climb my way up the sides as Charon turns and follows. "I want to be *alive*, Charon," I tell him bluntly. "And I want my daughter to be alive with me. Because to be alive is to be able to *grow.*"

The ship shudders to a stop. Charon stares at me in silence. I stare back at him in exchange. For a moment, all is silent. And then, like a flock of fluttering doves, the souls fly off the ship in a flash of silver. I look down and realize that we have landed on a dry beach.

Charon slides closer and then offers out a decomposing hand. In the gaps between his fingerbones, pale dandelions have started to bloom.

"You are a fool, Natalya Cermak." Charon remarks, bones rattling as he shakes his head. "A reckless, hypocritical, determined fool. Tell me, why are you so ready to throw your life away, and yet so adamant to keep it?"

"Do you know what my daughter's name is, Charon?" I ask. "Her name's Helen. Do you know what that name means, Charon? It means *the most beloved girl in the whole world*. It means *a woman whose face would launch a thousand ships*.

Even though there were dozens of other names I could have chosen for my daughter, I don't think I could have picked a better meaning than that. Because Charon, I would launch *ten* thousand ships. A hundred thousand. I would tear the stars out of the sky if they made her smile, I would burn the very world if she told me that she was tired of being cold. Compared to all of that, what's the price of one swim?" I smile then, as I take in the figure's expression. "There is nothing that I wouldn't do for any of my children," I tell him gently. "After all, they mean everything to me."

"I wish you luck, then," Charon murmurs eventually, a grudging respect glowing in his eyes. "I wish you well on the rest of your travels. Take care, oh Natalya Cermak. May it be a while until we meet again. And may your words hold as your journey prevails."

I look past him then, at the rest of the underworld. At the row of flickering flames that dance in winding paths through the fog and the mist that make up the barren fields. At the tall, darkened towers that stretch into the blackened sky, they loom with arching shadows. In the far distance, I can spy a dog with three heads pacing as it guards the entrance to the city.

I shrug my shoulders. Widen my stance. Anchor my feet so deeply into the ground that nothing can move me, neither flood nor fire nor frost nor hail. I take a step forward. And then a second. Until I'm flying down the track, backpack swinging behind me as I sprint through the barren fields.

(7)

BEFORE: HELEN

There is a Plum blossom that is growing along the cracks of my bedroom walls. I've been watching the branches unfurl for a while now, sat in my room for hours as ever so slowly the flower buds begin to bloom.

I've been thinking about destiny lately. Fate. What it means, exactly, when your name is switched out for something else. The cracks in my walls have grown wider, and flowers are covering the room in spots as they steadily start to pour in. Plum blossoms and roses. Violets. Daisies, daffodils, and narcissus cluster along my walls and smother my ceiling until I am nearly choking on their sweetened scent.

When I was little, my mom told me that there was something special about the blood in my veins. That I am the product of survivors. Toughness. The world is going up in flames, and Mother told me that I was born to blaze through it, to sear a path straight through hell and lead the rest of humanity to salvation.

She named me Helen because she thought it fitting that her child be named after the thing that she would one day vanquish.

And yet, my blood does not burn when it drips from my veins. I should know. I've examined it under microscopes, peeled open the valves that line the inside of my heart until I bled myself dry. Observed the fluid that flows between my atrium and aorta, watched as it swirled from blue into red at the contact with oxygen, and wondered what exactly it was that my mother thought made me so special.

"The time is coming when you will soon fulfill your destiny." The phrase drills itself into the corners of my skull as it whispers from the throats of men and creeping roses. "A tournament is coming, a chance to prove your worth." Mother watches, and the dog whines, and I move my bed farther away from the window because a part of me fears that the blossoms will grow down my throat in the middle of the night.

I sign up for the tournament. I don't know quite why, exactly. Just that I was born to burn like the dying stars that poets make wishes on, and a part of me fears that there is nothing else inside of me but this constant ache for perfection. I have been bestowed with the love of a god, and a part of me fears failing before his eyes.

When I enter the tournament, I go in with my bare hands. Watch grown men practice with their knives and their guns and see them stare back at this little girl who floats among their midst.

"Do you want a shield?" My first opponent offers. He stands across from me at the edge of a ring of sand while all around us, seats filled with cheering faces tower to the very heavens. I dig my feet down deeper into the dust. Pretend that it is someone else's name they call out when they present me in front of the ring. Someone better. Stronger. The people in the stands call for blood and guts and brimstone, scream at this man who hesitates before me with his axe shaking in his grip. I smile softly at him. Spread my hands out wide and beckon him closer with a twist of my fingers.

Inside the pockets of my jacket, seeds shiver and shake as they jump inside their lining. I force them to be still. Force myself to still. Stand there in the arena that screams with the voices of millions and tell the man,

"Everything will be alright." Stare deep into his eyes and widen my stance and promise, "You couldn't hurt me if you tried."

He swings his blade and slams it down in an arc towards my ribs. I grab the blade with my bare hands and *tug*. Nerves sear and fingers spasm, but I hold on tighter and *grip* the blade until blood runs down the sides of my palms. Startled, the man releases his grip. The pair of us stare at where the sword now lies in the sand, fingers still choking the blade from where my severed hand flops. I look at the end of my wrist, which now ends in a fleshy nub. Absentmindedly, I shrug my shoulders.

"Huh. That wasn't very handy now, was it?" Silence resounds through the arena.

Hesitantly, the man reaches once more for his axe. I kick it with my heel and send it skittering through the dust. It lands out of bounds with a dull thump. I hold my bloodied wrist up and look at it in the sunlight. "Oh well." I sigh airily. Recite silently the process for bone growth as I begin to walk towards the stunned figure. *Proliferation. Matrix Maturation. Mineralization.*

There's a sort of art, I think, that can be found in the light that bounces off pearly polished bone. In seeing the shadows threaded together to create twisting outlines of skeletal movement. Of weaving membrane and tissue and tucking them round and around in layers like a thick woolen blanket. There is a sort of art, I have come to find, that can be found in the science of anatomy. In taking the musty notes of rambling professors and using them to build a man.

The arena is silent as slowly, ever so slowly, I flex the tendons on my still-forming fingers. The stadium is quiet as steadily, ever so steadily, I begin to place one foot in front of the other.

Blessed Ones. Star Chasers. Fools. There are many names for those who choose to follow the paths of the arcane instead of science. Magic isn't inherent in the race of man, after all. It's a gift given from the Old Gods, granted in exchange for some object of equal proportion. Most people, if they have a lick of sense, rely on weapons or other forms of technology instead to help them fight. To see the use of enchantment in person is rare, an incoming trainwreck that you can't bear to look away from. It is a shooting star that is slowly going up in flames, snatching wishes on the edges of its points as it burns from the inside out. There's a sense of awe that can be found in watching those people who shine like stars. A sense of awe and yet also terror—nobody in their right mind would ever choose to make such a pact. For someone to sacrifice so much that not even Death seems to touch them – unease grows, and whispers begin to rise among the stands.

I watch as the man in front of me draws his shield and begins to back away. Draws his crossbow and fires it in three sharp blasts.

One.

Two.

Three.

I pull the arrows out, one from my brain, another from my heart, and a third from my spleen.

Smile softly as I repair the holes, keep on walking at that same even pace as my head flits through thousands upon thousands of ancient, yellowed texts.

The scary thing isn't that I fall to the ground, but that I get back up each time. The scary thing isn't that I dodge, but that I keep walking. In the end, it's not how cruel I am, how fast I run, or how strongly I strike. Throughout all the carnage, the thing that keeps the crowd frozen is the fact that I keep walking.

I walk faster.

I pick up my speed. Start moving quicker. Blood sticks to the sides of my skin as it dries under the rotting sun, and the man drops his shield with a curse and starts running, until the pair of us spin in circles around the roiling sand.

I walk faster.

The man draws out a gun. Fires off three quick shots.

One.

Two.

Three.

An eye. A lung. A knee. I keep moving forward, feel the bullets rattle against my bones until they fly into the palms of my hands. Shuffle forwards at that same unrelenting pace, rebuild retinas and mend branching bronchioles as gradually, ever so gradually, my leg straightens with a snap.

I walk faster.

He drops to his knees then. Stares at the crowd with tears in his eyes and begs them for salvation. Cries out to the dozens of planets that career in dizzying circles above our heads at night. He screams for Jupiter. Mars. Neptune. Everyone, Someone, Anyone. He drops to his knees and writhes in the dust, and he looks to the sky with bloodred eyes and in a choking voice begs for the divinities to come to save him. No one does.

No one can.

I move faster until I'm running, feet flying as I chase him up and down the track, slamming my feet down off the ground so hard that dust flies up at my footsteps. Come to a stop when I catch him.

Stare at him then. Watch how his chest rises, how he sobs and vomits as he writhes beneath me. Hear him mutter as he spits blood out of the corners of his mouth and realize that even now, he is still praying for someone to come save him.

"Everything will be alright," I tell him softly, as subtly, ever so subtly, a sound of chanting begins to rise from the thousands watching who sit in spirals around the ring. They are crying for his blood. "Do not be afraid. Tonight, you will walk home a living man."

"Finish him. Finish the weak one." I raise my eyes to the high heavens, gaze up at the sun and the clouds and the burning fury of a thousand shrieking voices. Mother sits in silence on the sidelines. I can't read the expression that flickers across her face when she looks at me.

I hold out a hand and lift the man to his feet. His palm dwarfs my own. I tilt my head and crane my neck to look at him. He stares down at the ground in shame, his shoulders hunching as he tries to cover his face. There is no honor in the weak. He rips his hand from my grip as if my touch might burn him, and races away towards the tunnels that lead back down the loser's gate. The resulting jeers aimed at his back would make the very angels weep.

I flex my arms. Roll my shoulders. Turn my gaze towards the opposite tunnel, and step into the comfort of its darkness. Let out a sigh and sink to the floor as my legs shake. Flowers are growing somewhere inside my throat. Slowly—*ever so slowly*-- they've started to bloom. I can feel roses, their thorns ripping open my insides as I try to breathe. Choke on the overwhelming stench of rotting narcissus. Pinch my nose and blink tears out of my eyes as desperately I root through my pockets and reach for the clumps of seeds that won't stop jumping. I pull them out and realize that they've grown.

Lying there, crumpled in my hands, rests a pair of vibrant rosebuds.

THE SWEETEST SONGBIRD

Once upon a time, in a kingdom where the wind crooned lullabies and islands swayed to the song of the sea, there lived a boy so skilled in singing that he could make the very trees pick up their roots and dance. Music was stitched into his soul, you must understand, and when he strummed his lyre or opened his mouth even the stars came down from the heavens to listen.

Many desired him for his music, and yet only one ever managed to capture his heart. Eurydice, a girl whose smile was bright enough to outshine the sun. The pair met each other one day along the banks of a silver river, and it is said that at the moment they held each other's hands, the sky sighed and blushed a rosy pink.

They were happy, and with them the world. Until one day, when walking through a field of blooming roses, Eurydice stepped on a serpent slinking through the thicket. She collapsed without a sound, and in that moment, the very world turned silent.

When Orpheus found out what had happened to his beloved, he did not grieve as other mortals do. Instead, he sang. He sang so sweetly that the birds in the sky forgot to fly and the moon wept and splintered into a million pieces. He sang until snakes slithered out of their skins and curious, ambivalent gods poked their heads out of the clouds and craned their necks to look at the weeping man.

The people whispered to each other, "I don't know what Orpheus could be thinking, refusing to mourn his bride in such a way. She's gone to the land of the dead. No one ever comes back from that; it's simply impossible."

And yet Orpheus refused to listen to their mutterings. He was the man who shattered the moon, who taught the trees to dance, and caused snakes to slither out of their skins. Things that were impossible for others were not even a concern to a man such as him. So he gathered up his golden lyre, kissed the ring that glittered on the limp hand of his lover, and began to walk.

The Underworld was no home for the living. Wraiths wailed and rivers whispered secrets in an effort to drown their swimmers. But Orpheus strummed his lyre, and at his sound the creatures paused. He sang songs of love and loss, of empty suns and memories echoing through lonely halls. Orpheus sang, and then the monsters began to weep.

Orpheus sang until his voice went hoarse, until his fingers bled from how often he strummed his lyre. When he could no longer lift his fingers to play his instrument, he stamped his feet to make a rhythm. When he could no longer sing without his throat bleeding, he whispered until the echoes of his rasps formed a chant. Eventually, word of this strange musician began to circulate through the Underworld, until it reached the king and queen of the darkened realm. His music was so strong that even Thanatos, a god unmoved by prayer or sacrifice, and Proserpine, the maiden caught between life and death, felt the pull of his music.

When Orpheus finished singing, there was a silence thicker than sorrow.

Proserpine's voice was as soft as fallen snow when she finally spoke.

"You may bring her back." She declared. But only if you look forward and never turn your head, not until you feel the sunshine of the world above."

Orpheus bowed, his heart beating like a drum against his ribcage. He turned around and slowly, ever so slowly, began the long, torturous journey back to the land of the living.

"...Orpheus?" The voice was small and timid behind him. "Orpheus, where are we going?"

Something was horribly wrong.

"...Why aren't you talking to me?" Orpheus flinched as Eurydice began to panic, chest squeezing tight as she struggled to breathe. "I missed you. You missed me, too, didn't you?"

"Please just look at me." Perhaps it was pathetic, but Eurydice knew that if only she could look Orpheus in the eyes, everything would be alright. She glanced down at her hand and realized with horror that she could see pearly bones peeking out of the gaps of her flesh. She was dead. And yet Orpheus, warm and soft and still breathing Orpheus, was alive.

Dead things were supposed to be gone forever. That was the law of nature, the one rule set in place before all others. What price must it have cost Orpheus then, what cost must her lover have given, to complete such an impossible task? Horrified, Eurydice felt her eyes begin to burn. Her throat tightened. Desperately, she forced herself to stiffen, trying to fight back the inevitable.

The tears fell.

Eurydice clenched her jaw and pressed her eyes shut. After a few steps, she stumbled into something warm and safe. That something held her close and drew her into a hug. A roughened hand carefully swept a tear off her cheek. When Eurydice opened her eyes, a rueful smile met her gaze.

Orpheus had looked back.

"You turned around." She stated, stunned.

"Of course I did." Orpheus agreed. "I heard you crying."

They sank to the ground holding each other, Orpheus cradling Eurydice in his arms, Eurydice with her hands around his neck. At that moment, the light from the entrance to the land of the living struck, and Eurydice vanished into a puff of smoke.

Orpheus crumpled, lyre tumbling from his hands. He did not wail, nor did he scream. He only sat silently at the entrance to the underworld, looking in disbelief at his hands, which had held the one he loved for a second.

Legends say that he wandered for ages after, singing songs too sad to be repeated in mere words. Birds fell quiet when he passed. Stones softened and began to weep. Trees bent low and bowed their heads in mourning.

Some say that the gods felt pity and killed him quickly before he suffered too long. That they let him reunite with his beloved up in the heavens among the glittering constellations, and there the pair sing songs of moonshine and starlight.

Others say he wanders still between the worlds, desperately searching for a song strong enough to give him a second chance.

Regardless of which version you believe, one thing is always agreed:

Whenever you hear music that makes your heart ache for something that you cannot name,

Orpheus has walked nearby.

(8)

AFTER: NATALYA

A girl is standing on the edges of the river Styx. I watch as she idly brushes a hand over a skirt made of beetle wings. She's waiting for someone; I realize with a start. The pearls on her fingers shimmer as she checks an old pocket watch. Her braided hair shines under the silvery moonlight.

She's beautiful. Beautiful in a way that I can't quite describe, after all, I've never been the best at writing. But I understand now how Orpheus could make the stones weep. I understand now why

Death was moved when he saw her face. It makes sense, how at her birth her very name came to mean desire.

She looks up. Watches me with eyes as soft as moonbeams and lips as sweet as starshine. I look at this woman before me, clothed in silver and softness and delicate butterfly wings. Gently, she holds out her hand and beckons me forward.

"Orpheus never made it this far, you know." She murmurs. In a world made up of dead things, roses still bloom as they wrap around her throat. The pale petals glow in the darkness. "Then again, I suppose everyone hurries towards death in their own unique way. Come with me, we have a long way to go." She seems tired as she walks. Thorns tear at her skin, and pearls weigh down her brow, and there is a sort of worn-down fury that echoes from her footsteps.

"I am sorry that he failed you," I call out. In front of me, the woman stills. Shakily, she lets out a breath.

"You seem to be mistaken; I am not Eurydice." She declares then. She spins around to look me in the eyes. There is a sort of grace to her anger. "But even so, I feel that I must tell you that

Orpheus did not fail, at least in the way you are thinking. You see, he'll always turn around, and she'll always be there, and just because he turned doesn't make it any less of an act of love; it just wasn't enough to save them either. Love wasn't enough to save them on its own."

Did you ever wonder why that legend is repeated so many times, why we hear it echoed through our storybooks even when we already know the last chapter? Because the urge to believe in a version where he achieves a happy ending is as internally human as a love that dooms itself every time. Orpheus failed in that he lost Eurydice." The woman states, with a furrow to her brow and tears in her eyes. "But if we keep telling his story, maybe one day Orpheus *won't.*"

"…I don't understand. What are you talking about?" Wryly, the woman shakes her head.

"In the end, the tale of Orpheus isn't really about a singular person." She explains. "It's about everyone who tried to be Orpheus, all those people who tried to go against a fate that they couldn't change and failed, and all those others who saw them fail and were inspired to get back up and think *maybe I will be the one who can make things different,* and so they go and try again. Orpheus' failure isn't the meaning found behind his story. The meaning is that one day, someone following in his footsteps might *succeed*." She frowns at my blank expression. "I thought you would have known this." She adds, confused. "After all, isn't the story of Orpheus the whole reason that you are even here in the first place?"

I start to reply, then stop, distracted as I take in the world that presses in on either side of the path. Far off in the distance, pairs of shadows race, their hands endlessly stretched to reach the other as they run up and down a sea of unending plains. They chase over hill and dale, dart through caves and curve around boulders, and hike up their robes as they wade through the streams that flow out from the river Styx. Left behind in the dust trail dozens upon dozens of glittering footprints, their shapes embedded in the glowing sands. Each time one draws close enough to catch the other, the person who is grabbed turns and slowly lifts their eyes. Hands wrench onto silken fabric with desperation and pull the other to a stop. And then finally, inevitably, worn-down fingers release their grip. And the race begins again.

"Who are those shadows?" I ask cautiously. The woman looks at where I point in pity.

"Those are the ones who failed. All the dozens of Orpheus's who lost their Eurydices." I'm silent, as I look at the sea of endless shadows. There are so many of them.

"Sometimes, you are a hero." The woman's voice is steady as she speaks. Her eyes are fixed on the flickering specters that race endlessly into the darkness. "You come in with a gun or a blade, and you force even Death himself to bend before you. Sometimes, you are the stuff of fairytales. Other times, you work a nine-to-five or stay at home and watch the children. How many times, if you could guess, do you think that you give up before your adventure even starts? How many times do you think that you listen to the failures of your predecessors, and choose to become a background character in your own story?"

"I'm not sure."

"Zero. In zero worlds are you a nobody. Regardless of whether you succeed or fail, there has never been an instance where you have not tried. You never go down without a fight. Never."

"This story has been told over millions of times," The woman murmurs, "in the pages of storybooks and frames of animation. It has been told from blaring radios, from computers, to typewriters, to that crevice in our minds where we keep thoughts hidden that will never touch a page. This story has been told over the course of millennia," The woman murmurs, "and it will be told once more here today."

Maybe it's foolish to believe that even though so many others have failed, I will be the one to succeed. That I am an exception, an anomaly to all the copies of this legend that have gone before me. And yet, if there is even the slightest chance that I can have my daughter back, I will take it. No matter how dangerous or difficult it may be. I *need* to take it. I tear my gaze away from the dead and keep walking. Follow my guide as she fades into the silvery tendrils of the creeping mist.

"Hey, mortal." The woman calls out, words tossed over her shoulder as she presses on. "I was wondering. The person you're searching for, what were they like?"

"She was a girl," I reply. "An awfully smart girl. So much better than I ever was. She enjoyed flowers, gardens, and old, yellow books. Her name was Helen."

A hint of wistfulness enters her tone. "I had a sister once, who bore that name."

"What was she like?" The Guide hums as she tries to think of an answer.

"I wouldn't know." She answers at last. "My mother didn't like us being together. Helen was always placed upon a pedestal, you know? A child of the gods. She was worth more than the presence of mere mortals. I used to hold her." Her voice is hushed, looking over her shoulders as she peers into the barren wasteland. "Late at night when no one else was awake. I used to sneak into her room at night and hold her, drag her into the royal gardens, and play among the dancing shadows. She was small. And lonely. They married her off when she was thirteen. She had a child by fourteen. Ran away with some fairytale prince one day and, well. I'm sure you know the rest. Sometimes I used to think that I'd see her hovering outside of my daughter's nursery at night, did you know that? They had the same fair hair and the same dark eyes. They were both taken from me at thirteen."

"My daughter died a couple of months after her fourteenth birthday," I say. Something is shining in the corners of the woman's eyes. I watch as the thorns burrow deeper into her flesh.

"How fortunate that you got to have an extra year with her." She whispers, smiling with tearstained cheeks.

"Who are you?" She looks at me with confusion. "I mean, I don't mean to pry, but there has to be a reason why you're my guide specifically. After all, wouldn't it make more sense for one of the ghosts down there to be my guide?"

"You wouldn't want those fools to guide you." Her words are sharp. Bitter. "All they do is cry and moan and beg. Simply speaking of their love instead of acting on it. They don't know how to succeed like we can. They don't know how to love like we can. Aren't you tired of begging, Natalya?" Her tone is careful. Pointed. Dark. She looks me in the eyes and bares her teeth and laughs. "Begging for scraps while all the others point and laugh? Don't you want to *fight* to get your daughter back?"

"My name is Clytemnestra." The woman murmurs. Looks me in the eyes as roses wind tighter around her ribs. "I am the shrieking fury of those who scorned the false gods. I am the vengeance that was promised to the house of Atreus. I am a woman who killed on behalf of my daughter, and thus was slaughtered by my son." She holds a shaking hand out, and thorns dig into the sides of her skin as blood drips from her fingertips. "I am known as the tragedy of the Greeks. Here, I will be your guide."

(9)

BEFORE: HELEN

Most people, when they watch me in the stands, assume that I don't get angry. Perhaps I don't, or at least not in the way that they envision it, all big and bright and burning.

I stand amidst the dust and stare at my next opponent. I'm tired. And sweaty. Their face swims under the hazy sky, and I wonder when all my challengers' faces started to blur together. The people scream under the blazing summer sun.

The opponent in front of me is angry. Angry in the proper way, all loud and furious with a voice made of thunder and explosions dripping from his roars as he pins me to the ground.

"They claim you are an angel." He mocks, laughing as he shoves me into the sand. The audience laughs with him. For all that they cheer me on when I win, they still love to laugh when they see me thrown around. As if there is something satisfying in watching a child be beaten for their entertainment.

The man grips me tighter, slams my face so hard that I see stars, and then pulls me up by my neck. My vision goes hazy as his grip tightens. "Death's angel, his precious, his sweet little plaything. I guess it makes sense that you keep chasing after him like an addict." I flail in his grasp, wriggle and writhe as my blood stains the edges of the ring. "Because you see this? This is the only love you'll ever get here among the living. Because the world isn't made for soft little things, and folks like you are better off dead."

He's wrong, of course. He's so, *so* wrong, maybe not about the world, and maybe not about my softness. But he is wrong about me not being loved. Thanatos cradles me like I'm his most precious treasure, and my mother watches me as if I'm her most valuable possession. They both hold me like I'm something worth clinging onto. Something worth more to them than anything else in the entire world.

My mother may be a bad person. And yet I do not doubt that she loves me, cupping me between palms that both protect and strangle in equal measure. And yet treasures cannot protect themselves. Treasures cannot hold value outside of the public eye. And the ancient parable still rings true that no matter how much of a treasure you are, there will be others out there who still consider you trash.

He snaps my head back and forth, and suddenly I realize that maybe this is what it means to be truly angry. To have your head clouded by hate and your heart by weariness.

It's bigger than mere destruction. Bigger than just bright and boastful and burning. My anger is hazy, all head swimming in the summer sun and bloodstained knees and metallic gasoline and disgust as I look at nearby bodies all lying haphazardly in a heap.

My anger is a match, not a flame, but a wick, all calm and poised and waiting to ignite. My clothes are wet as they stick to my sweaty skin, weighed down by something fizzing that sparks up sharp and impatient. The masses all jeer or yell or *laugh*, wild and cruel. They add more and more hatred to the pyre because maybe anger licks at them too, and they'd rather toss it onto someone else than ignite.

"I'm tired," I whisper lowly, glaring at my opponent out of the corners of my eyes. My skin is speckled with so many scars that they almost resemble beauty marks. My voice rasps out hoarse from where he crushes my windpipe.

"You're tired? Is the baby tired?" He laughs then, brays like a hyena as he slams me once more into the earth. I pick myself up with an almost deadly calm. Carefully, I stand up. Walk towards him, ever so slowly.

I feel a shudder, as tissue over tissue ripples across my bare bones to pave the way for newborn flesh. My body is a wasteland, all mismatched, broken parts stitched together with scarlet thread and pure grit because I am tired of being seen as trash. Of being a failure. Weak. Unlovable. My body is made from scraps of abandoned junk burning, forming smog and debris. Pollution that runs rampant, creating the ash in the wind, creating the carbon that chokes the planet, creating the very air we breathe.

"…The earth cries out as we make her bleed for us. Oceans of blood and rivers of pus, infected and decaying while the people do nothing."

She screams, and the people do nothing.

"You mock me," I call out, hands outstretched as I face him with a smile. "You mock me, don't you. You mock me and my god. Mock me and the souls that he protects, the ones under his domain." I smile then, all calm and jagged and just barely toxic. Let my eyes frost over. Raise my hands to the sky and then let them hang. My skin grows sticky under the burning summer sun.

"You people disgust me." I let my words hang, like a condemnation. An execution. Smile even wider and giggle, force my fury down with a teetering cackle. Slowly, ever so, I begin to sway. "What with your games and your arenas. Have you forgotten that we all die in the end?"

The sand beneath my feet is crying, but I ignore it. Ignore it like the rapid beating of my heart, like the twitching in my veins. Ignore it like how my lungs can sense that the very air is corrupted from the stink of the dead. No matter how desperately I try, I cannot filter out the stench. I let the earth rust over and bleed, decay, and rot as the soil weeps for all the bodies thrown into the streets until finally I can't take it anymore and give in to the heat.

"I ought to strike you down with lightning." I hiss, and the hair on the back of my neck prickles as I guide electrons to whirl and crash together. Up above my head, the clouds begin to crackle. Protons zing through the air until the very sky begins to sizzle in the heat. "Strike you down with the very power of the god you hold as higher than Death." Currents begin to swirl up, higher and higher, as the clouds above us darken. "Would you like that?" I ask, electricity sizzling as it rattles through my bones. "Do you want that?" I wonder, as with a flick of my fingers, light pours down from the heavens.

"I'm not going to do that," I whisper. Cradle the lightning between my palms and guide it towards the sand. The laughing has stopped. Silence rings out around the ring. Softly, ever so softly, rain begins to fall. "I'm not going to do that, because violence will never fix violence. There is a certain strength in being gentle. In looking at all the ugliness of the world and choosing to be kind instead."

"Weak." My opponent spits. His shoulders are shaking from a mixture of rage and shame. "You are weak, child, for not killing me where I stand. I warned you already, didn't I? The world is not made for sweetness, and soft little girls are better off dead." He draws his gun then. Aims it at my head and turns the safety off. "I will make sure you never make such a similar mistake again."

He shoots me in the temple. Shoots me as he lies there sobbing. I pull the shrapnel out with sticky hands. It drops to the ground with a sigh. Just one more drop to stain the sand.

I look at the corpses, all piled up in a heap in the corner. The earth cries from where it holds them. I'm tired. I'm so tired. The piles keep growing and the stands keep cheering, and it doesn't matter how many carcasses I bury, does it? Because the pile will continue to rise. I look down at the man and, holding out a hand, help lift him to his feet. He stills at my touch, at the lack of pain when I grip his palm.

"You're wrong," I tell him quietly. "And it's ok if you don't realize that yet. But you're wrong, and I'm not going to stop until I can prove that to you." I raise my eyes to the stands.

"To all of you."

(10)

AFTER: NATALYA

It's quiet as I walk through the underworld. Planets hum like buzzing bees, and shadows whisper as they trail kisses through my hair. Slowly, ever so, I begin to leave the sands of crushed stars. I follow my guide deeper into the darkened desert. Stare up at the walls of the city of the dead in silence as we march through the creeping gloom.

I take out a lighter and flick it until a flame flares up. Chase after my guide and watch as she marches ahead with long loping strides. She seems to float when she walks, almost like her footsteps are so light that they never touch the ground.

There's another river that slinks along with liquid as thick as bloodied ink. A sense of foreboding creeps up and down my spine. I listen as the river screams, waves slapping at the shore with enough force to split open skin. A faint hissing rises from where steam bubbles up.

"I didn't know that the underworld had so many rivers," I call out lightly. Stretch my shoulders and try to shove down the dread bubbling up in my chest. This beach is different than that of the one by the Styx. There are no stars here, or hopes, or dead man's wishes. I look at the beach and all I see is darkness. Like a void, waiting to swallow me up. I look out at the shrieking, blood-tinged waves. There is something deep inside me, something visceral and *human,* that is begging me not to step foot into that river.

"Oh, there aren't so many," Clytemnestra assures absentmindedly. The petals strangling her throat grow pink in the moonshine. "Only five, after all. And I hardly doubt you'll see all of them on your journey. Each man faces death in their own way and all of that. Still, it's interesting that you summoned this one."

"Which one is this?" I ask nervously. I try to ignore how few stars there are in the eternally night sky. Try to ignore the suspicious lumps hidden in the sand. Try to ignore how I can hear the waves screaming my name.

"The river of misery, the waters of wrath, the gateway to Tartarus." Clytemnestra grins. Holds her hands out wide and twirls, petals and pearls shining as she spins dramatically in front of the shrieking beach. "Mortals call it the spring that nurtures all violence."

"Why are we here, Clytemnestra?" I ask in the resulting silence. "I mean, if the underworld shifts and changes for each new soul who enters, why are we already in Hell?"

"Because this is where I belong and where one day you will be." Clytemnestra answers. She smiles, but it's more of a grimace. She bares her teeth and grins at the river. Not because she's won, but because she has already accepted her defeat.

"I don't know much about you or your world or your gods besides what I need to find my daughter," I argue, panic rising. Clytemnestra is silent. "But I do know that I don't deserve to end up in that water. I swear that I can be a good person, I promise I'm a good person. But even if I'm not, we're not here for me. We're here for my daughter.

And maybe I don't know much about how things work down here in the land of the dead. But I know that my daughter is the farthest thing from evil. She shouldn't be here. She should be up in paradise, somewhere safe and soft and surrounded by the angels."

"Oh, Natalya," Clytemnestra sighs, all pity and compassion and pale shining starlight. "Maybe you won't end up here in the Greek underworld. Maybe your home of the dead is something much different than mine. But can't you see?" She holds out her palms, then holds them out for me to see, and I watch how pearls weigh down thin fingers. "We have the same type of blood on our hands."

I pause and sigh. Stare into the darkness of the shrieking waves and let my shoulders slump. Beside me, Clytemnestra has stopped spinning. I look at her, and it feels like looking into a mirror, the edges of her mottled skin all cracked and distorted with thinly covered hatred. I suppose it makes sense how she normally haunts the shores here of the river Acheron.

Because every time she smiles, I can see the thin serrated points of enamel from a constant gnashing of teeth. Every time she speaks, I can hear the same slight rasp that echoes from a person's words because of a life of constant screaming. Every time I gaze into her eyes, I can see the poorly covered bags from nights when she grieved far too deeply to fall asleep.

What must it be like, I wonder as I look at my guide, to scrape away at your identity until all that people remember of you is your anger?

"Why are you looking at me like that?" Clytemnestra hisses. Her eyes narrow and her fists clench. I look at her in silence. "Stop, stop looking at me like that. Why do you act as if you pity me? I deserve this, I want this, I dug the coffin of my damnation with my own bare hands. I'm old," My guide emphasizes then. There is something ancient about her anger. Something mythic about her madness.

"Old enough to relish in the consequences of my own actions." She grips the roses wound around her neck and tugs on them until the thorns begin to cut off her circulation.

She looks small then as she stands there, all flushed and panting and defiant. She looks so small, as she stands there on the shore. And I don't pity her. Because I respect her far too much to offer something so condescending. I don't feel bad for her. Because I understand that it was her own choice to root herself on the bank of the Acheron. I don't feel pity, but I feel empathy. God, do I feel empathy.

"Sometimes I wish that I knew how to be kind." The words are quiet as they drift through the air. Clytemnestra looks up, tilts her head, and stares at me in confusion. Blood trails down her skin to drip into leftover footprints.

"Whatever do you mean?" She wonders. I sigh and look down at the mangled mess of my fingernails.

"I think I had this philosophy when I was younger that kindness is the difference between someone good and someone great," I explain.

"Sometimes I wish that I knew how to be kind." The words are quiet as they drift through the air. Clytemnestra looks up, tilts her head, and stares at me in confusion. Blood trails down her skin to drip into leftover footprints.

"Whatever do you mean?" She wonders. I sigh and look down at the mangled mess of my fingernails.

"I think I had this philosophy when I was younger that kindness is the difference between someone who is good and someone who is great," I explain. "That is the line that divides the strong from the weak. Because the weak do not have the option of mercy. If they refuse to harm, then they will, in turn, be harmed themselves. I used to teach that to my children when they were little, and I would repeat it over and over until the idea was drilled into their skulls.

I don't think I ever really had to do that with Helen, you know. She had always known, from a young age, how to be kind to others. Almost like it was instinctual or something." I smile bitterly then. Look out over the waves and force myself to take all the misery in. All the rage. All the hate.

"And I know that it's always the parents that raise their children, but I always thought that being around my kids made me want to be a better person. Sometimes," I confess voice lowered. "Sometimes when I look at my daughter, I wonder if I could have ever been as kind as she was when I was her age. I wonder if I could have been as good. I know I couldn't."

Clytemnestra is silent. Her shoulders slump, and I watch as her anger fades away.

"Did you know that I had a child, once?" She asks quietly. "Before my son and my daughter. I had a husband, too, before the one everybody knows of."

"I don't know your story, Clytemnestra," I explain patiently. "I only researched the landmarks that I knew were universal for most people who travel through the underworld. I don't know your husband, or the reason you're choked by roses, or what it means to remain stranded by the Acheron." My guide goes pale, and I press on.

"Clytemnestra," I emphasize, "I don't know your sins. So, if you want me to know, you're going to have to tell me ."

Clytemnestra pauses. And thinks. I can see her debating whether or not to tell me. To have the freedom of anonymity, or the honesty of confession. It must have been a long time since she had someone to talk to.

"Have you ever been in love, Natalya?" She asks at last. "I don't mean any of that silly Orpheus and Eurydice, let's get married and ride off into the sunset kind of love. I mean, have you ever felt *real* love?"

"I loved my sister, even though I was never really allowed to see her. Loved her not because she was some big mythical beauty blessed by the gods, but because she was small. Because she was soft. Her favorite animals were swans, and she loved to sneak out and see the city at night. She had an old map hung up in her room with all these little pins embedded in it, and she used to tell me that one day she would visit every single pin so that

114

she could see the world in its entirety. She used to beg me to go with her, said that she didn't give a damn if she sprouted wings and flew away so long as I was there to fly with her. I loved Helen because she loved me. Because we were a pair, through thick and thin. Hot and cold and small and tall, she was always dreaming of lands in the clouds, and I was there to bring her back down."

"I loved my first husband because he was grounded. Grounded like the earth, steady and solid, and when he told me that he would get me my happy ending, I knew without a doubt that he would make it happen. My father used to test him sometimes. Told him that he couldn't possibly think of marrying me until he had a ring made with pearls from the darkest depths of the deepest point of the ocean."

Clytemnestra smiles then. Fidgets with the pearls upon pearls that lie in golden rings upon her fingers.

"My Father said this to discourage him. Thought the man was silly and unsuitable and unworthy of marrying a woman of my standing. But that man went out with nothing but a net and a rowboat, and he gave me *ten* pearls, enough for a ring on each finger. He told me when he gave them to me, *I promised you a happy ending, didn't I? And I always keep my promises.*"

"We had a son. Asterios. And he was *beautiful*, all laughing smiles and dancing eyes. He liked it when I held him in my arms and when his daddy told him stories. He liked grabbing at the pearls I had on my hands and splashing around in waves at the beach. I called him Asterios, after the stars in the night sky. I called him Asterios because I wanted my child to grow up with his own little map taped up on the wall, with his own dreams and wishes that his dad and I could help him fulfill. I named him Asterios because I wanted him to fix his sights eternally on the stars. I wanted him to be able to *fly.*"

"Later, a man would come by the name of Agamemnon. He would come as an escort to his brother, who was trying to win my sister's hand, and I would beg my husband not to leave me alone with him. I would tell my husband that I didn't like the look that Agamemnon had in his eye whenever he watched me. That I didn't like the comments he would make whenever I passed by."

"My husband was strong, and my husband was great. After all, he was the only man I ever knew who could go and gather pearls from the darkest depths of the sea. My husband was powerful. But he was not the king of a strong nation. And Agamemnon was."

"It was late at night, when his soldiers busted through the door of my rooms and slaughtered my husband in his sleep. They took my baby, and they threw him out the window. Years later, I would still see the stain from where my son's head had bashed against the rocks."

"Agamemnon had paid my father a sum of 40 million denarii to slaughter my husband and take me as his bride. Agamemnon had met with my father one night, and they sat down to discuss the worth found in the lives of my husband and infant. I was married a week later."

"Sometimes, I wish that I wasn't someone men considered beautiful. I wish I was hideous, as ugly as a gorgon and with a glare just as paralyzing. I wish I was something people feared, instead of craved. Because maybe if I was ugly, my husband would still be alive today. Maybe if I had been born ugly, I could have kept my son."

"Slowly, ever so slowly, I began to let myself grow cruel. I allowed myself to sprout thorns, locked my heart away behind my ribs, and ground my teeth while I watched my new husband sleep."

"I had another child this time with Agamemnon. A baby girl. I picked her name with care and held her close as I rocked her to sleep each night. *Iphigenia,* I called her. *Strong born."*

"She had bright shiny eyes and soft little curls, and she used to love to play in the gardens, used to sing like a little bird and babble at the nearby brooks. She used to climb up high in trees whenever she played hide and seek with her siblings, and sometimes it would be nearly impossible to find her, until you heard her little voice giggling up there with all the chirping sparrows. *My little songbird,* I'd call her. *My sweet little songbird."*

"She screamed just like a songbird when her father cut her open with a knife. She screamed and wailed with tears in her eyes as he tied her to an altar and split her open like a sacrificial pig."

"The gods will not let us continue to Troy without a sacrifice." He had told my child, voice calm and steady as she tried to scream and beg. He'd taken off her gag then, and gently hugged her to his chest. She wouldn't stop screaming, Natalya. She wouldn't stop crying, and all she

did was beg over and over for her daddy to stop. She said that she was scared. That he was hurting her. That she didn't understand what was going on, that she was frightened and confused, and *please Daddy don't hurt me, I thought I was your baby.*"

Clytemnestra pauses. Shudders. I watch as the roses wind tighter around her throat, watch as ever so slowly the thorns begin to tear and choke.

"I used to wish that I had acted sooner." She confesses. "People talk about how swift my anger was, but I always wished that I had acted sooner. Because maybe if I had been quicker, if I had chosen to fight back and murdered him earlier, I could have at least still had my daughter."

"I killed my husband when he came back from the war. Killed him with an old, rusted axe and hacked and hacked until he was chopped into tiny pieces. I made sure to tell him as he died, that he screamed like a little girl. That he screamed like *our* little girl."

"Natalya," Clytemnestra murmured then, with a far-off look in her eyes. "Natalya, I am not a good person. I am a creature filled with rage, hate, and violence. But I am also a mother, and being a mother means doing anything to protect your children. Perhaps you are right in saying that only the truly strong can be kind. But I will allow myself to be weak so that my children can grow up strong. I will let myself sin so that my children have a chance at salvation."

I stare at her in silence. Take in the bruises, the scars, the delicate beauty shuddering over barely contained anger. I stare at Clytemnestra, and then I simply nod. I do not pity her. Nor do I particularly like her. But I understand. Because, like any parent, I would damn my soul for the sake of keeping my children safe.

"Are we going to go through Tartarus?" I ask quietly. My guide shakes her head.

"There is no need." She replies simply. Calm and still once more, as if her face was scraped from fresh porcelain. "Your daughter is not in Tartarus. We'll take the bridge instead."

I turn to look at the river again and notice suddenly how a bridge has materialized in the mist. I board it with shaking steps. Wood creaks under my footsteps, and I clutch at the railing as the planks beneath me bend and sway. I look down and stop. Stare.

There are people drowning in that river.

Drowning in rage, hate, and violence. Waves split open skin, and screams bubble up from where people throw themselves farther from the shore, until they lose themselves inside the river Acheron. The people keep swimming until they lose themselves completely in their wrath.

Clytemnestra tugs me forward. Nudges me along until I start walking again, until we move past all the blood and shrieking. Clytemnestra guides me until we move past the river and stand on the other side of the shore. I watch as her shoulders shake. As tears flood from her eyes, and the edges of her skin where thorns poke.

"I hope that you stay kind, Natalya." She murmurs then. "I hope that you are strong. As strong as you always wanted to be. Strong enough to move your kids throughout life without condemning yourself in the process. Natalya," she says, "I know I'm supposed to be your guide, but I so desperately hope that you are better than I am. From one mother to another, I hope you get your happy ending."

(11)

BEFORE: HELEN

"People are beginning to talk, you know." I'm silent as I sit there, look my mom in the eyes as I crumple the petals in my palms. She leans back against the walls of the echoing arena, holds out a hand made of scarred stitches, and pulls me to my feet. I take in her skin, all the grazed lines and swollen scars. Observe how one hand is made of flesh and the other of metal.

"…A cornered animal caught up in a trap will gnaw off its own limb in an effort to escape." Somewhere, far away in an overgrown greenhouse, a radio is babbling.

A person in an impossible situation can create a suit of armor from broken bones and a mask from mottled flesh. I look up at Mom quietly and drink in the lacerations that line the edges of her veins.

"They call you the beloved of Death, Proserpine." My expression is blank as she prattles on. "Queen of the underworld, they say that nothing in this life can stop you."

"People say a lot of things," I reply evenly. The flowers have started to tear from how tightly I crush them. I tune her out. Listen instead to the sound of unending shrieking that rises from the other side of the arena. The constant, nonstop screaming as people wail over and over again for more bloodshed. They guzzle violence up in the same way that pigs lick at slops. I grimace and, shaking my head, start to leave.

"Where are you going?" Mom asks, footsteps quickening as she darts ahead to stand by my side. Her fingernails reek with the stench of crusted iron.

"I want to get away," I answer curtly, hardly sparing her a glance as I leave.

"Somewhere far, far away from all of the ugly shrieking of this building." I cover my ears then, place my hands on both sides of my skull, and push, as if the force of my fingers can drown out the carnage. It doesn't. Mom stares as I push until blood comes trickling out of the corners of my ears. Somewhere inside the arena, crowds laugh as they watch a woman have her throat ripped out.

"Helen, there's something going on here. Something wrong." She warns, watching anxiously as people stream in and out of the stadium. I try not to watch her. Look around at the tall, stony walls of this place of violence and pray that I don't have to see the love fade from her warm, warm eyes. I can't stand to look at her expression. I don't want to see her stop being proud of me.

"Please listen, sweetheart," Mom tries, her voice turning soft. Too soft. It hurts more than the yelling. I shut my eyes as a headache bashes against the bones inside my skull. I can still hear the screaming, hear the bloodcurdling screaming as the woman begs and the slow, steady gushing as her life fizzes out. Her blood seeps through the sand and stains the soil deep down beneath it. Her bones glow like pearls as the vultures peck at her skin.

In the corner of my mind, I can see Thanatos watching, His face shuddering with a mixture of sorrow and *fury* as he cradles the poor, frightened soul ever closer to his chest. I wish that the people in the stands could see him. Wish that the others could realize just how angry these games are making Death. Maybe if they did, they'd know how to repent before it's too late.

"I'm getting worried about you…" I can plug my ears and shut my eyes, but I can't block out the stench of rot. Of arrogance. Of pride. I can smell the pile of corpses roasting under the hot summer sun, their flesh a faint, pinkish red under the wave of sticky heat. Sweat drips down my limbs, and it almost makes me want to tear at my skin, to itch and scratch until I am some pathetic, writhing *thing*. The dead are not supposed to be treated like this. They are meant to be mourned, to be loved, to be praised. Whether sorrow or delight, Death is not something to be laughed at. I don't care who they are; a person's death is not a mockery to be laughed at.

I stop. And let out a breath. Grasp the dancing petals that are flitting in and out of my fingertips. Burrow my feet deep into the earth. Pretend my toes are like great, long tree roots. Ancient, gnarled tree roots that are anchored down deep into the soil of this spinning planet which we call Earth.

I am sitting in a garden that I raised with my own hands. I am sitting in a world that I built from the ground up. Nothing can touch me here, not the rot, not the damp, not the noise, not the cold. No one can touch me here.

It's strange, almost. How angry I feel. I don't think I've ever felt this amount of emotion. Never felt such anger pool through the depths of my veins. Maybe that's just a side effect of my meeting with Thanatos. After all, I don't ever think I've felt quite as alive as I have before that meeting with Death.

"HELEN!" Mom finally roars, shaking me as she crowds my face. She's scared, I realize numbly. His hands are trembling. "Helen, I need you to *listen* to me, baby. What did you do?" My arms hurt from where she's grabbing me. She's going to leave bruises again if she's not careful.

"What do you mean?" I ask hollowly. It's hard to keep my thoughts together when my head is spinning. Spinning like how the sand is spinning, all hot and shivery and whirling under the burning summer sun…

"Don't act oblivious." Mom's started hyperventilating, mouth flopping as she tries to breathe through her panic. She's scared. Why is she scared? I'm doing what she asked of me. "I'm pretty sure I'd remember if my daughter was able to suddenly regenerate limbs and shake off gunshots. What did you give away in exchange for that power, baby? What type of deal did you make, and with whom?"

"Mommy, aren't you proud of me?" I tilt my head and look at her. "I'm *winning* now. That's what you told me to do." It's hard to pay attention to her if I'm honest. Hard to listen when all I can hear is the arena behind us cheering as metal slices into bone.

"Magic requires a sacrifice, Helen." Mother insists, frantic as she stares. "An equal exchange, a balance of give and take. Otherwise, the Gods don't consider it a fair bargain. What did you give up, Helen? What did you give up to cheat Death?"

Cheat Death? The idea is absurd. Laughable. How could anyone fool Thanatos? No matter what tricks a person may try to pull, they make their way into his arms one way or another. Memento *Mori. Remember your mortality.* All things succumb to Death in the end. I start chuckling, double over in giggles as tears start to pour from my eyes.

Silly, *silly* Mother. Out of all the gods, Thanatos is perhaps the hardest to deceive.

"Was it a memory? A dream? Some unfulfilled wish?" Mom begins rattling off possibilities, each one more outlandish than the last. "An artifact, a fear, some part of your flesh? I really hope you wouldn't be foolish enough to give away some part of your name…"

"They didn't take away my name, Mom." I choke out through giggles. "They gave me others instead. Proserpine. Kore. Izunaya and Aerecura. They gave me dozens of names, Mom. A thousand. Enough names that a person would go hoarse if they were to attempt to name them all."

"Why… why would they give you so many names?" Mother looks ill now, her face a seasick sort of green. "That's – that's practically impossible, Helen. Names are the things that define who we are as a person. People don't give away names unless it's a parent with a newborn. The Gods don't bestow names upon their followers; all they do is take. For a God to be so gracious with the regeneration and the names… You must have given them something important. So important that even the divine were stunned."

"I don't think I gave them too much." I counter, frustration growing. "I gave him my love, that's all. My loyalty. I need to show Durnon why the way they treat the dead is wrong, and in exchange, Thanatos will give me everything."

"I thought I raised you better than this." Mother hisses, eyes wild as she stares at me. "HELEN, I THOUGHT I RAISED YOU TO BE BETTER THAN THIS." Her hands are too tight, her grip too rough as she shakes me. "YOU STUPID, STUPID, *STUPID LITTLE GIRL*. How could you just throw everything away like that?" She's sobbing now, I realize numbly.
132

Mom's sobbing. I don't think I've ever seen her cry like this before, not since Dad died.

"You were supposed to be different." She wails. "You were supposed to be strong enough to survive, to be better than your brothers."

Marek. Pietyr.

Briefly, their names flicker through my head. Mom wails, and I look down at the ground in silence.

…I don't want to end up like them.

"I just…I just wanted to be loved, Mom." I croak out hoarsely. "I just wanted to be loved without everything hurting."

"*I* love you." Mother argues, yanking me closer as she stares deep into my eyes. "*I* love you more than anything else in the world. That's why I care so much about how you're doing, in your work and your studies. That's why I stay up late with you, training, over and over, until you can walk off anything that this world throws at you. I *love* you, Helen.

More than you can ever possibly imagine. You don't need some – some strange spirit in the woods to give you that. You already have that, here with me."

"I know that." I agree quietly. "I never said you didn't love me. I'm just tired of your love always *hurting* when I'm around you for long. I can't… I can't predict when it's going to be a good day or a bad day for you, and I'm so tired of having to creep through the house scared that anything I do is going to set you off, and I know you love me. But love isn't supposed to *hurt* so much." Mom's grip tightens, and I hiss in pain as her fingers poke into purpled bruises.

Mom shudders when she lets go of my shoulders. Stares at my arms and my legs with horror in her eyes and tries to categorize which of my wounds appeared because of the arena and which came from her. She starts to turn green and hunches over with her shoulders shaking.

"I need – I need to get some fresh air." She mutters at last. "Just… just stay there, ok? I need to… I need to be alone for a moment."

The sun burns from where it beats down across the surface of the pavement outside the stadium. Rays sear themselves across my skin with a smothering burst of heat, and I watch with a detached sense of fascination as Mom sprints behind a dumpster and doubles over to vomit. Somewhere, encircled by rows upon rows of jeering stands, a person is screaming. Somewhere, watching in the arena as more and more blood drips down to stain the sand, Thanatos is weeping.

"Durnon has been in shambles since the rise of the boys with hungry eyes." A stranger in front of me whispers. I blink slowly as I turn to stare at him, thoughts sluggish as my mind circles again and again to the events that are happening inside the arena. The man in front of me watches with a gaze almost like devotion as he drops to his knees, pleading. "The dead now roam freely up and down the streets. Prophets cry out from their altars that the Final Days are soon upon us. The animals that the augurs sacrifice have been found with flowers budding up and down the insides of their chests. Our people believe that Death has forsaken us. The king himself called you Proserpine," I do not like the devotion that shines from this older man's eyes.

"The nation looks at you and they see a child who stands in clothes of purest snow, unstained by the world's most savage violence. The people look at you, and they see a child who has stood amid slaughter and walked out without a single scratch. People look at you and see a Messiah. Do you not hear them, do you not see how they kneel when you pass by on the streets? How all the men you fight now bow like sacrificial lambs as they pray for the honor to be allowed at your hand the sweet caress of carnage?

They call you Proserpine when they watch you from their windows. Persephone. Kore. Queen of the damned, the very stars sing of Death's love for you. You should have heard them, Helen, heard them from where I was sitting in the stands." His smile stretches even wider. "They act as if you are a god. They speak as if your name will be spoken for all of eternity."

"I am not your god," I tell the man flatly. "Do not call me Messiah." I am tired. So, *so* tired. I want my greenhouse. Please, why can't I just go back to my greenhouse?

"They wish to make you a god, Proserpine." I do not like the devotion that shines from this man's eyes. As if I'm something divine, and not a scared little girl. I do not like the disappointment that is beginning to creep in.

"Even the gods are mortal," I tell him dully. "*Memento Mori*. Remember your mortality." I start to smirk then, lips curling back as I smile with just a little too many teeth. "No matter how hard you try, you cannot escape the end." My smile sours.

I think then of the plum blossoms that have begun to cling to the walls of my house. Of the millions of roses that have started to suffocate my small greenhouse. Arenas piled high with endless stacks of broken bodies and Death himself weeping as he stares at all the carnage, and I don't quite know what's happened, but my world is slowly dying. And I am so sick of having to mention death in nearly every sentence.

"I want to go home," I mumble. The man is silent, his hands shaky as he stares at me. "I want to go home!" I repeat, stomping my foot.

"But this is home." The man replies slowly, as if I am the weird one here.

He's wrong. This arena isn't home. This stadium isn't home; this place of sand and rotting bones isn't home. Home is a greenhouse. Home is a radio that never stops babbling. Home is the scent of damp soil after rain, where you can smell the flowers growing.

"I want to be loved," I mutter dumbly. My voice trembles, and slowly, ever so slowly, tears begin to build in the corners of my eyes. The man scoffs as he stares.

"What is adoration if not love?" He sneers. Foolish child, have you forgotten that people love all that is divine? Still, perhaps you are right. No one could honestly be expected to love such a selfish child. Our people are dying in the streets and yet you still squeal for more and more affection." I turn around and start walking.

"You would abandon your people!" He screams, all frustration and fury, and he marches up to me with his fist curled back as if to swing.

I stop and put my hands up. Turn around and look the man fully in their eyes and watch how even now they tremble. The flowers in my pockets start to shake.

"I am tired of this," I tell the one-handed man. "I am tired of hurting for the sake of your mindless entertainment." I pause. Inhale. Exhale. And then I scream.

They give me a trophy when I win the tournament. The king himself hands me a small iron crown, and he places it on my head with a proud grin. Chinks of gore are encrusted on the bottoms of his nails.

"Congratulations." He tells me with a smile. I go outside to the back of an alleyway and vomit. Sit down beside the rows of reeking trash cans as Thanatos settles beside my shoulder. We watch together as the sun beats down against the nearby pavement.

"I'm sorry," I whisper quietly. The medals hang around my neck like a noose. I can feel their ribbons cutting off my airway as they chafe against my skin.

"What for?" Thanatos prods. I start, and then stop. Start again, try to scrape the words off my tongue as I shudder and sob.

"I don't know. Everything, really." My skin burns from where it makes contact with the pavement. I dully watch as gentle pinks sizzle across my legs. My nerves are too exhausted to care anymore. "I'm sorry." I tell the shadow man. "I'm sorry I failed you."

"I'm sorry," I tell him again. The words taste like sugar, and they slip so easily out of my mouth.

"There is no need…" Death starts, but I cut him off with a shake of my head.

"No," I state simply. Cross my arms and pout at him as my lower lip wobbles. "Don't interrupt me. I don't care how you feel about it if you need to hear it or not, but I want to apologize for failing you. Just let me apologize." He opens his mouth but closes it again when I sniffle. "Please?" I beg him desperately, tremors jolting up and down my frame. "Please just let me get this out." Hesitantly, ever so hesitantly, he nods. I smile up at him. Smile big and wide, hold out my arms, and when he hugs me, murmur,

I'm sorry. I'm so sorry. Have I mentioned that I'm sorry? I didn't mean to do that, honestly, I'm sorry. You have to realize I'm sorry. Won't you forgive me? I promise I'm sorry. I'm sorry. I'm so sorry. You can't possibly imagine how sorry I am. I'm sorry….

"I'm sorry. *I'm sorry.*

I'm sorry.

I'm sorry.   I'm sorry.

I'm sorry.   I'm sorry.   I'm
sorry.   I'm sorry.   I'm sorry. I'm
sorry. I'm sorry.   I'm sorry. I'm sorry. I'm
sorry.   I'm sorry.   I'm sorry.   I'm
sorry. I'm sorry.   I'm sorry.   I'm
sorry.   I'm sorry.   I'm
sorry.   I'm sorry.   I'm sorry.   I'm
sorry.   I'm sorry.

I'm sorry.   I'm sorry.   I'm
sorry.   I'm sorry.   I'm sorry

I'm sorry.   I'm sorry.   I'm
sorry.   I'm sorry.   I'm sorry.

I'm sorry.   I'm sorry.   I'm sorry.

I'm sorry.   I'm sorry.   I'm sorry.

I'm sorry.   I'm sorry.   I'm
sorry.   I'm sorry.   I'm sorry

I'm sorry.   I'm sorry.   I'm
sorry.   I'm sorry.   I'm sorry. I'm
sorry.   I'm sorry.

It feels nice whenever I apologize. It feels nice, because then I have the chance at getting forgiveness. I love forgiveness. Like fixing things, patching them up with nothing more than a few words. Maybe if I say the words enough times, they'll fix things. My mom used to make me say 'sorry' seventy times whenever I needed to fix something. Then seventy times seventy. One time, when I apologized for two hours, she told me to stop. Said words don't mean anything. Said sorry can't fix things.

I'm not quite sure that that's true, though. After all, if you say sorry, then that gives the other person the chance to say:

I forgive you. Thank you for apologizing. It's so mature of you to be the bigger person. Don't worry I still love you.

Thanatos is silent after I explain this. Leans down to look me in the eyes and replies, "I would have loved you anyway. You don't need to say sorry for that to happen. You did nothing wrong, my child. I don't know why you keep insisting that that's what happened."

He sighs and rises to his feet. Tugs me up off the pavement and examines my legs critically. "My dear, you must learn to take care of yourself better. Humans shouldn't look so much like lobsters. Come." He demands. "There's something I want to show you."

He pulls me into the shadows of a nearby street sign when no one's looking and wraps the darkness around us into a pair of softened wings. The feathers are made of fluff when I reach out and brush them. Soft, with just a hint of down.

He twirls me around as he steps behind the street post. I spin and spin as all around us, glinting specks of sunlight fall and dust the edges of my lashes.

We dance, out there in the center of the square. Dance some strange old waltz with too many steps, and I'm laughing as I spin because I don't know quite why we're dancing, but sometimes it's fun to be ridiculous. Giggles spill out like bubbles, and Death's eyes crinkle in the corners when he catches me smiling.

He dips me again, and as we twirl up and down around the alleyway, the ground begins to soften, until with a gentle sigh we're sinking, deep down beneath the surface of the earth.

We float down into the underworld on Death's angel wings, float down as light and airy as the soap bubbles that soar in rainbow rings. I watch as the sun is slowly replaced by stars. The butterflies are by moths. The burning, scalding pavement softening into sand.

When we land, Thanatos pulls me into a marble garden. Rubies burn and diamonds glow, and I look up and down this garden made up entirely of metals and stare in awe at an enchanted forest blooming with golden branches. Thanatos does not stop and stare at the jewels. He walks through the mechanical woods without sparing them a single glance.

Hand in hand, we move through the garden before he stops and points.

There, growing amid the vibrant stones, a single flower blooms. The petals are white, with delicate, pink edges curling inwards as they branch out from their stem. I reach out and cup it in my hand.

Death takes off in a sprint, zooming through the underbrush as I stare transfixed at the delicate plant. He comes back with more petals, all pinks and whites and yellows that he cradles carefully in his arms.

"Helen, you are incredible." He whispers, dropping to his knees as he holds the flowers out in his hands. "Something extraordinary, a marvel I've never seen before in the entire universe. Look at these, please." His eyes are shining in excitement. "Don't you know what this means?"

"There are flowers blooming in the Underworld," I answer slowly, looking up in confusion. "I thought that wasn't possible."

"It's not. At least, not normally." Thanatos is twitching slightly, from where he holds the flowers between the edges of his fingertips. His eyes are bright, manic almost; pupils as wide as saucers as he looks down and smiles. "I've never been able to hold something for so long without it withering." He confesses stunned.

"What does that mean?" Thanatos looks up at my question. Gently, ever so delicately, he sets the flower down on the nearby marble. Taking me in his arms, he picks me up and spins. He starts laughing then, cheering and hollering as tears of joy start to trail down his cheeks. I grab onto the edges of his shoulders and laugh, look at the petals that lie spread out in front of me, and laugh until I too start to cry.

"Helen." Thanatos declares when he finally calms down. "Helen, my favorite miracle, it means you managed to make life bloom in a world only accustomed to death."

(12)

AFTER: NATALYA

The world is spongy, beneath my feet. Not dirt, not sand, but something else entirely, a texture that's sticky like bruised flowers or overripened fruit. I look down at the ground beneath my shoes. The land stretches out in a sea of violet clouds, thin whisps of fog drifting as they slink like serpents through the lavender light. Noises are coming from the fog. I can make out laughter – the type that swells up just slightly too bright, all sharp and brittle as it bubbles up from spasming chests. I can hear sobbing as well; low, choked-up moans that grate against my eardrums as they pick up in intensity. It's jarring, almost. Hearing the pair mixed together in such a fashion. The noises leave my head spinning, my palms sweating from where I jam them in my pockets.

And the smell, oh gods the smell. My eyes start to water, and I have to hold myself back from gagging.

It was sweet at first. The smell that is. Like vanilla, chamomile, and fresh warm milk. Then the scent turned bitter. Putrid. Rotten. The type that old flowers give off when they start to shrivel within their flowerbeds, all sour and pungent and wretched in their final moments.

I look up and take in the elegant, obsidian gate. The LAND OF ETERNAL SLUMBER. A nearby sign reads.

It always took a lot to put Helen to sleep when she went to bed each night. She was one of those kids who struggled to simply lie down, always flinching and startling at the sight of shadows lurking in her closet. At the squeak of the window shutters that she claimed reminded her of the rats at the sanitarium. I used to walk in on her mechanically scrubbing, late at night. Scrubbing at her hands in the bathroom sink until they were red, swearing that she was sure she could still see the blood crusted on them from where it had been spilled in the arena.

Often it would take hugs, cups of tea, and leaving a lantern lit on her nightstand. Counting sheep until she ran out of breath and sharing stories under the flickering candlelight.

It would always take a lot to help my daughter go to sleep when the night first began. As soon as Helen managed to close her eyes, however, she'd sleep so deeply that nothing in this world could wake her. It was funny, but also a little frightening. I'd stare at her, and it would look like a piece of her had died a little, as if all that was left stretched beneath her linen sheets was the shell of a corpse.

150

Perhaps that's why Hypnos rests here, not up in the heavens with the other gods of dreams but down in the ground with the dead.

Squeezing my eyes shut, I whisper numbers as I begin to count under my breath. "One, two, three…." Somewhere between swimming through the Styx and meeting Clytemnestra, I started counting the seconds I could go before feeling that "gut-kick" stabbing through my stomach whenever I think about Helen. Currently, the time is thirty-two seconds. Twenty-one before I have to take a breath and feel that ache in my heart again. Mornings are by far the hardest. When I have to wake up and face the reality that Helen's gone.

I have to remember that she won't answer anymore if I call her. That I *can't* call her anymore. That I can't – I can't wake her up in the morning. That I forgot to get someone to watch her garden when I set out on my journey, and now her flowers are probably withering away without anyone to watch them.

I should have gotten someone to watch them, her flowers.

I should have been able to watch *her*.

I should have noticed…

"Natalya?" Clytemnestra calls out carefully. "You're spacing out again."

"Sorry," I mutter, trying to pull my thoughts together. I just need to get myself together. Helen's counting on me to keep myself together. "What are we supposed to be doing again?"

"Entering the Land of Eternal Slumber," Clytemnestra repeats patiently. I nod and start walking, my steps mechanical as I focus on placing one foot in front of the other. I just need to get to Helen. I just want to see my baby again.

"Be careful." My guide warns. She reaches out a hand and yanks me to a stop. "Hypnos is the god of dreams and illusions. He is the Oneiroi, and yet at the same time the Dread wrought. He knows every single want, fear, and dream that you have ever had. Every hope, and every regret. He knows you better than you know yourself. Don't trust anything that goes on in there. And think of nothing other than why you are here in the first place. I will meet you on the other side."

Clytemnestra swallows, then. Places a hand delicately on the thorns that wind around her throat. Finally, she takes a step and vanishes into the mist. For a moment, I stop and listen to the chorus of cheers and screams. The stench of chamomile is so strong that it's nearly blinding, all cloying from where it clings to my skin.

I pause, and then I step into the mist. I'm standing in a room.

I think.

The silence is so thick around me that it feels like static, quiet pressing down so deeply that it leaves a visceral ache from where it hangs on my shoulders. Dust motes drift as slow as molasses from where they swirl around the room, their particles stiff as if the very air is dreaming. A suffocating haze blankets the room in smoke, particles of ash and something sweeter coating the back of my tongue when I open my mouth to breathe. It smells like lavender, sort of, and faint notes of pine. Longing, almost. The type of desperation that festers when forgotten for too long in the dark.

Helen used to love the smell of lavender.

Stained glass windows soar above my head from where they arc into the ceiling, the colored glass washing the room in a mixture of rusted reds and sickly greens. Helen's face stares down at me from every panel in the glass. I try not to look at them. I try to ignore how every image shows her dying, over and over again, as she bleeds out across stadiums and sanitariums and in the corner of her bedroom. Her gaze gets brighter every time I look up.

Ivory columns stretch to the ceiling in twisted spirals as they line the walls of the sleeping archive. Flying buttresses twirl beneath ribbed vaults, and the whole room is so dizzyingly grandiose that I have to close my eyes in order to fight back the nausea. Long, obsidian shelves stand in rows upon rows along the cracking tiles. Each one of them bears a label, categorized not by content or time period, but by feeling.

Dread.

Anticipation.

Wishes left eternally unfulfilled.

Sitting beside them on velvet cushions lie a series of broken toys. Porcelain dolls with shattered legs. Stuffed animals with holes slashed through their drooping stomachs. Action figures with their arms torn off and wind-up toys crying from where their limbs still halfheartedly twitch.

There's a banner hanging above the altar of the macabre temple. Words are stitched across it in shaky, childish handwriting.

You wouldn't have lost her if you'd been watching.

I tear the room apart. Start looking desperately for a clue, a hint, something that will help me find my daughter. Rip open cushions and flip over cases, smash open dolls until the porcelain shatters beneath my footsteps. Toys flop onto the ground in a sea of wounded bodies. My brain is spinning as I try to think. Time. I'm running out of time. There are no clocks on the walls. There never really are in dreams. Or so I've heard.

The walls start to pulse as I search frantically through the room. I need a clue. A hint. A key to this puzzle. No matter how frantically I move, I keep running out of time, wasting moments searching while my daughter waits, scared and alone, and- probably not confused.

No, she wouldn't be shocked, would she? I only have to look around the walls, take in the rows upon rows of stained glass, to see that my daughter has been hurt far too many times to count. My daughter has been hurt, over and over again, and I wasn't there to help. I couldn't save my baby.

I should have been there for her. Should have noticed that something was wrong, should have…

There's an old, weathered vinyl inside the heart of one of the porcelain dolls. I pick it up with shaking fingers. Look around the room wildly and realize that the writing on the banner has changed.

Insert the vinyl into the disc.

Do you remember now?

I look around the room. There isn't a radio, a record player, or a gramophone. There isn't a radio, until suddenly there *is*.

I stare in silence at where the gramophone sits on the edge of the altar. It looks like a normal record player at first glance. A thin layer of dust blankets the machine. The faded stickers have started to peel slowly from the buttons. If I didn't know better, I would have assumed that the gramophone had always been there, fitting neatly in place beside the notebook and flashlight.

But I know better.

I approach the gramophone with slow, careful steps. Place a hand on my knife, remember the words of my guide. *He knows every single dream and fear you've ever had. He knows you better than you know yourself.* For a moment, I expect the thing to attack. Grow legs and millions of beady little eyes. Leap off the desk and charge at me with a mechanical screech. Detonate. Anything, really.

I insert the vinyl and press the play button. The only noise comes from the snap of the lid as it closes. For a moment, all is silent. No sound plays, not even a faint purring as the machine awakes. Instead, the room begins to peel back and bubble.

There's a little girl sitting there when it finishes.

She perches on the edge of a rich velvet couch, twisting her hands over and over as she winds a ribbon around her fingers. Her nails are cracked and bleeding, the polish chipping off her fingers and falling in slivers at her feet. She's wearing my face, although I don't think my eyelids were ever peeled back like that. Her eyes are wide. Far too wide. Almost like she's scared to shut them.

A figure sits across from her, human yet at the same time *not*. Like someone had started halfheartedly scribbling ideas of what a man should be, and then drew something else on top of it. It's face is smooth, hollow; features bubbling under the skin like melting candlewax as it shifts over and over between a sea of faces. I watch in morbid fascination as the creature's jawline shifts, as flesh contorts and bone bubbles up beneath the surface.

No matter what form it takes, its voice remains the same. Soft and vaguely scratchy. Smooth, yet distorted at the same time. Like the thing is merely playing at being human, trying to force its voice to reach the same pitch that voices make on radio shows and portable speakers.

"Would you like a glass of water? Maybe a donut, some type of snack?" The girl sits there, eyes boring into the edges of the wooden floor. "Never mind, that's fine. We can go ahead and start if you'd prefer. Your name is Natalya, right? That's what your friends called you?"

The girl stares at the ground in silence, eyelids peeled back from where she refuses to blink. Her hands grip a pencil, nails digging into softened wood until graphite smears her palms. The creature sighs, air exhaling in a gasp of disappointment.

"Alright, Natalya." The man states eventually. "I'd like you, if it's possible, to walk me through the day of the incident." The girl hesitates. Another awkward pause, and then the man begins to smile. It's meant to be reassuring, I think. But humans don't smile like that. Humans *can't* smile like that, lips curling up to the corners of their eyes and displaying far too many teeth. "I understand, thinking of the incident can be quite traumatic." Silence.

160

"Sorry, traumatic means that it can be painful, such as causing you to feel all these uncomfortable, awful feelings and…"

"I know what traumatic means." The girl's voice is sharp, eyes hardly blinking. She looks fourteen, maybe fifteen. Had her voice really become that flat by then? That *dead?*

The interviewer giggles, chest wheezing and throat gasping as he jumps in his seat. His hands tremble from where he grips the edges of his seat. Eventually, he composes himself. Becomes calm. Professional.

"Alright, alright, that's progress. Improvement. Means you're ready to talk about what happened, doesn't it?" He's shaking. The man won't stop shaking, chuckles running up and down his frame as his smile grows wider. "Here's what's going to happen." He says, finally. "I'm going to tell you a story, about what I *think* happened. And you can chime in and correct me if I get something wrong. Sounds good?" The girl nods, limbs all robotic and stiff.

"It was cold. The middle of winter. You'd decided to go on a walk outside because you were tired of always being shut in the house, feeling all suffocated as you sat there by the fire and waited with your family for the bad men to finally find you." The man's voice is low, his pace slow. Almost like he's reciting a snippet of elegant poetry. "Your brother was dying, some sort of infection that was easy to catch but hard to treat when your family lived so far out in the icy wasteland."

Pneumonia. It was Pneumonia.

"Your father had set out earlier that month to try to search for a cure. Eventually, you found him on that walk. You brought him inside, and he gave the cure he had found to your brother. You sat with him at the dinner table, only he didn't touch any of the food on his plate." The man's face stiffens, smile peeling away to reveal the reddened gums underneath.

"You asked him, then, why he wasn't eating. It was rude of him not to touch the meal your mother had made after all. Not when food was so hard to come by in a place so cold. He told you he no longer needed it. That he didn't need much of anything anymore. He told you that he had found a spirit who would help him in the shadow of a mountain, and that so long as he was faithful, he would never want for sustenance again."

"It wasn't a spirit." Little Natalya spits. She glares at the man and crosses her arms. "They called it a god, but I know it wasn't a spirit. It was something else." The man pauses. Swallows.

"Right. Your father said that he had found *something* in the caves of the mountain. And he said that so long as you chose to believe, and accepted the cure, that you would want for nothing ever again." The man pauses. Smiles wider. "He said that you would never hunger again, only thirst."

Something shudders in the back of my mind.

"And so you decide to be quiet and listen. Trust your parents because they're bigger and wiser than you, and watch as slowly, ever so slowly, your family begins to stop going out into the sunshine. They stop eating as much and give the rest of the food to you. The colors in their irises erode until all you can see are the bloodied capillaries poking out of their retinas. They begin to rely more on hearing, walking around in the dark, as their ears prick up and point. They begin to change, physically and then mentally."

"No." It's a snarl, almost. A noise almost too guttural, too animalistic, for a child that age to have made. My fingers are hovering once more above the gramophone's dials. I jolt when I look up, and I back away instinctively when I focus back on the scene.

The little girl's looking at me. I didn't think either of them could actually look at me. Not when they're supposed to be projections.

Pay attention. She mouths, before turning back to face the shifting specter.

"No? I'm sorry, no, in what meaning?" The man's hands tremble as he picks up and drops his pencil, scratch marks ripping holes into the paper as he excitedly scribbles notes in the margins. "No, as in they still went out in the sunlight? Your mother still ate the breakfast she would cook for you? Your family was able to do more than just repeat the same daily actions as clockwork over and over? No, your parents were still human?"

"No." Young Natalya simply states.

"I-I'm sorry, Natalya." The smile drops. "I don't know how to help if you don't tell me what's wrong with the story. Maybe there's something, something you want to change…"

"They weren't the monsters." Brown eyes, dull eyes, stare straight ahead. I stare at the child. How is it possible for someone's eyes to be so wide? "*It* was."

"Right – Sorry. I'll, I'll just skip to the last part." The creature stutters out at last. His script is lost, the theatrical tone now shattered.

"Earlier, when we found you, you said there was a *thing* hiding inside your oven?"

"It wasn't hiding in the oven." Young Natalya answers, leaning forward in her seat. "It *was* the oven. Metal formed into flesh. Muscle. Skin. It came alive. I used to hear it whispering when my family fed the chimney ashes."

"Was this *thing* like the spirit your family called god?" The creature's hands clench into fists from where he grips his notebook. A part of me expects it to crack beneath his hands.

"No." Young Natalya whispers. She tilts her head until she's staring at the wall. The light of the projector flickers as the child's eyes grow bigger. "I used to wish it was. But – it wasn't holy. And it didn't want my family. It wanted *her.*"

The creature stops. And sighs. Scribbles more and more in the margins of his yellowed notebook. I hear him swallow. I hear him sigh. Inhale. And then exhale. Watch as he scribbles HER??? In large capital letters.

"I'm sorry Natalya, I believe this is the first time that I'm hearing about this person." He states, finally. "Who is *her*?"

The girl whispers under her breath. Takes a small, reddened ribbon and fidgets with it in her hands. Her eyes are vacant. Blank. Dull. Throughout the whole recording, I don't think I've ever seen her blink.

"Natalya?" The creature prompts, an edge of impatience cutting across his tone. The girl ignores him.

"Why didn't you save your mother, Natalya?" The words are sharp, pointed this time.

The girl whispers again. Sits up straighter in her chair this time. The blank-faced creature twitches, cracks appearing over its porcelain skin.

"Why didn't you save your little sister?" Something's growing, in between the cracks on the figure's face. It looks like mold, almost. Or spores of poppyseeds.

"Why didn't you save Helen?" The little girl's eyes are bleeding now, dark, scarlet tears gouging streaks into her cheeks as they drip down her face.

"Tell me, Natalya." The man is laughing now, skin sloughing off him in layers with each belly-shaking chuckle. "How many people are you going to try to save before you realize that you are the one who's hurting them? How many ghosts are going to haunt you before you understand that you have blood on your hands?" The creature's mouth unhinges, revealing rows upon rows of serrated teeth.

"Natalya?" She ignores the man across from her. Her eyes hardly blink. She raises them to face me. Her gaze is dark, hollow. The blood continues to silently drip from the corners of her eyes. Whispering, she tries again. "Natalya, what are you looking at?"

She's looking at me. Through the projector, through the screen.

"Run."

Softly, ever so softly, the ribbon flutters until it drifts through the screen and lands on the desk. I pick it up and look at it in silence. Wrap the fabric tightly around my fingers until it chokes off my circulation.

There's something breathing outside the room. I can hear it snarling, claws scrabbling against the walls as the thing draws closer. It would sound like a man if the panting wasn't just slightly *off.* I can feel the faint sense of needles prickling up and down my spine.

The thing is bulging in the side of the wallpaper. I can see the cartography charts twisting as the posters warp, smell a faint scent of iron as something oozes like sludge down into the floorboards.

I grab the notebook off the table. Snatch the recorder and wind the ribbon even tighter around my fingers. Stare in silence as the slime continues to ooze out of the deformed corner.

"Run." Young Natalya stated. I remember her eyes then, how wide, dark, and empty they seemed. How she held her eyelashes open with her fingers as if she was too scared to blink.

"Run." The little girl said, and I tear open the door to the room and sprint off into the darkened halls. A subtle click goes off when the door creaks open behind me, warping fingers peeling out of the wallpaper to hit the projector with a soft press.

(Recovered audio hard drive, fragment one of three.)

The noise of the tape recorder echoes throughout the hallway, bouncing off the floor and walls as it burrows into my hearing.

Experiment log oh-three-one, September second, five-oh-oh-six. Martin Russel.

I have previously reported the subject's improvement in her official case files, and the result of the pharmaceutical branch had been wildly enthusiastic.

The compound Sa-1202 has been launched immediately into phase three trials, showing noticeable improvements in clarity, appetite, and regrowth of the pineal gland.

What I'm recording here is completely off-record. I believe that I'm going to keep it that way. The subject has consistently alluded to the existence of a creature, "The hungry one", that for all intents and purposes appears to be completely psychological. The widely held opinion, of course, is that the "hungry one" is a sort of trauma-based coping mechanism, a way for the subject to disassociate from the actions and violent tendencies of themselves and others, to attribute such tragedies to some diabolical 'other' that is separate from the subject. This same coping mechanism has been found to prevail in several other members of the incident, claiming that they themselves have become monstrous as a way for the cerebral cortex to avoid associating themselves with the tragedy of such prior actions.

That's the assumption that they're sticking with, and the current hypothesis is that with the Sa-1202 working so well that Natalya — redact, backspace, the subject, can comprehend her past actions as being her own. They believe she has been cured.

I no longer believe this conclusion to be the case.

(Remainder of file corrupted.)

(13)

BEFORE: HELEN

The sky is storming outside the greenhouse. Rain pelts down in sheets of hail, and trees stretch their branches up desperately into the heavens. I watch as stems uncurl, flowers opening as they frantically slurp at the droplets. It's been a while since the Earth could drink something other than blood.

I sit there quietly and watch through the glass as water pours down. Life trickles into the soil through a series of crystal droplets. I can feel it settling in the atmosphere, taste it on the tip of my tongue as raindrops plop onto the edges of the grotto with a series of soft clinks.

A slow knocking starts at the door to the greenhouse. A woman is standing there. Her hair plasters itself to the sides of her face as she waits in the pouring rain. Her black pointed heels begin to squelch as they sink into the mud. And yet the woman keeps her head held high. Raps at the edges of the glass door with a professional demeanor. I freeze. Back away quietly until I hide behind a cluster of potted ferns. Blow out my candle with a sigh and frantically begin to look for Thanatos.

"I can see you." The woman calls out. She stares at me through the glass as the rain steadily continues to pour outside. "Proserpine, right? I've been looking for you for a while now. Could you please let me in? I have some important matters that I wish to discuss with you."

"I don't know you." I bite back, my limbs curled up and shaking. She found my greenhouse. A stranger found my greenhouse. And maybe that's a silly thing to get all worked up about, but this was a place where I could be safe. Somewhere warm, and inviting, and protected. I've trained in here and I've hidden in here, and whenever something scary would happen, I knew that I could just close my eyes and pretend I was standing inside the comfort of these thick glass panes, embraced by a sea of roses.

The woman flashes a badge, then, all neat and crisp and signed with a dark iron crown that stands out as she waves it in the air. I feel a sense of dread slowly start to rise. A feeling of unease, sort of like a mouse that just discovered it's been caught in a trap.

"I serve on the national department of wellbeing and domestic affairs." The stranger explains. "Proserpine, your skill in the arena has granted you the honor to be employed in the service of our beloved government."

I look out then, at the shadows behind the woman. Hiding in the bushes crouch a swarm of armed men, their weapons shining as they surround the greenhouse. The metal of their guns gleam silver in the pouring rain.

"Tell your men to put their guns away, and then I'll let you inside," I tell the stranger dully. It's mainly just for the sake of formality, anyways. Having them lay down their guns won't stop them from charging if I choose to decline whatever the woman wants. I remain calm, despite this. After all, those men would need far more than bullets to take me down.

And yet, there's a part of me that shudders at the thought of them shooting up my greenhouse. Of glass walls shattering while flowers lie crushed in the dust from being trodden underfoot. My radio being smashed and shattered into pieces, broken notes spilling out weakly as the soldier's scream. The men can shoot me all they want; in the end it wouldn't really make a difference. Still, I will not stand by and watch as they destroy my greenhouse.

I sigh and let the woman inside. Hand her a blanket and curl down on the floor across from her. A part of me wishes that it didn't feel so much like giving up when I let her in.

"I thought that I told you people already, I'm not going to play along with your little games. I am done with pointless violence." My voice rises as I stand and start to pace. "I don't care who you are or what you think you can do; I'm not going to stand there while people chant for more and more bloodshed."

"I'm not from the military, if that's what you were fearing." The woman's response is quick, her face unreadable as she sits across from me. She pulls her lipstick out of a leather handbag while she talks, pursing her lips as a rich red, the color of rubies, coats her mouth.

"Though heavens know they must have already tried to sink their teeth into you. After all, a child with your gifts would leave anyone with a brain drooling. But don't worry, I'm a healer. We don't engage in violence; our purpose is to help, not hurt." For the briefest moment, a flicker of emotion crosses her face. Adoration. Pure, devoted adoration.

"Could you imagine the benefits that your gift could bring? The potential for cures and future vaccines is endless. How much pressure can a human body withstand before it collapses? How much water can a body hold before collapsing?" Her eyes grow wider as she rambles. "What about skin grafts, or organ transplants? Could cloning individual cells allow an amputee to receive a fully functioning limb? Can you stop someone from aging, shock someone's heart back into beating? The possibilities are simply endless."

I sit there frozen as she rambles. It feels too good to be true if I'm honest. The possibility of being able to use my powers for good, to show how precious a person's life is. To save someone, to truly save someone. It's one of the main reasons that I focused so hard on my training. Yet I still find myself having to ask,

"How would you find out the answers to those questions?"

"Why with experiments, of course." She answers. Her smile has far too many teeth.

So that's why she brought so many men, I realize. She's going to turn me into a lab rat, a science experiment. I suppose I can't blame her in the end. After all, I experimented on myself too.

"Will it hurt- those experiments of yours?" I ask quietly. No matter how much I try to tell myself it's for the greater good, there's a part of me that's still scared of getting hurt. The woman stares at me, then. Stares at this child, whom she has asked to be offered up on a silver platter.

"Perhaps." She answers. "But this time, your suffering will be for a purpose. You will save the lives of millions. Your name will go down in history as one of the greatest martyrs of your time. You will suffer because anything of value includes suffering. But Helen, you will be known as a *hero.*"

I'm not entirely sure if I believe in heroes anymore. At least, not the ones that everyone else seems to believe in, all brave and strong with bright shiny guns and cocky grins. I'm not sure if I believe that there really are heroes in this land, given the way they are marketed in those arenas. And yet, a part of me still wants to prove myself wrong. Wants to become a hero and save everyone. I want to take down the entire system with nothing more than a smile and outstretched hands.

The woman in front of me is asking for a sacrifice. She wants me to go and lie myself down on a stone-cold altar, present myself before her like a lamb willing for slaughter, and offer up my flesh for the sake of science. It sounds cruel. And sick. And wrong. But isn't that what I've already been doing?

"Okay," I tell the woman then. A part of me is proud of how little my voice shakes. "You can take me to the scientists."

The woman smiles and, standing up, pulls me by the hand. Her palm is so big that it covers mine. Leads me out of my greenhouse, past the rows of armed guards. We walk into the woods through the pouring rain. I look back once. At the place where my greenhouse stands. Look back, and then look forward. The sky continues to wail above my head.

The building is tall when we finally approach it. Tall, and blank. Sterile. Clean, in the way that the floors have been scrubbed so hard that holes have begun to rot through the beams. White, in the way that there is simply an absence of any other color. Fluorescent lights flicker overhead as the woman slowly leads me to my room. The very air reeks of bleach.

The room is plain. Bare. A small operating table rests in the middle of the floor. Linoleum counters line the walls, filled to the brim with beakers and flasks. Medical tools shine under the cheap lighting like pairs of metal fishhooks.

On top of the table sits a large, plastic tub. Rats squeak from where they lunge at the sides. Their little paws scrabble as they try to escape.

"I don't understand," I ask, confused. "Why are there so many rats?" The woman simply smiles and reaches for a pair of gloves. "I mean, I thought that I was going to be the experiment."

"Oh, of course, sweet Proserpine, you will, you don't need to worry." The woman soothes, as slowly one by one the scientists begin to march in. "We'll use you soon enough. It's just easier to pick something that isn't human to practice on first. Builds up muscle memory, or something of that sort. Desensitizes the brain."

They brought in rats from all over the country and gathered them into a big round tub. Then they brought in fleas. And I never felt so much pity for a creature as small as a flea before, but the poor things were shaking and trying to tear off their very wings to stop their flight. Can you imagine that? The creatures were in so much pain that they vomited and tried to claw off their very wings so that they didn't have to move anymore.

And then the fleas bite the rats. And I watch as the rats get these giant, swollen bumps. The spots are round, and swollen, and filled to the brim with pus and fluid. They cover up every single inch of their skin until the poor balls of fluff could hardly see from where the bumps had bubbled up over the eyelids. The bumps grew around their mouths and climbed down their throats, and when they reached the insides, all the organs turned to fluid. They liquified the organs. Rotted the poor rodents from the inside out.

It takes weeks for the rats to fully die. Weeks of trying to sleep while the creatures scream as their throats slowly start to liquify. Weeks of trying to eat while the rats tear off their oozing skin with dripping claws. It takes weeks for the last one to finally die. And after a while, a part of me wishes that it were sooner. Because after a while, life just became too much of a burden for those soft little creatures.

They make me organize the files when they finish with the experiment. Make me separate and categorize the research, as if in its own way the action is its own sort of threat.

This is what we did to the rats. This is what we will do to you next.

I'm typing up the conclusions to the experiment when I finally see it. Typing paragraphs on an old computer with fingers shaky with nerves, with grief, with sorrow, with helpless anger. I'm recording the blood consistency of the last living rodent when I finally see it at the end of the lab report.

I see what they did with the bodies of those poor, poor rats.

I get up and start walking. Vomit into a nearby trash can and watch as the vomit stains the precious, sterile cleanness of this place.

Slam my feet into the cracking tiles as I march, hands shaking as I clench them into fists. Inside my pocket, a pair of seeds begins to dance.

I hunt through the hallways until I find the woman. Rip open doors and claw through walls as easily as if they were made of paper. My fury is rising, the longer it takes to find her. My patience is growing thinner, the longer she hides.

"Can I help you?" The physician stares at me as she sits in her chair. If it weren't for the shaking of her hands, I'd think she was perfectly calm. My skin itches as I stand there. A scraping, guttural itch. My veins twist as I stop and take a breath. There is something bitter and ugly blooming inside my throat. I can feel its thorns burrowing down deeper as they scrape the insides of my skin. A part of me is scared of what will happen if I let it crawl out of my mouth.

"Can I help you, Proserpine?" The woman repeats. I close my eyes and take a breath.

"I saw what you had them do with the rats." I hiss, disgust rotting me from the inside out. "I saw what you had them do with the bodies of the dead rats." I cut her a glare then. Choke down my fury as I continue.

"You dropped the carcasses into the grain mills. Silos. Dropped them from airships, and the bodies fell into the wheat fields of people who would starve because they had nothing else to eat. Then the fleas infected the crops, and the rats rotted in the nearby rivers, and then the plague started killing *people*, Doctor. It started killing people by the thousands because they had nothing to eat, nothing to drink, and people watched as their children dropped around them like flies, and you just *sat there* and watched, didn't you? You killed thousands with the toxins for no other reason than to see them die."

"It was a worthy sacrifice." The woman replies calmly. "We needed to figure out how the disease would work on a man. How it would evolve, and how it would spread." I grow silent. Still.

"You lied about the goals of this corporation," I say finally. Betrayal hangs heavy in my gut. *Idiot. Stupid. Foolish little girl.* "You handle plagues and diseases, sure. But you never really cared about a cure, did you? You just wanted to make bioweapons." The woman is silent. Serene. She looks at me without a single hint of guilt in her eyes and simply shakes her head, sighing.

"My child, have you ever wondered why our nation clings so strongly to fairytales? To poems, artwork, and music displaying our courage? Have you ever wondered why the military continues to serve as the backbone of our society, or why we as a people have always been so desperate to preserve our legacy?" Her lips curl down into a sad smile. "It's because we are dying."

"Everyone dies." I counter blankly. She shakes her head softly, pulls out a map, and shoves it into my hands.

"No, not us as individuals, our *nation* is dying. Ever since its birth, our country has fought for the right to survive. To exist as free men. Look at your maps. Do you not see how we stand at the center of a battle between two vast empires? Our domain is small and isolated, cut off from access to the eastern mountains. If we were even a little weaker, we would be entirely overrun. Our people would be enslaved and our children stolen away. Look at your history books. In the five hundred years that we have been a country, only in twenty have we been at peace. How do you think that we have survived, Proserpine?" She leans in close, her eyes wide as she peers into my face. "By training up our military. By making our small numbers the best army that the world has ever seen. By understanding that it's a dog-eat-dog world out there, and if it's between me and the enemy, it's sure as hell not going to be me that walks away in defeat."

"Is it cruel? Perhaps." Nonchalantly, she shrugs her shoulders. "But if I have to commit atrocities to make sure that my children will grow up without fear, then I will do it without a second thought. There's a reason heroes always have weapons in those stories of yours, Proserpine. Always carry guns in holsters and swords strapped in sheaths. Because being a hero means that you protect the people you have sworn to save. It means getting your hands dirty so that the people you love can keep theirs clean."

"How many of those wars have been started by us, though?" I ask, voice rising. "How many of those wars have been waged against each other inside Durnon, various factions led by power-hungry men convinced that they can satisfy their greed with bloodlust?"

"I have seen your arenas." I spit. "I have stepped into the sands of your stadiums and watched as people held votes on whether strangers should be allowed to live or die. I have seen men slaughtered for nothing more than the sake of entertainment. Tell me, was that honorable? The work of a hero?" My voice drops. "Was that for the good of our nation?"

"I have seen the bodies," I tell the woman. "I have seen the bodies stacked up in pyramids on the side of the road, their flesh rotting as they bake in the summer sun. Is that honorable? I have learned to fall asleep to the sound of unending screaming, unending wailing from mere rats unable to give a proper voice to their suffering. I have seen *animals* display more humanity than any single man who works here at this building. Tell me, is that for the good of our nation?" I stand there, panting. And wait. For an answer. A response. My vision swims, and I try to blink back black spots as I lean in the doorway.

After a pause, I scoff. "One day, you will be face to face with whatever saw fit to let you exist in the universe, and you will have to justify the space you've filled." The woman stays silent. Ever so slightly, a faint smile begins to creep across her lips.

"That's it," I tell her then. "I'm leaving." I turn to walk away and stumble as I lean on the doorframe.

"No, you're not." The woman counters. She crosses her legs and smiles as the room around me begins to spin. "Or I guess you can try. You'll probably make it quite a way, I can imagine. But not far enough."

"What are you talking about?" I hiss, doubling down as a searing pain shoots up and down my chest. My heart is spasming. My legs are shaking as they struggle to hold me up.

"The infection. Can't you see, child? It's already spread across your immune system." I start laughing then. Double over, gasping, and throw my head back. Laugh until tears pour from my eyes. Laugh until my chest aches.

"Do you seriously think that a small infection is going to stop me?" I ask wheezing as I try to catch my breath from laughing so hard. "I have survived stab wounds. Gunshots. I taught myself to breathe with only one lung inside my chest. One time, I dismantled my heart and rebuilt it just to see what made it tick. You think a few sniffles are going to put me down?"

"No, I don't think that the plague is going to keep you down." She smiles then, her glasses flashing as her eyes twinkle. "Proserpine, you are such a fascinating individual. I don't think anything, not even a bioweapon, could seriously hurt you. But I do think that it will slow you down. Enough for us to catch up if you try to make a run for it."

I sink to the floor. My ears are ringing. Bursts of light are blooming along the corners of my vision. I clutch a hand against my stomach. Try not to imagine the organs liquifying on my insides.

"No matter how far you run," The woman coos, "we will always find you. No matter how well you hide, you'll always come back."

The woman stands up. I burst for the door, legs shuddering as I struggle to keep upright. Tear a hole through the wall and simply jump, desperation overriding any shred of common sense as I struggle to run. I will not let myself be hemmed in in a maze of winding, sterile hallways. Will not let myself scramble like another rat in a trap, hands feebly scraping at the walls as I try to run.

I want -

To feel the sun on my face. To breathe in air that doesn't come from a filtration vent. To burrow my shoes into the soil and grow still like the trees do. I want to smell the flowers. I want to hear the birds sing.

I want –

To run and run until no one can catch me. To climb a mountain, or see the sea, or touch a cloud that hangs down as fluffy as sheep. Would it be soft, do you think? Logically, I know that they're made up of pollution and hydrogen dioxide particles, but I like to think that a cloud would be soft.

I need to stop thinking about clouds. Need to focus my energy on simply running, slam my feet down one after another as I tear into the undergrowth. I need to focus on escaping and concentrate on getting as far away from the facility as possible.

But I'm so tired.

I want to focus on the clouds. Sit down, hide, and simply watch the clouds. Hide away from the rest of the world and watch as everything simply falls into place. I didn't... I didn't want this. I didn't want to be a hero. In the end, all I really wanted was for someone to love me.

I hide myself under a thicket of shrubbery and stare at the sky with half-lidded eyes. Glance at my skin and notice how already my flesh has begun to erupt in boils. Watch the clouds drift over the sun, their shapes shrinking and stretching as they form an endless swarm of butterfly wings.

I lie down and watch the clouds as I feel the strength slowly pour from my body. Sit and watch the clouds as the search parties begin to approach. Allow myself to relax and close my eyes, to slump against the ground and simply rest.

Soon, soon I will be the Proserpine everyone expects me to be. I will march across the land of Durnon and put an end to all the suffering.

Soon, I will be the hero, the savior sent to bring about a happy ending.

But for now, I am Helen. And I am allowed to be tired, and soft, and rest. For now, I am Helen, and I can wait for a couple of seconds.

(14)

AFTER: NATALYA

(Recovered audio hard drive, fragment two of three. September second, five-oh-oh-six. Martin Russel.)

The EEG records from exposure therapy reveal flaws in the initial assumption. In severe infections, microorganisms circulate throughout the bloodstream. Antibiotics create a hostile environment, forcing bacteria to hide in low-vascular areas— segments of liver, lung, or intestine—where they build protective barriers, reproducing and occasionally escaping to cause systemic infection when their numbers drop. This is called an abscess.

That is what is going on here.

They say that 'the hungry one' isn't real, that 'the hungry one' is just a figment of Natalya's traumatized imagination. They are wrong. 'The hungry one' is real, and if they would run another Technetium or MRI scan I might even be able to point out that exact area of the brain, those exact neurons, where it lives. It isn't a creature of flesh and blood, it's electrical signals. A mutation and overgrowth of the parasympathetic nervous system. It's everything we've been trying to cure, coalesced, hidden away in a shadowy corner pretending to be dead. Those autonomic reflexes – warming her skin, constricting her pupils, slowing her heart rate – those are its efforts to camouflage itself and its host. It knows we're monitoring. Measuring. Watching. It- it is hiding.

(Remainder of recording corrupted.)

There's another room, this time. A small one. I have to stoop to avoid the ceiling from scraping my head when I stand up. I slam the door behind me, press my ear against the panels to listen for the sound of heavy breathing.

There's nothing.

Not even white noise, that faint buzz that always arises from static and ticking clocks and all other forms of background noise. I don't hear the thing behind the door when I listen.

I try to tell myself that that thought is something reassuring. Slowly, I look around the room.

The barren room looks back, dust smothering the furniture as strips of wallpaper peel off the walls. The furniture is small, and the wood on the bunk bed is rotting. A couple of children's drawings flutter from where they rest halfheartedly nailed against the walls. In the center of the bed, a small stuffed animal flops. A paper airplane sails down and lands on the corner of the moldy bed. Hesitantly, I reach out and touch it, unfold the mildewed edges, and stare at the faded writing.

[] Do you remember now?

The bed is where it's always been. So is the chair, decomposing quietly in the corner. Rotting paperbacks litter the floor. The creased spines are ripped out. I walk around my childhood room, listen to buzzing flies as cold light filters through window cracks. A sense of comfort stirs in my chest, though it's much too wrong and far too late.

There's always something special about being back in your childhood house. Even if the house hasn't been your home in a while now.

I reach out and touch one of the drawings, the yellow page tearing slightly. My fingers trace over smudged charcoal, follow choppy lines done in that familiar style from where I was convinced I knew how to draw. Rushed. Frantic. Sloppy.

There's a monster, drawn on the page. It's got big, sharp teeth and coal bright eyes that glow from where it pokes its head out of the chimney. It would look like a human if there wasn't something just slightly off.

I'm not sure exactly what was off about it. What made it clear that the thing staring back from the other side of the page wasn't quite right. It could have been the nails; how yellow they were. Not sunshine yellow, not cigarette yellow; but translucent, almost. Like there was something decaying just below its fingertips.

It could have been its ears, how they swiveled around like those of a bat. It could have been the chunks of hardened pus that dripped and bubbled under the cheap costume of a thing it called a skin. I don't quite know what it was if I'm honest. It might have been a monster. But it was most certainly not a man.

Underneath the picture is writing. *My* writing. Yet the penmanship looks too cold to be written by a child. Too… neat. Orderly. Precise. I could just be uncomfortable, I guess. After all, I know that I wasn't the one who wrote this, despite how much the author might be pretending otherwise.

Sometimes, I think I'm scared of growing up. Daddy says it happens to everyone, though. He said that we should be proud of what we've gone through because that means that we are still alive. We survived the cold. And the genocide. And the hunger. He said that these are our battle scars, that they mean we survived what others could not.

Sometimes, I'm scared that we didn't really survive. That we're just pretending, playing make-believe here in the cold and sleet. I miss being able to play in the sunshine.

I miss being allowed to leave the house.

[] <u>Do you remember now?</u> The paper airplane taunts from where it splays unfolded on the bunkbed.

[] <u>Maybe you remember now?</u>

I stagger back as the room shifts, floorboards sliding and jamming back together in shades a little bit too dark, the wood slightly more weathered. Faded paint peels down the sides of the walls in uneven strips, the wallpaper beneath a rustic red that's unsettling familiar. A hungry fire gurgles from where it licks at the nearby granite.

I'm standing in a kitchen. My parents' kitchen. Anxiously, I reach for the lighter inside my pocket. The flame sparks up with a hiss, and I watch the shadows warily from where they slink between the corners.

If I didn't know better, I'd say that they're watching me.

I grip the lighter tighter as hands reach out and wrap around my shoulders. Carefully, almost lovingly, the fingers reach out and begin to pet the edges of my hair. The skin is slightly sticky from where it brushes against my scalp.

"Everything is temporary." The thing wearing my mother's skin whispers, her voice soft and cloying as she continues to stroke my hair. "This was just one of those things."

I try to tip my head back, and as I inhale, the smoke from the fire chokes. It's soaking up all the oxygen, and the world around me spins in the suffocating darkness.

Outside, the winds howl, and shells ring out like falling stars as they light the ice on fire.

Outside, it is cold. And damp. And dark. The ice is melting under armored footsteps, the snow grinding down into bloodied slush. But here, here it is warm. I exhale again, and the embers sear themselves against my eyes.

"Everything is temporary." The thing wearing my mother's skin croons, as the cold wind roars. As the fire pop, pop, pops and fingers slip in sticky sweat.

"But not us, Natalya."

"Never us."

There are maggots in the meat in the bowl on the kitchen counter. Fat and white and squirming as they worm themselves under the reddened chunks. I watch as they wriggle, watch them shiver and pulse as their bloated bodies splash around in the gravy.

"Mom," I know it's not my mother, that's looking at me with such a loving smile.

That the thing in front of me can't possibly be my mother, with her roughed hands and too bright eyes. Her smile is too warm, too bright, too *present*. Like someone had forgotten how a parent might smile and was trying to recreate it from memory. Even the room is too hot, the flames dancing so high in their fireplace that the heat feels suffocating. "Mom, we're going to die if we don't leave this house soon. Mom…" my voice cracks "Mom, I'm scared."

"Nat-bat?" The thing that wears my mother's skin asks at last. "Baby, what's wrong?"

The spoon in my hands shivers as I hold it, my hands shaking. I wasn't holding a spoon, or at least I don't think I was. I was holding a lighter. *I know I had a lighter.* And yet, it's a silver spoon that I'm gripping in my hands.

The food on the counter gurgles, the maggots bubbling as they worm deeper and deeper beneath the rotted flesh. I look down at the spoon in my hands, rub my fingers against the ridges in its handle so I don't have to look at the thing wearing my mother's smile. I want to say no. I want to ask what is in the soup. But I never do.

Sometimes, I have dreams that there are maggots in the meat Mother cooks. The food would rot in my stomach, and I would rot along with it, and Mother would nibble on my corpse until the bones grew pearly white.

I blink, and the room changes. I look down and notice the blood dripping from my fingertips. Somewhere in the shadows of the room, a baby wails.

I'm in a nursery. One I built with my husband from the ground up with nothing more than our hands.

There's a cradle in the center of the room. The crying is coming from inside it. A part of me wants to go and look inside it, wants to grab the whimpering thing and hold it close. And yet I'm scared. I'm so, *so* scared. Because my sons are somewhere safe, far away from here, and it's been a long time since my daughter was an infant.

The crying continues, the wails wet and gasping. I take a step, and then another. The white bedding begins to turn beneath my outstretched fingers, blood dripping from my stained hands and turning the sheets scarlet. My heart is screaming at me to look inside the cradle, hands itching to pick up the poor little thing and cradle it close. I want to hold it. I need to comfort it, rock it back and forth the way I used to…

But my sons are safe, bright and alive and far, far away from this place among the rotten. My daughter was small, yes, but she was far too big by the time she died to ever fit inside a crib.

I don't know what's crying inside that cradle, but I know that it's only pretending to be my baby.

A part of me still wants to pick it up, in spite of that.

(15)

BEFORE: HELEN

Some days, I pretend that I am already dead. That my flesh is already rotten. My skin nothing more than a sack stretched over decaying bones.

I stay inside and simply rot in my bed. Clutter accumulates around my room, a pile of clothes and stethoscopes, medals and books, and constantly decaying flowers, and everything is just *too much*. On the bad days, I grow tired. I sleep until I'm too tired to sleep. I lie there staring at the cracks in my ceiling and wonder what it would be like to simply stop moving.

A pair of vultures has gathered to perch outside my window. They crane their necks and bend their heads as they wait.

"I'm tired," I tell Thanatos. He's silent from where he watches in the corner. Softly, ever so softly, he sighs. Holds out a hand. My palm shakes in his grip.

A part of me worries that I'm being too greedy, with how desperately I look for him. How much I need his hugs. Sometimes, I get scared of asking for too much and having him leave. I can't handle having him push me away.

"I'm a failure." I sob out quietly. Death reaches out his hand and strokes my hair. Cradles me close and shushes me softly as I break down in his arms. "Death, I'm a failure. And I'm sorry. I'm so sorry."

"I thought I told you already that you don't need to apologize to me, little one." He murmurs soothingly.

"But I'm useless." I protest angrily. "I mean, look at me, Thanatos. I can't even get out of bed anymore." I stare at the ceiling as tears continue to pour from my eyes. Outside, the wind wails. I have learned to morph the very clouds, and now whenever I cry, the sky cries with me. "I can't fulfill our promise." Death keeps his eyes fixed on mine as the rain slowly freezes.

His eyes soften. I want to suffocate in that softness. Let it smother me up, hold onto me forever. I just want him to want me.

"I will always love you, Helen. Forever and always. You are more precious to me than anything in the whole world. You do not have to prove something to be lovable. Even if you failed, I would still want you."

"You wouldn't get tired of me?" I have to check, worry twisting in my chest. I may be thirteen, but I'm not naïve. "Not ever? Never leave me? Never throw me away, or decide I'm not worth keeping? My voice trails off. "You'd never hit me, would you?"

"*Never,* Helen." He hisses and *oh*. There is something so strange about seeing the god of gentleness start to rage. "I would never lift a hand against you. I would never leave you. Because you are my child. And that means you are dearer to me than anything. How could I grow bored with my own child? How could I ever let you go once you were mine?"

"They've started having me work with the scientists." I choke out with a sob. "They said that I didn't need to fight in the arenas anymore, that I could just stay and practice with the doctors instead. They said I could be a healer." I wail. "They said that my existence could amount to more than just mere violence." Thanatos holds me tighter as I cry into his cloak. His bony hands stretch out and wipe away my tears. "The Royal Physician himself visited my house," I add with a sniffle. "She promised that I could bring my family honor without ever having to kill again."

210

"I'm so tired, Thanatos." I gasp out. "I'm so tired of feeling scared. And trapped. And I'm trying so hard to be a good kid. I'm trying to help people. But Death, I'm so tired of wanting to die." I feel a shudder wrack my insides. "I can't even *die* anymore, Thanatos. At least, not permanently. My cells keep being rebuilt over and over, and no matter how many times the physicians poke at me, I keep being reborn, and it's not fair, Thanatos. I can't even die to escape anymore. Why would you give me a gift so cruel?"

Death hugs me tighter, and with a flick of his hand, we are sitting in a gazebo, on the edge of a mechanical garden. Flowers bloom as they smother up the windowpanes, and a radio warbles from where it merrily sings.

"… The Monster's gone.

He's on the run.

And your Daddy's here.

Beautiful,

Beautiful,

Beautiful,

Beautiful Girl…."

When I was little, back when the only form of death I had witnessed was the type discussed in old, battered books, I used to think that dying was instant. I believed that endings were clean, the flat line of a heart monitor or faint gasp of a final breath. I've learned differently since arriving here in the sanitarium. Endings aren't sudden; they're gradual. They creep in through the small things: the subtle cough that rattles deep inside your lungs, the pockets of stillness that seem to gather in the corners of your room like dust. Death is something that rots you from the inside out. It blooms under your skin, softly growing, until one day you wake up and realize that the end isn't something you can run away from – it's inside you. That it has always been, patiently watching, waiting for your heart to slow and your body to fail.

"It's fascinating how the virus evolves." One of the scientists murmurs. He takes a chunk of my skin and observes it critically with a pair of tweezers. "Even with Proserpine's antibodies, the virus continues to mutate. Even a single vaccination could cause the virus to be terminal. See how it attaches itself to the lymphocytes?"

"Most extraordinary is how easily the pox spreads." Another one comments. Glasses glint and pens flash as they continue writing. "It affects animals and plants alike. Already, the rivers tested have turned nearly solid from the poisoned fish floating in piles, belly up. Imagine if we could transform the disease into spores? Or gas? Our army would be unstoppable."

They call me Proserpine. The name feels clinical as it drips from their lips. *Proserpine.* They don't call me by my real name, my human name. They don't call me Helen. Because Helen is just a girl, while Proserpine is a god. It's strange, really. How dehumanizing their devotion feels.

I sob from where I lie there strapped onto the operating table. Paper sheets crinkle from where unknown hands pin me down. My head is hazy, and I look around with scattered thoughts as the room wobbles. I drift in and out of memories, float through arenas and operating tables and graves in the Underworld, and I don't quite know what's going on anymore. Time shifts and warps until my brain goes numb like cotton.

Throughout it all, Thanatos watches. He holds my hand, marks the physicians by their faces, and whispers with a softened voice promises of their eternal damnation. He does not leave my side.

He holds my hand when the men start screaming. Squeezes my fingers soothingly while the men beg and wail and cry. Covers my ears while they throw themselves down on the floor and writhe like the fleas did, gouge holes out of their arms and legs, and scream scream *scream* as they begin to scrape at their own skin. Above our heads, the sky begins to cry tears of blood. I look on numbly as the

214

scarlet stains the soil. The earth slurps it up eagerly. The liquid rises until eventually the men begin to drown in their own blood. They begin to choke on their own vomit.

"It is a mercy for them to die." Death whispers lovingly. Grabs a radio and raises the volume until I can no longer hear the screaming. Takes a candle and a match with an almost painful gentleness to his eyes. Lights a flame. Shuts the slaughter away behind a pair of blinds and hugs me tight. "This way, they are spared judgment from all the abominations that they would have created at a different date."

I let myself relax while the world rages outside. Sit there in the room and breathe. Rest a hand on the wooden planks that make up the floor and pretend that I can feel the beating trunks they once belonged to. Carefully, ever so carefully, Death begins to braid flowers into the curls of my tangled hair.

Eventually, the screaming dies out. The sanitorium goes silent. Thanatos sighs and then relaxes.

"Just a little longer, little one." He assures me gently. "You're doing so good for me, Helen." The bones that make up his fingers spasm from where he grips my hand. His head is tilted, ears pricked almost like a dog as he strains to listen for the noises in the hallway. "It won't be much longer now." He adds after a pause.

Gunshots begin to go off, over and over again. Footsteps begin to race through the halls, their sound echoing in a series of thumps. Above my head, the AC unit wails, its metal screeching as it whirs back to life.

"HELEN!" That's… that's my mom who's screaming. Desperately, I try to drag myself off the bed. I want - no, I *need* to get to her. I need to see my mom again. I need her to hold me like she used to, so she can let me know that everything's going to be okay.

The door doesn't open as much as it is ripped off its hinges. Steel caves inwards, screaming like the metal is alive as it's ripped off its hinges. Mother stands there panting, skin-stained red from where the blood cakes her arms. Her eyes are bloodshot. Her hands are shaking.

Our eyes lock.

Somewhere behind her, I can hear my brother laughing. *Marek.* It isn't joy, at least it doesn't sound like it is. The sound is almost feral in its intensity, a cackle wild and sharp as he begins to hunt. There's a hunger in him that seems to seep into the cracks of the linoleum tiles, pooling beneath his footsteps as he stalks down the scientists.

Marek's shadow stretches tall behind him, darkness prowling up the walls, silver teeth smiling from a grin in which there should only be darkness. Before the storm of bullets can even properly die down, he's already grown bored of using his guns, throwing the weapons to the floor as he snatches at the scientists with his bare hands.

"Helen." Mother croaks out, voice hoarse as she drinks me in. *Helen.* Not Proserpine, not Kore, just Helen.

"Oh, *sweetheart.*" Her hands are shaking as she reaches out and tugs me into her arms.

Marek slams a security guard into the doorway. Bones crunch. The man flops, useless, as Marek turns. He looks at me and waves. His fingers are just a little bit too long, his smile just a tad too bright. He cocks his head, ears perked, listening. I feel the world tighten as it closes in around me, the hallway squealing as walls sink in and doors squeak open. Marek giggles. The overhead lights flicker. By the time they come on again, there's nothing left where my brother stood but a pair of bloodied footprints.

A part of me knows, deep down, that the hunt is over almost as soon as it's begun. Marek prowls along the hallways, and Thanatos slips between the shadows, and there is something about the brightness in their smiles that causes the hairs on the back of my head to stand up.

"Helen?" Mother calls out again, voice cracking as she tries to get the words out. "Helen, let's go home, ok? It's time to go home now."

THE FOOL THAT FELL

Once upon a time, in a land of ivory palaces and wine-drunk seas, there dwelled a prince named Theseus. He was crafty, strong, and far too sure of himself.

He slaughtered the Minotaur. He defeated the Amazons. Soldiers called out his name on the battlefield, eyes wide in devotion as they dropped to their knees before him. Enemies would see him riding closer, the glint of his armor blinding from where it burned with the flames of hellfire, and they would know fear. Beloved Theseus. Clever Theseus. Child of the Avenging Tide, He was a being considered more God than man, something greater than the mere mortals that scurried underneath his rule like ants.

Perhaps it makes sense that Theseus's downfall was foretold long before he ever picked up a sword, let alone set off to fight the Minotaur. It's easy to believe you are untouchable, after all, when the poets claim that nothing in this world can touch you. (And yet at the same time, I suppose he really should have known better. The gods are jealous creatures after all, and they do so love to break the little haloes that fools claim as their own.)

And so when his friend Pirithous suggested, "Let us steal wives from the gods," Theseus smiled and accepted.

"I'll take Helen of Sparta," boasted Theseus. A woman whose beauty was more of a curse than a blessing, a face so sweet it drove men to madness.

"And then I shall take Proserpine," added Pirithous, meaning the Queen of the Dead herself.

And like two fools in search of conquest, they descended into the Underworld, believing they could outwit the gods.

The world beneath the ground was quiet, with wraiths pausing from their wanderings among the wasteland to turn and stare as the heroes walked past. Getting up, they began to follow the men, sneaking closer so steadily that the pair had to take turns looking backwards. First, it was one. Then two. Then twenty. Despite how stealthily the heroes crept or how fast the pair ran, they couldn't escape the millions of watching eyes.

They found the temple to Thanatos carved from bone and cadmium, its walls sighing with forgotten prayers. No soldiers. No watchdogs. The doors swung open upon the slightest touch.

Inside the temple, two marble thrones waited.

"Gifts," proclaimed Theseus. "For heroes such as we."

They sat.

And the ground swallowed them whole.

The thrones were traps. The marble clung like mold to their skin, as if the Underworld itself had grown hungry. They could not stand. Could not move. Could only stare across the vast throne room at where Proserpine approached slowly, silently, with eyes filled with... I wouldn't say mercy, exactly. But definitely pity.

She stared at them with eyes as soft as Winter's frost, snowdrops shivering from where they clung to her shoulders in unease. Although the flowers winding around her skin shuddered, the goddess herself was still.

"Why have you come?" she wondered.

"For you," claimed Pirithous, foolishly.

"To prove I could," confessed Theseus, honestly.

Proserpine turned to the darkness watching in the corner. "They are yours now," she stated with a shrug.

And the darkness whispered back: "Yes."

Time does not tick in the Underworld as it does in the world of the living. Instead, it drips, feeding on memories rather than the passage of the sun. Days passed, then decades, and the two friends did not age so much as wither. Their thoughts grew thin. Their names faded and rusted until they wore down like river rocks.

Until one day, another man entered the realm of the dead: brave, golden, and stubborn.

Hercules.

He pleaded for Theseus's freedom, claiming that one mere mistake compared to the host of the prince's victories should not condemn him. He spoke of honor and justice, listed the dozens upon dozens of deeds Theseus had done to benefit his people.

The Gods may be many things, but they honor courage.

And thus, Theseus was released.

But when he started towards his friend, Pirithous, the stone hardened. Proserpine held out a hand.

"Only one can be set free."

Theseus stared at his friend who had once dared to take a goddess… and stayed silent.

He returned to the land of the living, but his kingdom had changed. Instead of worship, people walked past him without a second glance. Statues of him were cracked and forgotten. What worth was his legacy then, Theseus wondered, if no one could remember it? What use was his former glory when he had faded into obscurity?

He stayed for a while. Then wandered. Then vanished.

Some say he became a ghost, haunting the stadiums where athletes crash and burn for a momentary glimpse at glory. Others say he sits by the edge of the sea, watching ships pass as fishermen gossip, and wondering when he stopped being someone worth talking about.

Regardless of the different endings, all soothsayers whisper this before closing out the man's story:

If you ever feel clever enough to cheat Death, or brave enough to overpower the gods,

Remember Theseus.

The man who entered the Underworld believing he could steal from the divine and left with nothing but silence in his hands.

Because the Dead do not care how famous your name is.

Only how honestly you carry it.

(16)

AFTER: NATALYA

(Recovered audio hard drive, fragment three of three, September second, five-oh-oh-six. Martin Russel.)

I wasn't supposed to return to this case, to be honest. Was supposed to keep it closed off, all locked and shut up and left to rot with the other files in the back of the storage shed. I was supposed to forget about the girl with the dead eyes. Forget about the child with the supposedly cured virus that I knew was still alive.

In light of recent events, this order has changed. I've had to dig up my audio files. Been forced to find my old notes and compare them with past data. But I now know, with unfailing certainty, that this belief has changed.

The subject had two sons. Became a mother. After years of perceived fertility issues, the subject bore children. And those offspring are producing the same symptoms seen in the people on the mountain.

Polydipsia. A shrinkage of the pituitary gland. Signs of iron deficiency are directly countered by an overgrowth of calcium in bone marrow. Enlargement of the frontal cerebral cortex and an excess of auditory signals that produce echolocation. An improved autoimmune system, erosion of pigment in the irises, advanced metabolism, the list goes on. The point is that the Sa-1202 failed in stopping the infection from the mountain. And now the virus is spreading into Natalya's offspring…"

I cradle the infant carefully in my arms. Rock it quietly and hum until it slowly stops wailing.

"The subject had a daughter, later. A changeling child found weeping alone in the forest. Although it's rather unprofessional of me to do so, a part of me wonders what exactly Natalya had been thinking, taking it home. Maybe she had hoped that at least this way she could have one child who was normal. If so, she has been sadly mistaken."

"It's alright," I whisper softly. "It's alright, you don't need to cry. I'm here. I'm always here."

"Which is crueler?" The recording asks then. *"To have a child with a rotting mind, or one with a decaying body? To see your selfish wish for a son create a monster, or watch as your daughter's body breaks down under the weight of suffering for others?"*

It's a little girl that I'm holding in my hands. Dark curls flop as her crying slowly quiets. Her hair was black before she dyed it. I don't think I remembered just how dark it was. It's still soft, though. My daughter has always been so soft.

"They call it the curse of Eve, at least that's what the theologians say. The pain of watching your

*own sins bleed into and corrupt your children. The curse of Eve, tell me, **Natalya,** how does it feel to realize that your blood flows within, poisoning their veins? That you damned your children to a life of suffering before they were even born?"*

I sit down in a nearby rocking chair and hold the infant tighter as all around us the world spins. Slowly, the sound of screaming starts. Shrieking ghosts and morphing faces, and the very world twists and turns, but I hold my baby tighter and rock her softly. Sing a little lullaby and watch as she coos.

"I don't know what you're trying to do," I say to the screams and the shrieks and the host of nightmares here in the land of dreams. "I don't know what your goal is, whether you're trying to scare me away or cause me to break and falter. But there is nothing you could do," I state, "to make me leave my daughter."

For a while, the voice is silent. The screaming subsides, and the spinning pauses as the voice from the recorder thinks. Slowly, ever so slowly, something begins to bulge out from the flaps of faded wallpaper.

I watch in silence as the thing begins to ooze out from beneath the flaps of the painted wall. Hold my baby closer and watch as something similar to oil spills out and begins to writhe at my feet. It's faceless, in the way that the thing has so many faces that they blur together. It's tall, in the way that it stands just slightly larger than it should be if it were human. A dark dress coat shapes over its spindly shoulders. A tall, gentlemanly hat stretches to completely encapsulate its forehead.

"Hello Natalya. Do you know who I am?" The creature murmurs, eyes half lidded as he stares at me. His voice crackles like logs on a slow-burning fire, pitch slightly distorted as if whispering from a radio. I watch poppies bloom like spores across the surface of his skin. "My name is Hypnos." A sleepy smile spreads across the chthonic deity's face. His bones continue to grow until his hat squishes the top of the ceiling. "I believe it's time that we had a talk."

"Yes, I quite think so." I stammer out, and then reflexively widen my stance. Hypnos smiles, and then with a wave of his hand, the room changes, a table and chairs neatly resting on a rug of spinning stars.

"I do not hate you, Natalya." Hypnos starts, cubes of sugar clinking in his glass from where he pours himself a cup of tea. "Do you know that? It's important to me that you know that."

"Maybe." I shrug my shoulders, stare at him warily as I pull my teeth back into a smile. "But you still want me to fail. Otherwise, you wouldn't be sending me through all those nightmares."

"Is it a nightmare to remember Natalya?" He murmurs, poppies flaring as they burrow and bloom along the layers of his skin. "Still, I suppose that isn't important. After all, we aren't exactly here for *you*, are we?"

"We're here for my daughter." I agree. Make sure to emphasize that last part, look him dead in the eyes as I say the last two words. *My daughter. Mine.* Hypnos's nostrils flare before he feigns disinterest and looks away.

"Yes, Helen." He states calmly. The scent of poppies is beginning to make my head spin. "Ruler of Helheim, queen of Hades. Proserpine. Persephone. Explain to me, please, foolish mortal, why exactly you think that you'll succeed at Stealing Lady Death from the dead."

"Because she's- she's my daughter." I stammer, flustered. "She was young and full of life. She didn't deserve to die."

"Do you think anyone ever believes that they deserve to die, Natalya?" Hypnos replies softly. "Warriors, sick, the old, and the young. No one truly believes that it is their time to fall until it finally comes. Helen herself was unique in the fact that she never quite feared dying. She made that deal with

Thanatos even after being made aware of the consequences."

"She was a child…"

"A child who was old enough to grasp the repercussions for her actions. No, not merely understand them. In fact, your daughter craved them. She wanted to die. Natalya," Hypnos looks up then, with a gentle sort of pity in his tone, "did you know why Helen would possibly choose to enter that sanitarium?"

She wanted to die. It's weird, hearing the words stated so bluntly. That was- that was my baby. My baby wanted to die. It's strange to look back and try to remember if there were signs. There must have been tons of them. Dozens. The trouble going to bed at night, her constant isolation, the constant cuts and bruises marking her skin, even though no one had been with her. The way she was just a little bit too eager to be her nation's martyr, just a little too excited to imagine her death having some sort of meaning. In hindsight, I should have known better. I thought that I was giving her space, letting her have room to breathe. Instead, I failed her. I failed my little girl.

"I know that she was desperate." I croak out eventually. "And I-I know that she was tired."

"Then you never really knew her." He sighs softly. "Not before she made that deal with Thanatos. You never really knew her when she was small, did you?

"I was with Helen when she was tiny, you know." Hypnos continues.
"Really, *really,* tiny. I used to watch her waddle around your family's garden when she was far too young to properly walk. People begin to dream as soon as they're able to think, and I do so love to visit children and wrap them in dreams. There's always something soft about them when they sleep. All fluffy clouds and dancing unicorns and bright sparkly rainbows. Children's dreams are always such beautiful things, and I do so love to watch the kids smile when they see them."

"Helen was unique from the other children in that she was able to see me when she slept. Perhaps she was more attuned to the spirits, and as such, she was more skilled in dealing with myth and magic. Either way, she saw me. And instead of being frightened by this utterly grotesque-looking person," Hypnos laughs deprecatingly as he gestures to his shifting form. "She was enchanted instead. She called me *Mr. Flower Man.* I guess she saw all my poppies and thought that I was obsessed with botanical plants."

We used to spend nights together, constructing whimsical labyrinths here in dreamland. The most beautiful gardens, Natalya, you simply wouldn't be able to imagine the brightness of the flowers or the softness of the trickling streams. I spared no expense, drew on all my creativity and power to make her smile.

And yet, my creativity was eventually not enough. I was forced to watch as she grew sicker, her skin pale and eyes red from where she used to cry herself to sleep at night. I watched as my child suffered. I watched as my baby was hurt.

They call me the god of dreams, you know. Hypnos, the ruler of nightmares and wishes. I am the gentle kiss of morphine, the sudden rush of ecstasy. It is I who bears the keys to protect each soul's fear and hope."

For a moment, Hypnos pauses. He inhales, breath shaky as he looks down and stares me in the eyes. Slowly, ever so slowly, I watch as the god before me begins to cry.

"I... I can help with nightmares, Natalya." Hypnos states. "But I can't help anyone when they're awake. I can craft wishes, but what am I supposed to do when I encounter children so broken that their only wish is to disappear from existence?"

"Did you ever wonder why it was *you* who found Helen when she was all alone in that terrible building?" The deity asks desperately. "It's because *I* sent you there. Not Thanatos. *I did.* Because Thanatos, in spite of all his efforts, cannot be anything other than death. And I wanted my child to wish for something other than dying. I was so tired of watching her dream of dying."

"*You* were the one who sent me?" I repeat, staring at the being in astonishment. "But I thought you were trying to stop me, with the series of dreams and memories."

"I am tired of watching my little girl be hurt." Hypnos declares in response. "And perhaps it was dark and perhaps it was cruel, but Natalya, I wanted you to grasp just how evil the world you inhabit is. That if you don't have anyone to rely on, it will inevitably break you. I wanted you to remember, mortal." Hypnos confesses. "Because only then can you understand just what type of place you're choosing to bring Helen back to. I want you to think about whether you really want to bring your daughter back to a life of pain. Here in the underworld, she'll never be hurt again."

"Maybe you're right in saying that the world I live in is fallen." I agree, relaxing as I look up at the god who towers above my head.

"Maybe you're right in saying that life is cruel and will break a person if they're not careful. But Hypnos, Helen is not alone. She has a family, one that loves her no matter how big her dreams or potential may be. She has a family, who will be there for her through every scary and terrible nightmare."

"And so maybe it's true that the world is decayed and rotten and filled with corrupt people. Maybe the world is so wicked that your most horrific nightmares pale in comparison. But no matter how dark the night is, the sun will always continue to rise. There will always be another day. A day where Helen can *grow*, can laugh, cry, smile, and rage, and no matter what happens, she will have a home to return to. She will have a family to return to."

Slowly, ever so slowly, Hypnos's still expression begins to crack. A tear slides down the edge of his pale cheek. And then a second. And then a third. More and more tears begin to drip from his eyes until the god seems to almost shrink before me, transforming from a massive divinity into a wretched, weeping thing.

"I… I helped her?" He asks uncertainly.

"You did," I assure him. "All you have to do now is let me pass and bring her to life again."

"I don't know if that's a good idea," Hypnos whispers. He shrinks and he shrinks until he pools into a tear-shaped puddle at my feet. "What if, as soon as I let her go, she gets hurt again? What if she gets worse? Reality can be a terrible, cruel place to go through."

"What if she gets better?" I ask him, tone growing wistful. "What if she learns what it's like to laugh so hard her stomach hurts? What if she learns what it's like to chase fireflies at nighttime, or stay up late enough to watch the sunrise, or swing from a tree she has seen grow since it was a sapling? What if she heals – smiles for nothing more than the sake of smiling, accomplishes a goal she never once dreamed of reaching? Hypnos, I know you're scared of life hurting her, but what if Helen was able to give life meaning?"

Hypnos grumbles. Sighs. He lets out a deep breath as he pauses and deliberates. Eventually, he pulls himself together into a vaguely humanoid form and nods.

"You have made good points." He concedes eventually. Flicks his fingers and waves an ivory door into existence. "Go through that exit and you'll find your guide waiting on the other side. Only do me one favor, why don't you?"

"What is it?" I ask with one hand on the handle. I open the door and stare into the endless black void.

"Make sure she's happy, Natalya," Hypnos begs. "Let Helen know that I want her to be happy."

(17)

BEFORE: HELEN

It's quiet on the car ride. Marek fiddles with the mirrors as he looks out the windshield, floors the gas, and takes off down the beaten roads, dirt flying up as the tires flash. It feels strange riding in a moving vehicle. Especially one like this, all big and strong and unlike the spindly little automobiles I've seen in cities. I lean my head back against the seat. Feel seatbelts tighten as they wrap around my chest. Watch Mom out of the corner of my eye and spend the rest of the time simply staring as the trees race past. And then fields. The car races on for miles upon miles, until pine gives way to palm, and we start driving alongside a swamp. Until the forest by the sanitarium is swallowed up by marsh.

"I thought witches were supposed to ride on broomsticks," I remark after a while. Keep my eyes fixed on the window, catch glimpses of Mom's face reflected in the windowpane. She looks straight ahead, a tired grin creeping in as she fondly shakes her head.

"Good thing I'm not a witch then." Marek chuckles, bloodied hands curling as he adjusts the gear shift. "Could you imagine how uncomfortable that would be?" The engine roars as we accelerate.

I look down at where the engine purrs under my feet. Glance in the trunk, where knives, guns, and axes lie all carefully bundled up next to ransom papers.

"How'd you learn to make this thing so advanced?" I ask, trying desperately to crack the tension hovering over us. Marek chuckles again, that odd little laugh from the sanitorium rattling inside his chest. Mom hasn't stopped staring since she found me. Her eyes are wide—far too wide. I don't think I've seen her blink yet.

"What do you mean, how did I make this thing so advanced?" Marek teases. "It's a car for goodness' sake." I stare at him in silence. "Wow, you really need to get out more, Helen. I mean, I get that Durnon's not as technologically advanced as some other countries, but there's no way you don't know what a *car* is."

"Marek, stop teasing your little sister." Mother rasps out. She gives him a sharp look, then goes back to staring at me. "Not everyone gets to just go gallivanting around the world whenever they wish. Basically, think of it as something similar to your gift, sweetheart." She explains gently.

"So this technology is just another type of magic?" I ask cautiously. I shoot Marek a look, wonder what type of God he must have bound himself with to make metal come alive.

"Depends on what you think magic is, I suppose," Marek answers. "After all, magic is merely some sort of secret that people don't fully understand here in the universe. I can drive a car, which is essentially a collection of metal parts welded together. I can use a lighter, which causes a spark to flare up just from a single click. However, there are certain things I can't do that I'm sure you experience so often that they become a part of your everyday life. I know that I, for one, can't just magically make the sky rain."

His voice lowers. "I can't take a bunch of body parts and suddenly bring them back to life." He turns back to look at the road when I go silent. In the quiet, I can feel the metal walls slightly vibrate and shake.

"Where are we going?" I ask after a while. Keep my eyes fixed on the window, catch glimpses of Mom's face reflected in the windowpane. She looks straight ahead, a wry grin twitching at the edges of her lips.

"A safehouse. I already sent messages to your brothers." She responds, bloodied hands curling as she clenches them into fists. "Marek responded a little quicker, obviously, but Pietyr should be at the house when we get there." The engine roars as we accelerate. Marek's arms shift as they turn the steering wheel. Tattooed stories spill across his skin in a mess of ink.

"We're not going home again, are we?" I say then. A statement more than a question. I look out the windows one more time. Watch as the last of my known landmarks slowly begin to slip away, growing smaller in the distance. We pass the edges of Durnon without much of a fuss, Mother reaching into a compartment and fishing out stacks of paperwork to give to the border patrol. I'm not sure what was in those papers, but whatever it was was enough to keep the men from looking too closely at the little girl slouched in the backseat.

"No, we're not." She agrees, voice hardening as she shifts in her seat. "I don't want any of you three in Durnon, or anywhere that *thing* can touch you."

Thanatos. The name is blistering in its absence. I stiffen, fingers itching as I dig them into my palms to keep from screaming.

Mother wants me to get rid of him. Thinks that he's unhealthy for me, that it's not right for a girl to cling so desperately to a thing like Death.

"I'm sorry." Mother blurts out when the silence gets too thick. I blink, turning away from the sunroof to stare. "You shouldn't have had to go through that. Any of it."

"It's not… your fault." The reply is stilted. Automatic.

"Actually, it is." Mom insists. "But even if it wasn't, I'd still be sorry."

We drive until the sun rises. Keep going until it sets. Get out a couple of times, move around, and shake our legs, and when Mom parks the car to go into a local tavern, I freeze and wonder if I should run away. My purpose is in Durnon. My purpose is my people, whom Thanatos promised would one day be saved by me. I should know better by now. A hero in a story never gets rescued. Especially not by someone with blood on their hands.

"Hey Helen, are you coming?" Mother calls out, pausing. I stare into the woods, all wild with fireflies and creeping shadows. Watch the trees as they shift and slowly breathe. Feel their roots flex and curl beneath my feet. I could always go back home. I could always return to my greenhouse.

"I'm coming," I reply instead, eyes still fixed on the woods as I chase after her.

I don't know where Mom is taking me, but I hope it's somewhere warm.

It's dark outside by the time we reach the old, stone cottage. Ivy creeps up the sides and nestles against painted shutters. There's an apple tree, and a garage, and a shed filled with just enough guns to successfully take down a minor government.

I follow Mom inside. Watch as she hangs up her coat and takes off her shoes. Lights a fire and gets out a teapot as she slowly brings water to a boil.

She makes pancakes. Flips the batter in the pan, and I watch as the butter melts. The syrup burns from where it sticks to the back of my teeth. Mom grabs a first aid kit and sets it on the table, lines up salves and bandages in neat, even rows.

"Do you think I can see where they hurt you?" I jump at the sound, then turn to look at the silhouette standing in the stairway. He's quieter than I remember, Pietyr that is. Quieter, and yet at the same time *not*; some type of static seems to follow and warp around his breathing. He comes down the stairs carefully, shadows winding around his ankles like as he kneels down to look at my arms. His hands are gentle when they reach for mine.

"You scared me, Pietyr." I whine, trying not to flinch when he bends my wrist. "How long have you even been standing there? We need to get you a bell one of these days or something."

Pietyr laughs, a small, muffled chuckle that bounces off of the floors and bookshelves. For a second the sound hangs, a faint harmony that makes the woodgrains swirl and the candlelight fuzzy. I blink a couple times to stop my head from spinning.

"Good one Helen." His voice lowers. "But seriously, show me where they hurt you." He sighs when I stiffen. "I know it's a touchy subject, but I need to see so I can patch you up."

"They couldn't hurt me," I respond hesitantly. "I'm fine."

"You can cut the bullshit," Mom responds, voice stiff as she grips the spatula in her hands. "I read the files they kept."

"They couldn't hurt me anymore than I can handle." I amend. I show Pietyr my arms, roll up my sleeves and point out the lack of scars that should scrape my skin.

"They still hurt you, though." Marek insists, voice firm as the door slams shut behind him. He's not laughing anymore. "You know that, right? They still hurt you, even if you grew from that." I still, then. Stop and stare, as something ugly begins to squeeze the back of my throat.

"I'm sorry, Helen." Mom's crying now, hands trembling as the spatula shakes in her grip. Tell me what you need," she begs, "and I'll do everything I can to help you. I'll do whatever you want."

"Whatever I want?" I echo. Mother nods, her expression warm. And soft. Safe. I could be – I could be safe here. I don't have to hurt myself or others for the sake of mild entertainment. I don't have to walk through life alone except for the lingering dream of death. I could be happy here. I could – I could be happy.

"This is it, Helen." I look up at the sudden voice. *Thanatos.* The room freezes, Mother stuck in a smile as the flames in the candles pause their dancing. "You're done. You can stay here, here with your family in this cottage by the sea, and you can finally rest in peace. You can have your happy ending.

A person will be inspired by the actions in the arenas. They will look at you and your determination to pursue mercy instead of violence. They will learn the power of peace instead of pain. And they will let that peace carry them on to change the corruption found in Durnon. They will see you as a symbol, an inspiration, a girl who went out before thousands screaming for her death and offered them nothing but love in return. You can stop here, Helen." Thanatos offers. "You can stop here and receive your Happy Ending. You have become a symbol of my power, and as such, our bargain has been fulfilled. You can rest now, my child."

"Can I rest?" I ask him hopefully. I imagine a greenhouse, nestled contentedly beside a rolling sea. A family that loves and cares for no other reason than me being me. A future where I live until I'm old and grey. A life where nothing ever bad happens. A place where I don't have to sacrifice the things I love to reach a good ending.

"Anything," Thanatos affirms, watching me with pure adoration in his eyes. "You can have anything, oh darling child of mine. This is my gift to you."

Time unfreezes, and I watch as steam rises in tendrils from my smooth teacup. Watch as the candles flicker, as Natalya's eyes twinkle when she smiles at me.

"Do you ever sit down and read fairytales?" I ask quietly. Let my fingers run over the wooden whirls on the table. "Do you believe in heroes?" Mom pauses.

"I think that sometimes Durnon is a bit too focused on glorified legacy and other silly ideologies." She responds at last. "I think you, of all people, would know the danger that comes from that. Still, there is something nice, I think, in being able to believe in something."

"I don't quite know if I believe in heroes anymore, especially after all the things that I saw in the sanitarium," I confess. I look up, then. Stare out the sunroof at the heavens. Watch the millions of shrieking stars twirl as they dance along the morning sky. "But when I was strapped there onto the operating table, I used to wish that a hero would come save me."

"And instead, they just cut you up all over again." Mom's voice is harsh. Sharp in its disgust.

"Instead," I correct, "You came." Mother stills, her hands clenching as they grip the steering wheel. I go quiet and turn back to looking out the window.

"I don't know if I quite believe in fairytales anymore," I continue, pausing as I think back on everything and nothing all at the same time. "But I think sometimes the most important things in this life can be found by trying to emulate them. After all, just because true heroes don't exist doesn't mean that they never will. Maybe I could be a hero for someone. Someone who needs me as much as I needed you.

If I stop and end here, then nothing in the world will have really changed. The stadiums will still swallow children. Bloodshed will stain the floors of sanitariums. If I stop here, then all my suffering will be for nothing." I look down at my hands, trace the lines of jagged scars that I kept on my skin. Not because I was unable to heal from the wounds that had caused them, but because they were signs of how far I had come.

"I was given this gift of mine for a reason." I continue. "And being able to help people, to show them that there is more to life than this constant violence, that is my reason. I want to tear down the stadiums. I want to shut down the sanitariums. I want to walk alongside the roadside and bury all the corpses."

I think of my greenhouse then. My safe space. My home. "I want a place where I know that someone would miss me when I was gone. Somewhere where I can be valued not for my actions, but for simply being me. Somewhere where my worth did not rely upon how much blood is stuck on the palms of my hands. I need to overthrow my government. I need to fix things." I tell Mom desperately. I start begging, voice catching as I struggle to force the words out. "Please don't let everything I've gone through so far be for nothing. I can't have suffered this much just for nothing."

"Absolutely not." The words are sharp and decisive. Mother sets her knife and fork down with a clatter, the metal clattering as it strikes the table. "You're thirteen. You're *thirteen*, Helen. And those people whom you are so desperate to save went and turned you into their little lab rat. They can all go rot in a hole for all I care. They don't deserve to have you as their martyr."

"You've read my files, haven't you?" I ask then. Mother goes silent. I start to smile then, let the edges of my lips curl back as I keep talking, "You've heard the names they've called me throughout the city streets. Persephone. Proserpine. Death's Beloved. *Messiah*. I've walked through stadiums packed with slaughter without retaining a single scratch. I've survived horrors that your mind couldn't possibly imagine. Do you think that makes me *weak*, Mom? I've already lived through the worst things imaginable. All that's left for me to do is decide whether it actually means something."

"I'm not saying you're weak." Mother bites back. "I'm saying that it's not worth it. I've buried enough bodies in the past to know what dreams like yours lead to. Don't you dare ask me to bury my daughter, too, to watch her kill herself for people who would turn on her in a heartbeat."

"I don't…" A part of me knows that if I go through with this, I will die shortly after winning the war. Thanatos mentioned it in his deal after all, the words a dark crimson from where he swore them in an oath. *You will show the others why they are wrong, and then you will join me in the spring.* It's strange, looking back on it. Half a year ago, I think I would have done anything to join Death faster. And yet, looking at my family gathered around the dinner table, I feel my eyes begin to burn. I don't…I don't really want to die anymore.

"You won't have to." The words are soft, yet they cut through the room like a knife. I look over at where Pietyr sits in the corner, his expression still as he fidgets with a worn-down coin. "Marek and I can handle it." The room starts breathing. I can sense it, somewhere deep inside my bones. The walls pulse and twitch over and over, candlelight warping as they move in tune to a pulsing heartbeat. The drink in my brother's mug smells sweet yet at the same time terrible, like it could melt my brain if I drank too much. Casually, Pietyr leans back and takes a sip.

"I'm sorry, did you not hear me?" Mom asks, voice rising. "I said that none of my children are going to sacrifice themselves for people who don't give a damn if they live or not."

"You can't keep burying your head in the sand, Mother." There's something mocking, almost, in Pietyr's tone. The coin glints from where he spins it between his fingers. "Eventually things are going to end, one way or another. It's already bad enough that they got their hands on Helen. Do you honestly think that this could end any different way?" He smiles then, lips curling back to expose his teeth. "Sooner or later we have to stop playing games."

(18)

AFTER: NATALYA

The first thing I see when I leave the mist is Clytemnestra. She stands with her back to me, staring out into the eternal dusk. Her hand is stretched out, fingers trailing over a tall, withered tree whose rotted branches still bloom with fruit. The wood shivers beneath her touch.

"Are you all right?" I call out hesitantly. There is something still about her gaze. Something that makes her seem young, even though I know she must be older than most myths.

"Do you ever wonder why trees are considered to be the main tool for temptation?" She asks, nails digging deeper into the papery bark. "Tantalus and his hunger, Eve and her curiosity, Idunn and her youth. Why is it always a tree specifically that proves such a great source for desire?" Slowly, ever so slowly, Clytemnestra begins to scrape at the tree. Until splinters worm their way through her fingers. Until holes begin to appear in the sides of the decaying trunk. Until Clytemnestra's face drips with salty tears.

There is a plaque attached to the edges of the tree. The copper is rusted, a once-bright orange now a moldy green.

ELM OF FALSE DREAMS

"I wouldn't say that trees represent temptation necessarily," I respond hesitantly. "Rather, they represent life. The North Men and Yggdrasil, the Scots and Crane Bethadh, the Bodhi of the land of the East. Power, strength, and wisdom, trees can often be seen as symbols of goodness. And yet, sometimes merely living isn't enough for some men. They begin to desire more, dreaming at night of things that can fulfill their insatiable hunger. And yet, for some strange reason, their hunger is never satisfied. They begin to rot like their dreams do, husks trapped inside living flesh, pouring everything they have into this dream of something more that they eventually lose themselves. They sacrifice everything, only to achieve nothing in the end. I don't know what you saw in the realm of Hypnos, but Clytemnestra," I continue, "this tree is dying. This dream of yours is rotting. And there is nothing you or I can do to change that." The words taste bitter as I scrape them off my tongue.

Clytemnestra pauses, hands still wrenched into the rotting bark. Slowly, ever so slowly, she begins to break down and cry.

"I know." She sobs, wrenching her hands from the tree as if the touch burns her. "Believe me, I know."

We begin walking again until the land of Hypnos vanishes from view. Until the rotted elm becomes merely a blip in the distance. The crooked moon shines in the sky with a soft, gentle light, and I watch Clytemnestra's face as it begins to harden. Eventually, we reach a fork in the road.

At the edge of the land of Hypnos lies a sea composed of three rivers, lapping constantly against either side of a sheer rock that glows pale in the fading moonlight. Although the waters touch, they never intersect. Behind each river lies a gate that stretches up to touch the stars in the very heavens of the sky. They seem to bend and warp around the edges of the horizon, swallowing up the shadows and keeping the wandering ghosts inside.

"Behind us is the river Acheron," Clytemnestra explains, holding a hand out and pointing as she describes each clashing sea. "Follow the wailing waves, and eventually you will find yourself drowning in the fires of Tartarus."

"To the left is the river Lethe. Try not to touch the water, or else you'll forget anything before the moment you set foot upon its shore. Lethe separates the land of dreams from the children of Nyx: centaurs, gorgons, harpies, hydras, chimeras, and many more. It is the home of every benediction and abomination, a land consumed by the accumulation of childhood wishes."

"The Lethe is crueler than the Styx, you know. Crueler than the Acheron, or the burning of the Phlegethon. Because all those other rivers can do is kill you. But the Lethe can take away your whole life."

"To the left is the river of weeping, Cocytus. We will sail down that one until we reach the domain of Cerberus."

"With all due respect," I interrupt, "Do we *have* to specifically travel down the current labeled as the river of weeping? I mean, isn't there a better option? I thought all paths would eventually lead to Helen."

"I mean, I suppose so…" Clytemnestra replies hesitantly. "But as misleading as the name sounds, the Cocytus truly is the best option. It is a river of recovery, not retribution. It is the path of healing from woe, of recovering from grief. It will lead you to feel grief, because any soul who willingly travels across its shores is fundamentally fueled by an all-consuming sorrow. Even still, it is better to remember and recover than to shove the pain down and forget."

I turn to watch the three rivers, watch the water writhe and boil as it bashes up against the lone white rock. No matter how close the waters intermingle, they never unite as one.

Clytemnestra waves her hand, and with a flick of her wrist, a boat materializes out of the shadowy mists. A small rowboat barely big enough for two, with sides of polished ivory and oars of pearly bone.

"Are you coming?" my guide asks impatiently, muscles straining as she shoves the boat into the river. I turn to help her. Despite how heavy the boat is, it barely sinks into the water.

The Cocytus stings whenever it touches my skin. Bitterness coats the salty spray and tears open my flesh whenever I pull the oars too hard. A part of me wonders if this is how my daughter felt.

Clytemnestra points out several landmarks as we travel down the salty stream.

"Alongside the river Cocytus lies a path known as the dividing road. All freshly dead must pass along it. There they are judged by three wise kings: Aecus, Rhadamanthys, and Minos. All spirits are given three days and three nights to plead their case before them. Depending on which judgment is placed before them, they are either imprisoned in Tartarus, ferried to Asphodel, sailed to Elysium, or born anew on the shores of the Lethe.

Past the shores of the river Lethe lies a meadow known as the Vale of Mourning.

Layered with rows upon rows of exquisite gemstones, the meadow is considered a land of exquisite beauty, a type of sight that brings the viewer to tears upon seeing it. And yet no matter how vividly the riches shine, they cannot bring a single spark into the inhabitant's eyes. Wealth is useless, after all, for soothing grief."

There's silence, as we pass the shore of weeping wraiths. I think back to the beach beside the river Styx, where I had flung coin after coin at the retreating back of Charon. None of that money, no matter how much of it I had thrown, had been enough to make him even turn his head.

I look at my bag then. All my supplies and preparations, each item carefully added after hours of research. Is any of it enough? Do I have anything I can rely on?

Orpheus had a harp, but the strings couldn't help much when his voice stopped singing. Theseus had a sword, and yet it lay there lifeless when his arms became paralyzed.

Hercules had a variety of weapons, and yet he chose to use his bare hands when it finally came to taking Cerberus.

"I need you to be honest with me, Clytemnestra," I ask hesitantly. "Do you think I have a chance? At saving my daughter, that is." Despite how much I try to block it out, my mind keeps wandering back to the Land of Hypnos.

"Do you know, Natalya, how it is that most men hunt whales?" She replies eventually. I frown and shake my head.

"In stories, yes. And perhaps if you count looking at a couple of pictures." I answer. "But I was never close enough to whales to ever consider hunting them."

"The most popular way to hunt whales is by killing the child first." My guide explains dully. "They throw a harpoon at the baby, because it is weak, and it is soft, and its flippers are far too small to help it swim away. As the child screams and flails in pain, the mother stays by its side. She is physically incapable, or so it seems, of leaving behind her baby. That's when the second harpoon is thrown, this time at the mother. The actual target. The pair dies together, and the hunters smile at the extra food.

Whales, you must know, are awfully intelligent creatures. The mother knows that she herself will certainly be killed if she doesn't abandon her baby. And yet she never does. She chooses to stay there and die with her child. She chooses to comfort her child in its final moments, even though she knows it will lead to her own death in return." Clytemnestra trails off and stares into the bitter water.

"I am a human, Clytemnestra," I interject then. "Not a whale. And even if I were, you're misunderstanding the situation. I'm not trying to comfort my daughter; I'm trying to save her."

"Orpheus went mad after he failed." My guide murmurs then. "Went mad and wailed until his very screams tore him apart."

I cringe slightly, the imagery of Orpheus's death causing goosebumps to rise across my flesh. Helen used to scream like that. She used to wail over and over, mouth flopping open like a gasping fish as she struggled to breathe through her shrieking. It used to annoy me, to be honest. I'd shake her and scream back, blast loud music, bang on pots, and slam doors until she finally stopped. Her little shoulders would hunch, back doubling over as she curled up in a ball and tried to block the noise out.

I just wanted her to stop crying, to understand that the world is a cruel, dark place that doesn't give a damn regardless of how loudly you cry or whine. I'd thought that if I could somehow make her stronger, she'd be able to survive where I couldn't. And yet…that notion of screaming until you tear yourself apart… I wonder if Helen ever felt like that when I yelled at her. Perhaps I didn't break her, not completely, at least. Maybe my daughter was always doomed to die, tied too deeply to my country's corruption to be anything more than a martyr. But I gave her a reason to believe that she was all alone, and in the end, that's all that matters.

"I'm not Orpheus, Clytemnestra." I remind her. Some part of me is guilty for that. It would be easier if I were the one always screaming. "I'm Natalya."

She looks at me then. Really looks at me. She studies me with her sharp, dark eyes, and as she stares, the thorns on her skin shudder and tremble from where they twitch.

"The truth is I don't know, Natalya." She decides at last. "Is that the answer you want? After all, I think I know better than anyone just how much the Muses love tragedy. I know just how many failed souls haunt the lands of Orpheus. I know how even the heroes who boast of beating death always fall into misery in the end.

And yet, if there was anyone who *could* succeed, I think that it would be you. Because you have something that the other heroes did not, despite their magic, skills, and weapons. You have a mother's love, and that is something that will keep you moving until you drown the world in hellfire."

A Mother's love. The words feel hollow, even though Clytemnestra says them with such conviction. Mothers don't… Mothers don't hurt their children. Not without a good reason.

… Is there ever a good reason?

I'm not sure if there is. What I do know is that sometimes mothers can treasure their children and still hurt them. That they can love and yet at the same time hurt the very souls that they were entrusted to protect. I know I did.

Maybe… maybe Helen didn't deserve to have me as a mother. Maybe I've already failed her, time and time again, up there in the world above. But if there is one thing that my daughter deserves, it's a chance at life again.

The chance to grow, to not merely survive but also *thrive.*

My skin burns, reddened sores forming from how tightly I grip the oars. I grit my teeth and force myself to row faster, blisters popping open in agonizing bursts. If there is even the slightest chance that I can save Helen, then I will row until my arms pop out of their sockets. Even if the Underworld swallows me whole. Even if I'm not worthy to bear the name Mother at all.

(19)

BEFORE: HELEN

The new house Mother picks is an old stone cottage that rests on the edge of the nearby seaside. I stare up at it in silence as Marek and her drive away, off to stockpile supplies or collect information or some other secret plan they'd spoken about in whispers when it was late enough that they thought I was asleep. I go out and sit on the front porch when they drive off. I can't see the sea, not from where I'm sitting. But I can hear it murmuring from where it ripples in the distance, can smell the sharpened salt when I breathe in too deeply.

It's quiet from where I sit. Hills roll on in endless rows of minty green, clovers, shamrocks, and moss creeping beneath my toes as I get up and move towards the back of the house. There's a creak of a portable radio, and a beeswax candle that I found in the kitchen. I cradle each of the objects carefully in my hands. In the distance, shadows dance, large whimsical patches of darkness that creep behind the barriers of a nearby forest.

"What are you trying to do, my darling child?" Thanatos asks curiously from where he watches. I go into the shed and grab a shovel and a rake. Throw on a pair of battered gloves as I make sure not to mess with the guns.

"I want to build a garden," I tell the shadow man. Flick my fingers and watch as strands of ivy begin to wind around the stone and mortar. Trails of Wisteria flow around the edges of emerald, green shutters. "Mom said I could do anything I wanted, and right now I want to build a garden." I dig my fingers into the earth. Rip out a series of spiky weeds that are strangling a patch of shrubbery.

Death sits down and watches passively as I work and sweat under the cooling sun. There's a certain chill in the air now that nips at exposed skin, no matter how brightly the leaves burn. He takes a string of flowers and quietly braids them into a crown. The type that girls wear on Midsomer, roses, dandelions, wisteria, and morning glories, all braided together until they form a regal coronet. Carefully, he places it onto my head.

"I am sorry, my child, that you lost your greenhouse." He says softly. I stop and freeze, hands shaking and throat gasping. The weeds I clutch tremble in my grasp.

"It's alright," I murmur eventually. "Well…no. It's not alright. But I understand that I needed to leave in order to achieve my destiny." The weeds wither, from where I choke them in my grip. Thanatos remains silent. Slowly, ever so slowly, irritation begins to bubble up inside my chest. I force it back with a grimace.

"Have I ever told you how much I adore you, Thanatos? I think that I would give up practically anything for a shred of your affection." The words are bitter. Resentful. There is something dark and ugly blooming beneath my skin, and I can feel its venom stinging as it oozes from my mouth. I try to push it down without much success. Try to make Death understand; let him know *I love you so much. So, why did you have to put such a huge burden on my shoulders?* Death is quiet, from where he sits beside me. Looks at me with a soft expression and murmurs,

"It's ok to be angry, Helen." I stand up and stalk away. Stomp down to the seashore, feel my eyes burn at the sting of salt on the wind. I watch as the waves slam up against the rocky shore.

The coast here is different from how it is in the underworld. The shore is made of rocks instead of sand, calcified hunks of obsidian that scrape against the cliffside, keeping me grounded on my feet. They aren't soft, like the sand of dying stars. In fact, they aren't particularly nice-looking. There's a certain ugliness to them, something born from a constant battle with the waves that leaves them scarred yet still standing.

I take a step, and then another. The seawater closes around my ankles, and then my shins. A spray of foam slaps my face and blinds me, eyes tearing up as I blink back salt. I close my eyes and move forward. Stretch my hands out in front and grope for the rocks like a blind man. My feet sting from where they scrape against roughened pebbles. I take a breath, and the ocean slams into the warmth of my open mouth.

"You're desperate." I startle and open my eyes. There's nothing in the water, not even a stray speck of seaweed. The sun burns from where it boils up above my head. I can't see a single seagull drifting through the sky. *"Ask for*

anything, little girl." The strange voice murmurs. *"Ask for anything at all."*

"I'm not desperate," I argue back then. "And I'm not little either." I pout and cross my arms. Blood has started to pour from the scrapes on my legs. It makes my skin grow sticky, and the ocean warm. Absentmindedly, I watch as the cuts continue to ooze. There's something strange about how blood can turn nearly clear when mixed with enough water.

"Still, you must want something." The voice insists. *"What do you want in exchange, oh girl of a thousand names? What do you want in return for what you have given me?"*

"What exactly have I given you?" I ask suspiciously. Start to move backwards as I step out of the sea. Deals are rarely good after all when you don't remember what you've given.

"Life." The voice croons, its tone soft and sweet. My shins sting. I stare down at where my blood lies trickling towards my feet.

I stop. And pause. Remember a night when the sky was storming, when my hands bled as I crouched by a broken rosebush.

"I have already given up my life," I answer softly. My voice is gentle. Delicate. I look out at the hungry sea that licks at my skin and sigh. "I have already given up my life," I repeat. "To a different being, who asks for a different cause. I have given up my life for the lives of my nation. And no matter how much I love or hate that promise, I have made my decision."

"Do you regret your vow?" The sea whispers. *"I could give you something else, free of charge. After all, your blood has already paid any possible debt."*

For a moment, I pause. I think of a world where my veins were filled with saltwater instead of choking vines. Where I did not have to breathe the pollution that chokes my country's streets. I think of a world where I could shed my skin for scales and simply exist, here by this little cottage and garden beside the seaside. I think of a world where I don't have to hurt in order to get my happy ending.

I heard a story once. About a girl who chose to move from the sea to the land. A girl who fell in love with the sun and clouds, who was willing to give up her voice and gills in order to breathe this same polluted air I hate so much. I turn once more to the voice in the sea.

"Did you ever – make someone feel, when she moved, like she was walking on knives?" I ask hesitantly.

The waves murmur as they rush forward and then dart back. The salt shrivels up my fingers as I wait. I pull them out of the water and simply look at them, twist my hands over and over in the sunlight as the August heat warms the edges of the shore.

"Beauty," The sea decides at last, *"is pain."*

"And didn't she lose everything afterwards," I wonder, "and turn into seafoam?"

"Love," The sea declares, *"is worse."*

I lower my hands into the water. Watch as the sea swallows them up, dark waters tugging deeper and deeper. When I lower them farther, they vanish entirely.

The sea waits. And I wait with the sea. Watch as the tide draws out, and the voice begins to grow impatient.

"She asked for a soul, didn't she?" I call out, finally. Dig my feet into the sand and stand there planted. Anchor myself to the ground and hold myself still as all around me the world spins, the very planet that I stand on is nothing but a giant rock careening wildly around in orbit.

"You already have a soul of your own, little girl." The sea admonishes.

"I know." I sigh. "Oh, believe me, I know."

I used to be confused about why it was that Thanatos had chosen to give me the gift of cell manipulation. That when I went crying for love from the god of death, he chose to give me power over life instead. I think I get it now.

Because sometimes love is allowing someone to grow, instead of ending things when they're hurting. Sometimes love isn't the gentleness of morphine, but soft hands cradling your own as they cover wounds in antiseptic. Sometimes, love is forcing someone to keep walking, encouraging them to push on even when they beg so desperately for rest.

Death offered to me his love, and loving someone means that you want them to be happy in things that exist outside of yourself. Death offered to me his love, and that means that he gave me the tools and encouragement to create my own happy ending. Because in the end, no matter what happens, I will die and join him for eternity. This fact isn't special, after all; anyone can die. But not everyone can live, and that's what Thanatos wanted for me.

I go back to the house on the side of the sea. Burrow my feet into moss and shamrocks as I close my eyes and breathe. Grab a shovel and a rake. Head towards the weeds that gather around the sides of my house. I get back to gardening. I get back to living.

(20)

AFTER: NATALYA

Eventually, the boat runs ashore. My feet sink into softened stardust. The boat vanishes into a puff of smoke once both feet are on the ground, its wispy form floating upstream as if guided by an unknown wind.

There is a path that winds past the beach and through a nearby meadow. I begin to follow it on slow, shaky footsteps. Slowly, ever so slowly, sand gives way to grass. I freeze once I notice the flowers smothering the nearby ground. Remember the poppy spores that seemed to bloom like acne on the skin of Hypnos. I may not know much about this underworld, but even I know that there should not be life here among the dead.

THE FIELDS OF ASPHODEL, a sign nearby reads. The plaque is rotting, strangled by the creeping stems.

"Are you coming, Natalya?" Clytemnestra asks impatiently. The rose that curls around her throat seems to stretch and shrink as she breathes.

"Why are there flowers here, Clytemnestra?" I murmur cautiously. "Why are small pockets of life still growing, even in the land of the dead?" My guide smiles then. A small smile. A sad smile. The type where you instinctively know that the answer to the question will be worse than never knowing.

"Some things, Natalya," my guide replies, "are better left unknown."

We walk in silence among the fields of flowers. ASPHODEL, the sign had said. The plants flicker and glow like fireflies as they sit there, bioluminescent petals opening up to face the empty sky. It would almost be pretty if the sight wasn't so wrong. What type of flowers bloom in a world of dead things?

Tiny planets buzz and whir as they flit through the air. Galaxies twirl around the sky as they stretch and burst like fireworks. Between the glowing plants flock the dead, their veils a tattered grey as they drift past in aimless pacing. They seem like ghosts, almost. But at least a ghost has enough love to haunt something. Here, the shades wander lost without a home, veils covering their heads so completely that even their faces are forgotten.

"I do not like this place." I hiss out through chattering teeth. The air seems colder here, frost nipping at my skin until my very limbs go numb. "Clytemnestra, I think that I would almost prefer Tartarus to staying here for eternity."

I can't see the faces of the shades as they walk. It's a stupid thing to comment on. After all, most funeral services prefer to leave the heads of the dead covered in closed caskets.

But I can't see their faces, can't hear their voices, can't even tell their skin color. Their smiles, wrinkles, hair, and eyes are all gobbled up by their ashy robes. All their memories, fears, hopes, and everything else that made them human have simply been removed. Erased. There is nothing left of them from when they were alive. All that remains is a floating corpse.

"Do not be a fool, Natalya." Clytemnestra bites back, misery and envy warring across her features as she watches the nearby dead. "After life, one of the highest privileges is the ability to rest. To be able to move on from all the pain and tragedy. To shed behind your flesh, and then your mind, and let your spirit drift among the clouds of the heavens with your family beside you. To become a star, so that your very existence becomes the stuff of wishes."

Clytemnestra is openly sobbing now, peering through the nearby ghosts as if searching for someone. It could be her husband. It could be her children. Whoever it is, their mind is now long gone. Whoever the person is that she's looking for, she'll never find them.

That knowledge is what makes the fields of Asphodel so terrifying. Because what kind of cruelty must it be to have your existence so completely erased that not even your own family could recognize you?

I stare intently at the veiled faces all around me. Is my daughter among them? Is my daughter here, and I'm just too blind to recognize her?

Silently, ever so silently, the figures drift past. I can't tell if she's among them or not.

Even after everything that has happened: all the memories we shared and all the trials I faced on this godforsaken quest. I still can't tell.

I start walking faster. Move through the fields so quickly I'm nearly running, my speed increasing until I reach a full-out sprint. Clytemnestra trails behind me, her shadow stuck as she stares into the void. Slowly, her eyes catch on my fleeing form.

"Clytemnestra, I want to go," I call out then. She ignores me, eyes still caught on the drifting figures. "I want to go *now*," I repeat, stomping my foot and crossing my arms like a petulant child. Panic is starting to sink in, and anxiously, I dig in my bag until I pull out an old pocket watch. What if – what if there's a certain limit on how long ghosts stay ghosts? What if I'm too late and my daughter's soul fades into the stars, losing her humanity as she drifts for all eternity?

The clock is dead when I look at it. Dead, like everything else here in the underworld. I shake it, but the hands refuse to budge. I shake it harder, until metal shavings begin to flake off in my hands. The hands refuse to move. No matter how hard I try, I can't bring the clock back to life.

"Wait just a second, Natalya." My guide murmurs, voice hoarse from crying as she looks out around the field. "Just, just give me a second, why don't you? I mean, you understand, you're a mother just like me and…"

"No, you're not like me, Clytemnestra." I hiss, hands shaking as I clutch the broken clock in my hands. "You are dead, along with your children. What is done is done, your story is closed. But mine is not. I can still save my Helen."

Clytemnestra freezes. Turns slowly to stare at me. Her face has gone bone white. Her thorns have sunk into her skin so deeply that they have fused themselves to her flesh.

"What did you say to me?" She calls out with a still voice. Her eyes are blank. Suddenly, I realize just how frightening the woman standing before me is. How tightly composed her anger must have been, impatiently simmering as it warmed the Acheron.

"I said," I repeat snarling, "that at least I can save *my* Helen."

The world goes quiet. Freezes. Turns slow, like molasses. I watch as Clytemnestra's face turns red like a bush of bloodied roses. See how her hands grow white as she curls her fingers into fists.

"You should be careful, mortal," She hisses, "about what words you speak next."

I turn around and start walking. Place one foot in front of the other. Clytemnestra splutters and stammers incredulously.

"Are you really just going to walk away?" She asks disbelievingly. "I'm your guide!"

"I don't have time to start a conversation with you, Clytemnestra," I call over my shoulder, breaking into a jog as I move down the path. "After all, it would only be a waste of time. I need to save my daughter."

"Natalya, wait!" She cries out frantically, eyes shiny from recently shed tears. I urge myself to move faster, follow the winding road in front of me as I weave between the specters.

I have decided that I'm tired of the underworld. Tired of this journey. I'm tired of listening to the dead spin stories when I could be moving even faster to reach my baby.

I want to go home. Home, to my cottage by the seaside, with my son and my daughter and a day that always rises. Home, where growing is a norm instead of an anomaly, where I can wake up each day and be content with nothing more than the sake of being alive. Home, to my library filled with books that my husband used to try reading in outrageously terrible accents. Home, to where my dog is waiting curled up by a nearby fireside.

I am sick of death and its coldness and emptiness. I'm too awake to crave the relief of dreams, too ambitious to be soothed by empty condolences. The sooner I find my daughter, the sooner I can go home.

I run until my legs give out. Run until my sides are racked with stitches and I struggle to breathe through gasping lungs. When I can no longer find the strength to run, I walk. When I can no longer walk, I crawl.

There is something to be said about the strength of the indomitable human spirit. How even when the world seems stacked against us, mankind continues to press on. The power to keep on fighting when all appears lost, to rise above our circumstances and overcome the odds. It's the power that Hercules used to shoulder the weight of the sky in the palms of his hands. It's the motivation that encourages Sisyphus to roll a boulder up a cliffside every day, determined to reach the top despite the impossible odds.

I am not Hercules. Neither am I Sisyphus. I'm not some great big hero that comes in with a sword and emerges triumphant amidst a blaze of glory. I'm not a hero, like the legends of old. But I'm a mother. And like any parent, I will stop at nothing to protect my child.

As I crawl between the end of the fields of Asphodel and the edge of something else, I feel my hands begin to burn, and my legs sweat. My muscles are an achy, bloodied mess, and yet I push myself forward, dragging my resisting body behind me as I crawl through the dirt. Determinedly, I force my lips into a grin. There is nothing that will stop me, neither rain nor frost nor hail nor fire. My name is Natalya Cermak. And I will stop at nothing to save my daughter.

(21)

BEFORE: HELEN

The world is colder when I get up in the mornings. The tree leaves burn in a series of golds and oranges and frost begins to skitter over the ground whenever I go outside. My garden blooms, a final surge of color before retreating to sleep underground. My arms are sore from where I stand opposite Marek panting. It's cold outside, but my skin burns from the effort to keep myself standing.

"Again." Marek singsongs, crouching two paces in front of me. His smile lowers as my legs buckle. I look up with watering eyes and notice how there's no hesitation in his expression. "Now." He prods in a gentler tone. I stagger to my feet with a grimace.

I swing a fist. Marek dodges. He leans to the left, and I pull dust from the air and send it swirling. Sand spins around my brother until he is nearly choking on crushed shells. I dig my feet into the ground and feel the earth open beneath our feet. Marek laughs, as the sand fills his eyes. As weeds sprout out of the ground and wrap in circles around him before slithering towards his throat.

"That's my Helen," Marek croons, head tilted to the side as he smiles back with big, sharp teeth. The vines shred like paper from where he rips them apart in his hands. Leaning forwards, I watch as my brother's back hunches, eyes bright as his fingers spasm and pop. He tilts his head, and I have to fight the urge not to flinch. "Are you ready to have *fun yet?*"

296

Pietyr watches us from the sidelines. Dark eyes narrow as he observes the pair of us in our movements. I pause and watch as Marek crawls towards me. My lungs are spasming, and my sweat has nearly stuck my eyes shut. It's been around three hours since we started training.

Marek raises an axe and I duck as he brings it down. Air whistles past as the blade misses. I move back a couple spaces and clutch my arm tightly to my chest. Double over wheezing and feel the edges of something beginning to poke from my skin. Marek pauses. Watches as I struggle to breathe. A look of frustration enters his eyes then.

"Helen," It's weird, hearing Marek's voice sound so serious. "Helen they're not going to just let you lie there on the ground like that. There will be no mercy, in the people of Durnon. They will try to kill you if you go through with your plan."

He raises his axe again, but I ignore him as he lifts it for another blow. I tap down deep into my energy reserves, the sugar leftover by insulin in my pancreas, and *consume* until my body nearly begins to cannibalize itself.

I need a weapon. My hands are not enough, not after hours of fighting. I need a weapon, and a part of me mourns the fact because it feels like an admission of defeat to want one in the first place.

But I remember the screaming of rats that filled the walls of the sanitarium. I remember the piles of corpses rotting as they lay on the roadside. I remember Thanatos holding me in his arms, his voice oh so kind as he murmured,

"It is a mercy to kill them."

And I don't want to fight, don't want to hurt, or maim, or kill. But death is not the worst thing that can happen to a person. And if I have to defend myself so that I can pave a way out of this cancer that plagues my nation, then so be it.

I grab my femur and focus inwards until I can feel the blood vessels throbbing within it.

The capillaries beat to the same sluggish tune of my own pulse. Marek begins to drop his axe. The blade glints from where it starts to arc. I ignore him. Focus inward on the bone aching in my upper thigh, and slowly begin to build it in my hands. Quicken the process, until cartilage grows and hardens under my hands. Until I grip a copy of the bone in my hands like a club.

The axe swings down. I raise the femur to meet it and feel my arms shudder at the impact.

Marek swings again. I focus on the blade. Scrape off excess cells and marrow, until the thing begins to sharpen in my grasp.

Marek lunges at me again. I bat him back and refine the blade as I clutch it between my fingers. Perfect it until the edges are sharp, a sword of solid bone that pulses and twitches as I guide it through the air.

I can *feel* the blade, now. Like it's still attached to my body, an extension of my arms. Can feel how it hardens under the calcifying cartilage. How the longer the fight drags on, the stronger it becomes. It is a blade formed from the cells of my own body. As it flies through the air, it feels like a phantom limb.

Marek bats the sword away. It shatters on impact. I go sprawling in the dust. Blink blackened spots out of my blurry vision and notice with a start that my legs are shaking. Gently, ever so gently, He pulls me up into a sitting position. Hands me some water, then pours it for me when I am too weak to even drink. I have exhausted all my body's energy, even the ability to keep my head up.

"You're getting better." Pietyr calls out from where he sits on the front porch. He goes inside before coming back out with a bottle of water, placing the metal in my hands as he motions for me to drink. "But you need to stop burning through your energy so quickly. It takes much more fuel to recover from a hit than simply blocking it."

"I don't like fighting." I mutter resentfully. Tears of exhaustion bubble up and

I start to sob as I reach out and grab my brother's shirt. He shushes me then. Reaches forward with a hug and squeezes me tightly.

"I know, Helen." He agrees, guilt hanging in his words. "I know how horrible it is. But they're not going to just let you walk in and suddenly run things. If there's anything you need to know of Durnon, it's that they never go down without a fight."

"I know." I wail tiredly. "I know that. But people won't take peace seriously if the only way to get it is through violence."

My brothers are silent, as they stare at me. I can't- I can't read their expressions.

"They're going to die either way, Helen." Pietyr states blankly, static crawling up and down my arms like millions of tiny, hungry centipedes. "Does that make things easier for you to accept? They *hurt* you. And so if you don't stop them, if you don't end things on your own terms, then Marek and I will." The leaves start spinning from where they drift, colors swirling and morphing as they spiral from yellows into oranges, from golds into deep, rusted reds. Stars flare up in the corner of my vision, and blood begins to drip and coat the fallen leaves. I shake my head and the fuzziness stops. Pietyr smiles. Sometimes I forget that no matter how careful, how poised, how *controlled* he may seem, he is just as hungry as Marek.

Pietyr pauses, and hums under his breath. Stops, and thinks for a couple seconds. The beach is silent as I watch him. Unnaturally silent. Almost like the waves are scared to splash too loud and risk catching his attention.

"The weapon was a good idea." He says at last. His tone is lighter, and he smiles at me encouragingly. "I've got to admit, I wasn't expecting you to literally grow an extra bone out of your skin and try to beat Marek over the head with it. That was honestly one of the most horrifying things that I think I've ever seen in my life." I smile weakly as he chuckles, and the world begins to twist. "There was the problem of it being too brittle however, it broke much too quickly to ever hold up in a fight. What type of strategy do you use in your fighting?"

"I try to touch the other person." I answer, voice hoarse. "I try to grab onto any patch of exposed skin and sap their energy from them. Make them too weak to stand. Too tired to fight or run. And then I leave. That way, I don't hurt anyone more than I need to."

"What about when you can't touch them?" Pietyr presses carefully. When they're wearing armor, or tactical gear, or something else that makes it hard to reach their skin? What about if it's a long-range fighter, and they come at you with a gun or a bow or a spear?"

"I keep marching." I respond. "I keep walking. It doesn't matter in the end: how fast or strong or skilled I am. In the end, I win because I never stop walking."

"That's nice, Helen." Pietyr says. "But even if you have a higher stamina than most of us, you still get tired. Otherwise, you wouldn't be flopped all over this couch right now. What you need is a weapon. Something you can use to defend yourself with as a way to conserve your strength. And something that can last much longer than mere bone can. What you need," he snaps his fingers "is a good blade."

My brothers let me rest, away in my room for a few hours. Enough to let me heal the aches in my muscles, the exhaustion in my bones and the tiredness of my brain. While I rest beside a cup of tea and a couple storybooks, Pietyr paces around the kitchen and begins to plot.

He drags me out to a scrapyard, junk piled up around me in towers as I stare at the piles of nearby trash. He takes me to the place where old machines come to die, their metal rotting under the harshness of the snow and sun.

The moon has started devouring the sun, in the distance. I watch as Pietyr takes out a worn-down coin and flips it, grooves and scratches bubbling under the dying rays. He turns to stare at me when he notices how still I am.

"What are you doing?" He asks then. A mix of worry and frustration lacing the edges of his tone. "Go get yourself a weapon."

"But I don't know where to find a weapon." I shoot back, looking around at the decaying scraps.

"Then make one." Pietyr declares simply, as if the solution was obvious. As if I could suddenly wave my hands and materialize a weapon from thin air. I look around the ground at the twisted metal groaning at my feet. The torn open shells of those things called cars that seem to bleed under the dying sunlight.

"I don't know anything about making weapons," I confess, then, my voice small as I notice how endless the junkyard is. "I don't know what type of blade I need, or what materials, or what procedures, or…"

"Learn how then" Pietyr states with a shrug. "I'm sure you can practice on some of the tools in Mom's shed. And don't worry, I'm not going to leave you all high and dry. I'll help you make one."

I stare at Pietyr in the light of the dying sun. Leaves fall down as bright as embers, and something is burning inside me deep within my bones. The outstretched lighter hisses in the stillness.

And then I turn once more to look out upon the junk yard. Take in the twisted chunks of metal and steel, the mutilated rubber and dripping gasoline. I burrow my feet deep into the cracks that line the ground beneath my feet. I focus inward. And then, taking off into the labyrinth of trash, I begin to hunt.

(22)

AFTER: NATALYA

The towers are closer now when I exit the Fields of Asphodel. Close enough that I can touch. I press my hand up against the obsidian stone. The material is cool beneath my fingertips. Cold enough to burn, cold like the frost of an unending void.

"The sound of a cat's footfall." A shadow behind me croaks. The voice echoes as it bounces off the darkened walls; a sound neither old nor young but rather separated from the whole matter of time itself. "The roots of the tallest mountains. A woman's beard. Sinew from a bear. Fish breath. And lastly, spittle collected from birds. These were the ingredients used to create the darkened watchtowers of Erebus, as well as the chains of the terrible hound."

"Who are you?" I ask the voice then. Spin around and search through the empty darkness. Silence is the only thing to answer. I turn back to the wall. Crane my neck and squint up at the watchtowers. Carefully, ever so carefully, I raise my hand once more to the darkened walls. Maybe if I can just climb over the towers, I don't have to face the thing guarding the front gate.

I don't quite know what you would call the thing that stands outside the doors to the darkened walls. Perhaps a dog would be most accurate. After all, it certainly sounds like a dog. It smells like a dog. It even looks like a dog, if you ignore the fact that dogs normally don't have three heads. If you believed that it was usual, perhaps, for canines to be around fifty stories in size.

I can handle the size. I can handle the three heads. Hell, I think that I could even handle the strange sort of immortality that arises from being unable to kill a thing that's already dead. But fighting the thing would be a hassle when I could just climb over the wall. Hesitantly, I begin to climb.

"Natalya, stop." A second voice calls out. Clytemnestra. I don't bother looking at her. Don't bother wasting my time listening when the very underworld whispers my daughter's name.

"You would dare to steal Hel from Helheim?" A man made of memories and morphine once asked me.

I would. Oh, how I would. So long as the dead quit slowing me down with their mindless chatter.

"You know, I'm starting to get really sick of being told what I can and cannot do," I call out through gritted teeth. "Charon and his

Styx, Hypnos and his dreamland, it seems as if the very underworld is conspiring against me. I am going to get my daughter back, no matter how many times you all tell me no."

Clytemnestra stands there doubled over, panting, her eyes tracking mine with an almost frantic light. The bottom of her dress is tattered, and her feet are streaked with mud and grass stains. Despite this, she continues to run forward. Until she's grabbing me by the hand. Until she's tugging me off the wall.

"I know that." She exclaims breathlessly, yanking me down and dodging my flailing limbs. "Gods above, I know how stubborn you are. But look up." She jabs a finger into the sky and glares as I cower under her gaze. "Look up, you impatient fool, and view with your own eyes what guards those wretched towers. Do you really think you could survive against those things?"

At first glance, they had appeared to be nothing more than chunks of hardened stone, twisted sculptures deformed by the abundance of darkened shadows. I had assumed that they were some type of gargoyles, like the ones that guard mortal palaces and religious buildings. Curling snakes dripped from their scalps in tendrils, and leathered skin folded in a pantomime of wrinkles. Their hunched-over backs revealed exposed rib cages bent into the forms of outstretched wings. They looked like a nightmare of an old woman, leftover scraps from some hungry abyss.

They're watching me. Watching me with eyes gleaming in onyx and jade and malachite, and there is something so *ugly* about the creatures perched on the spires that they make even the gorgons appear beautiful.

"They're known as the Furies." Clytemnestra's voice is quiet. Afraid. And I have never heard my guide afraid, but I can now hear the fear shaking in her voice. Can see the terror trembling in her bones. "And they- they are the things that tormented my family. Natalya," she looks at me then, voice still and eyes serious, "if you trust me even a little bit from this time that I have served as your guide, then take the way of Cerberus. Do not climb the walls."

"There is a reason that sometimes even death is considered a mercy. Take another path. This way will only end in suffering."

"Why are you helping me?" Clytemnestra startles at the question. "I mean, I angered you in the fields of Asphodel. So why do you keep offering to help me?"

The woman pauses. Thinks. Wonders over her words, hums and deliberates as she struggles to figure out what to say.

"I'm not doing this for you, if that's what you're asking." She says at last. "I'm doing this for your daughter, and perhaps myself to a certain extent. For too many years, I watched as my children were hurt because I stood back and did nothing. I watched as one by one, I failed to protect the people I love most. Maybe if I help you save Helen, it can help ease that guilt. Perhaps I could be someone who saves, rather than curses. Maybe by being your guide, I can make a difference and change things."

She stretches a hand into the pockets of her dress made of beetle wings. The silvery wings shimmer from where they flutter in the moonlight. She rummages around for a couple of seconds before pulling out an old, jagged axe.

It's the type of axe that you read about in fairytales, all large and ornate and covered in bright glittering jewels. Although comically oversized, the blade seems to glide as it flutters between Clytemnestra's practice swings. As the metal arcs and cuts through the shadows, a strange scream begins to resound from the jagged weapon. It is the sound of something breaking, ripping at the seams as my guide's blade slashes past. If I didn't know better, I would say that Clytemnestra was cutting the very shadows into pieces.

"We will have to be quick." My guide advises, her grip tightening as she holds the blade in between clenched hands. "Very quick, as quick as you possibly can. We cannot possibly surprise the hound with stealth, and so we must use speed."

I draw my gun then. Feel the metal shiver between my fingers as I check the safety. My sword presses against my side, and I can feel a rush of adrenaline that pulses through my veins.

There's something *itching* inside me. Something that scrapes along my veins and grates against my stagnant muscles. It whispers in my ear when I'm tired, and it snarls from where it clings to my shoulders, and it tells me that I can get everything I want if I just push a little harder. It's been with me from before I first set foot in the underworld. Before I even packed my bags and left my house.

It's been with me since the day I saw my daughter lying there dead in the ground.

I lick my lips. Pull my face into a grin. Widen my stance and get ready to sprint. My hands are itching for the chance to rip and tear and *hurt*.

For too long have I been stuck on the sidelines of my own story. Made to beg like a dog and grovel on my knees for some chance at salvation. I am tired of pleading. Tired of asking oh so sweetly. Tired of having to debate my own daughter's life as if it were ever something worth debating in the first place.

"At my signal, you run." Clytemnestra orders. The dog is now staring at us, drool leaking from its waiting jaws like weak, old, rotten pus. It can sense my bloodlust. Can smell my rage.

I take out my bullets and shove them in the rifle's magazine. My hands are shaking, eagerness and anticipation making my pulse race. Position the magazine just inside the magazine well and then rock it back.

"On your mark." My guide begins. Six eyes. The creature has six eyes. There are twenty rounds in my Barretta that can be fired before I need to replace the bullets. My fingers tremor from where they lightly hold the trigger. Carefully, I raise the butt of the gun until it's resting between my shoulder and collarbone.

"Get set." Clytemnestra orders.

I point the gun right at the monster until the target is placed on its massive, awaiting eyes. Bend my knees. Plant my feet shoulder-width apart. Raise the gun up to my eye level and listen to the tiny *click* that rings out when the safety pops off. My hands aren't shaking anymore. My fingers aren't trembling anymore. I feel myself relax, an icy calm washing over me as I lightly brush the trigger.

Clytemnestra wants me to run. Wants me to flee with my tail tucked between my legs, run like a cowardly dog as I beg at Thanatos's feet.

And yet I made myself a promise when I tucked my daughter into bed at night. I made a promise to my daughter when I braided dandelions into her curly hair and danced with her on sunny mornings. I made a promise to my daughter when she was still new to a life where love could be a thing of safety instead of something to be feared.

Clytemnestra wants me to run, but I've never been good at running. I've never been good at taking the easy way out, especially when the situation involves my family.

Clytemnestra's about to speak again, the word *go* resting on the tip of her tongue. I force myself to inhale. And then exhale. Release the nerves pent up writhing beneath my itching skin and steady the target pointing at Cerberus's eye.

"Move." My guide orders.

It's funny, really, just how deadly gunpowder can be. The fact that something as insignificant as specks of dust can create destruction if sparked by the right catalyst. *The rage of the gods,* stories have often called it. *Araktelos. The vengeance of the damned. Rumors say that the powder was made from the ground-down bones of those too angry to die.* Perhaps it's fitting then that it is a gun I use to face the undead hound with instead of a more common type of weapon.

These people took my Helen from me.

I wonder how they'll react to the taste of hellfire.

(23)

BEFORE: HELEN

On average, the typical frame of a car is made up of a mixture of iron and steel. From that single car, the amount of steel used is so great that the resulting pile eventually weighs around nine hundred kilograms. I stare down at the scraps laid in front of me, the metal cold under my hands as I lug it in pieces back to the house by the sea.

I've started studying chemistry when I find time to practice. When I first began, I read how everything that has ever been created can be classified under the same core elements.

There's something beautiful about that thought. Poetic. My skin is composed of the products of spilt starshine, and the blood in my veins contains the same oxygen found in the air I breathe. I can break down organs into tissues. Tissues into cells. Cells into molecules. Molecules into atoms. And within each of those atoms is an element.

It is the addition of carbon that makes steel so much stronger than iron. Bound tightly between the two elements found on the periodic table, carbon gives the steel something that iron could never achieve on its own: durability. It's able to withstand more damage than any other piece of metal used inside a sword. It remains unchanging in the face of strike or stab, can survive frost and hail, and remains unyielding even as the world around it bends. When owned by a proper swordsman, a blade made from high-carbon steel will never once lose its edge. It's also the only way that I can fuse my gift into the edges of the weapon: Thanatos only granted me control over organic and still living objects.

I gather the steel from the skeletons of disassembled car parts. Despite its size, the metal is light when I carry it in my arms. I bring it down to the nearby seashore, Nestle the steel between obsidian rocks, and holding out my hands, begin to focus inwards.

Steel is made up of iron and carbon. Iron, like the hemoglobin in red blood cells. Carbon, like the gas expelled from the lungs when a person exhales. Steel is a metal made up of iron and carbon. It is a metal formed from the same elements as my body and the body of the universe. It is me, and I am it. We are but two organisms made of the same parts left to exist on this chaotic mess of a thing we call a planet.

In order to mend steel, you must melt it. Hold it over burning charcoals and watch as it succumbs to the intense pressure that cooks it. See how it neither breaks nor shatters. Only becomes the form most needed in that exact moment.

I watch the metal burn from where I torch it in the sand. Watch as oxygen combusts when it gobbles up fuel. Watch how the steel warps and bends from where it begins to take shape in the iron shavings.

There is something addictive about the heat as it burns on the beach. Like dizzying supernovas that pulse and twist as they careen around the heavens, jeweled colors that sear the back of my eyes whenever I shut them. The buzz of lightning, electricity fizzing like sour candy under my tongue as the flames lick the rocks.

It feels like comfort, this process of burning. Nostalgic. I feed the embers memories of sizzling metal slides, gasoline-fueled lighters, and fireplaces that would constantly blast hot air in the winter.

I add charcoal. Melt the metal in a clay boiler and watch as the steel warps and bends, forming curved ridges on the sides. Take the blade out and watch it cool into something frigid, cold, and unbreaking in its creation. The metal darkens, its surface changing the brightness of magma into something black. And steady. The blade seems to whisper as I try a couple of practice swings. It seems to murmur, as it cuts through the air with a near-silent hiss.

From the flames of Hell I have been molded. Molded to rid the choking itch that burns and strangles my nation.

"It needs a name." Mother murmurs as she makes a handle for the weapon. Her fingers are deft and skilled. She wraps strips of green leather around a handle made from my bones and etches curling vines around the surface of the blade. "After all, all truly great blades bear at least one. Names give weapons souls, bring them a type of life and recognition that exceeds even the battlefield."

I stop and pause then. Look at the blade silently and think of what to call this weapon of mass destruction. There is no real love felt for this thing in my hands. Not when I know what it was created for.

Thanatos materializes and examines the sword with a critical eye. Nods his head in quiet appreciation. Reaches out a skeletal hand to stroke the edge and asks me softly,

"Are you alright, my child?"

"I don't know what to name it," I reply hoarsely. Hope that they think my tone is a result of fear instead of disgust. My skin crawls as I hold the metal, cells itching as I resist the urge to claw off any part of my body that the object touches.

"That's alright," Mother responds. "Sometimes it can take time to think of the perfect name."

"I had a child, once." Thanatos tells me, "He named his blade Revenant, a word that means one who comes back from death. He named it as a way to give a name to his new calling, the first word on his path to writing a new legacy. I'm not sure if that knowledge is of any help to you, but it can give you some ideas at least."

I stare once more at the chunk of metal that I hold in my hands. The chunk of metal that *I* made, born from fire and ash and fragments of my bones. I think for a couple of minutes.

"Requiem." I decide then, my voice steady. "I want to name the sword requiem."

A mass for the dead, a sword that sings the memories of those it slays for all eternity. A sword that binds itself to the lives of those it takes, that grants them mercy instead of prolonged suffering. I look up at Mom and realize that she's grown silent.

"That's a beautiful name." She murmurs eventually. I force myself to grin.

"Thank you," I respond simply before heading back into the house. Thanatos trails after me like an extension of my own shadow.

"Are you alright, my child?" He asks when I lock myself in the bathroom. I look up at him from where I sit curled in the corner, my shoulders shaking.

I'm starting to struggle to get air into my lungs. The tile counter looms above my head, and I shrink down smaller as the bathroom begins to shift and warp. I feel dizzy, suffocated.

There's blood pounding in my ears. I can hear it beating, a wild BA-dum ba-DUM. My hands are shaking. My hands are shaking. And I can't feel my feet anymore. The world is closing in on me, growing oh so tight and suffocating, and I don't think I can breathe anymore. There's a tight pressure building up around my chest, and I don't think I can breathe anymore.

Thanatos is talking, but I can't really hear him over the sound of blood pumping through my ears. Can't understand what he's saying, when the world is caving in around me, and my hands refuse to stop shaking. I start sobbing. Bile rises in my throat as I hunch over the pale white tiles. Everything's spinning. My head hurts. My head *hurts* – there's an icepick drilling itself straight through my skull, and I think I forgot how to breathe air into my lungs.

"Can you tell me what's wrong?" Thanatos asks, his voice calm as he sits beside me. Slowly, ever so carefully, he begins to approach me as if I were a baby animal, his motions soothing as he reaches out a hand to grab my own.

I try to speak up. Try to tell him then, why the thought of killing someone makes me want to vomit my guts out. That I'm afraid to look a man in the eyes and hear him scream like the rats did. I don't think I can bring myself to actually hurt someone. Violence doesn't come naturally to me, and because of that, I'm going to let him down.

Just like I always do. No matter how hard I try, I can't stop letting people down.

I try to talk, but it's hard to speak when you can't get air into your lungs. I start crying even harder, look away from Death's concerned face, and try to hide the way my shoulders are shaking. I'm letting him down.

"I can't, I can't do it, Thanatos." I muster out then weakly. I look in the mirror and stare at the person staring back. My crying stops, words trailing off as I stare at the girl's bright, shiny eyes. She doesn't look like me. The girl in the mirror doesn't look like me. There's something wrong – no *distorted* about her appearance, and I can't tell if it's the wrong shade of hair or just slightly too large eyes, but I don't recognize that girl in the mirror.

Carefully, ever so carefully, I reach a hand out and shakily trace it across my cheek. The person in the reflection does the same. And yet, their fingers are slightly too long. Their cheek is too soft in the dim overhead light.

"Thanatos," I ask him then, refusing to tear my eyes away from the reflective glass, "who is that girl in the mirror?"

"That's you, Helen." Death cautiously answers. "That's always been you." He pauses. Waits for me to answer. To make some sort of comment or response. But I can't. My throat is still too choked up.

"You know, sometimes Helen," Thanatos adds gently, "sometimes when a person is really upset or scared, they tend to forget what they are supposed to look like. They discover that they cannot rationalize the world around them, and so their brain imagines instead that everything is a dream. Strange things often happen to people whose brains believe that they're in dreams: objects distort and skin shifts, and senses jumble in such a way that a person could very well feel mad if they're stuck in that dream for too long. It's called depersonalization."

I keep looking in the mirror, and slowly start to slow my breathing. Perhaps it is wrong to take comfort in the idea that I am someone else. That it is not my face but another girl's, who looks back from the other side of the glass. That the real me is someone far, far away from here, safe and warm and inside an old, overgrown greenhouse.

"I'm not a good person, Thanatos." The words feel strange as they roll off my tongue. Strange, in how easy they are to admit. "I'm weak, and selfish, and a coward. I can't be the hero everyone wants me to be. This is me giving up, Thanatos." I admit. "Because I can hurt myself just fine, but I draw the line at another person."

"But Helen, you've already *been* fighting." Thanatos counters, his brow furrowing in confusion. "You entered into arenas and battled dozens of people. Isn't this way better? At least now you'll be fighting to end things, instead of only furthering the cycle."

"Is that- Is that what you think I did, Thanatos?" I feel sick as I sit there, my stomach churning as I look at him. "Just fought for *nothing?* Hurt all of those people, watched them beg and scream and die for *nothing?* I did it for you. I did it because I loved you, because you told me that you needed me, and I so desperately wanted someone to love me."

"No! No, of course not, little one." There's something itching beneath my teeth in the crevices of my gums. I feel feverish, almost, my flesh hot and sweaty. Desperately I begin to pinch myself, tug at my cheeks and wiggle my tongue in order to feel *something,* to wake up WAKE UP and snap out of this swirling confusion. Everything's too loud – I can hear the sink steadily dripping as the water falls in a pit PAT pit PAT and the door is squeaking and Thanatos is talking but I CAN'T HEAR HIM, can't hear him over the growing static buzzing in my ears. I touch my face in an attempt to ground myself, but all I feel is skin.

"…That's what I need you to understand, do you know that Helen? You were a scared, quiet, *lonely* little girl born as the product of a broken system. It's not your fault; no one taught you any better. You just wanted to be loved, didn't you, baby? You just wanted to love without everything hurting."

"You said you wouldn't let anything hurt me." I choke out, vision swimming as I slowly start to cry. "You said that nothing would hurt me, either in this world or the next." My tongue is swollen, all thick and floppy, and it's hard to push the words past, but I try to anyway. "You lied." My head is spinning, all dizzy as the world around me swims, but I try to get the words out, try to speak because this is important, Thanatos needs to know because otherwise that means he was fully aware of everything that the stadiums and the scientists were doing and he chose to put me through that anyway. "You– you told me that you loved me." I wail hysterically, tears in my eyes.

"Of course, I love you, Helen." Thanatos agrees, and I feel myself crack as a piece of me starts to die inside. "You are.... Little One, you cannot even *fathom* just how dear you are to me."

"My mom says the same thing, you know." I keep my eyes focused on a crack in the tiles as I talk, stare at the ground so that I don't have to look him in the eyes. "She said that she *loves me,* that she doesn't like hurting me, but she just needs to make sure that I am stronger. That I wasn't weak and died young like my father. That I had *so much potential,* and one day I was going to be an even greater hero than she could ever be. She said…she said that she *wanted to protect me,* that the world is a cruel place, and she had to hurt me so that by the time someone else did, I could learn to walk it off."

"My mom *loves me.*" I sob to Thanatos, "She loves me so *very much.* But she doesn't know how to love something without breaking it." A sniffle, and then in a quieter voice. "Sometimes I think you're the same, Thanatos. I mean, you can hide behind a bunch of changing names and faces, but that doesn't change the fact that in the end, all you'll ever be is Death. I don't really mind, though. My mom doesn't know how to love something without breaking it either."

"Do you want to know something funny, Thanatos? When I said that I wanted to be a hero, that was a lie. I never actually wanted to stand in that arena. I never wanted to go to that sanitarium. I never wanted to fight an entire nation, or forge a sword, or learn how to turn death into a mercy. In the end, I never really cared about anyone else, all those poor souls who suffer while I stand back and watch. Ultimately, I just wanted someone to love me. Wholly and unconditionally, I just wanted someone to love me without everything hurting. I'm so tired of everything hurting."

"A wise man once said that true courage is not the absence of fear, but the triumph over it." Death answers at last. "Helen, there is no shame in being afraid. After all, you would have to be a fool not to be."

"And yet, there is a reason that people who ignore evil are just as wrong as the people who commit such crimes. Over the course of history, evil has only been allowed to succeed through the silence of those who should have spoken."

"You are young, Helen. A child going against an institution that is thousands of years old. And yet, I believe that you already understand what I am saying. There is a reason that you use the past instead of the present to describe the things you wanted. I fully believe that in the beginning, you didn't want anything more than to simply be loved."

"But when you were given the chance to walk away and live a quiet life here in this cottage, you chose to become a hero instead. When you were granted the option to break your vow with me as you stood there in the salty sea, you chose to turn once more back to the land instead. You call yourself weak. Selfish. A coward. Helen, when I look at you, I see that you are anything but. Because when time and time again you are given the option to walk away, you choose to stay and fight."

For a while, I am silent. I stare at the girl in the nearby mirror and realize how dull her eyes are. How scarred her skin is. How empty her smile. And yet, the girl in the mirror is still smiling. Her eyes may be dull, but there is still a fire lit within. Her skin may be scarred, but there has always been a sort of pride felt towards those marks. A sense of accomplishment, of growth. I look at the girl in the mirror and realize that although she is breaking, she has not given up yet.

I stand up then. Pull myself to my feet. Slowly, ever so slowly, the image of the girl in the mirror begins to feel like my own. Her nose is my nose. Her hands are my hands. Her smile is as soft as mine is. She is me, and I am her. There is nothing shameful about that fact.

"If I am going to fight, then I am going to do it on my own terms," I tell the shadow man. "Not with a sword, but with my bare hands." Quietly, he nods in approval.

"How are you going to do that, my child, when already you struggle to fight against one person?" He asks curiously. I reach into my pockets and wrap my hand around a small, sharp needle.

"Have you ever wondered, Thanatos, how an evergreen tree can keep its leaves even when faced with the coldest winter? Or how any plant, for that matter, gains energy simply by staying still?" I hold the pine needle tightly between my fingers and rub my hands around the waxy coating.

"They do it by using photosynthesis, a fascinating technique where trees take sunlight, carbon dioxide, and water from the air to give them the energy to not only stabilize but also grow.

Inside each plant cell are small organelles called chloroplasts, which store the energy of sunlight from various light waves. These chloroplasts contain a unique pigment enhancer called chlorophyll, which takes in the solar power and converts it to the system's growth hormone, which maintains a plant's need for food and sleep.

By mimicking and utilizing the chloroplasts found inside a pine needle, one of the few plants that stays green even through the winter, I can reduce my need for sleep and exhaustion, thus giving me higher stamina."

"Helen, if you fail…" Thanatos starts hesitatingly. I cut him off.

"Failure is not an option, Thanatos." I look at the girl in the mirror as I wind plants in bracelets across my skin. Pine needles. Holly locks. Magnolia. Plum Blossoms. Roses. My hair begins to darken, yet at the same time, it lightens. The thickened thorns that live in my lungs begin to shiver in delight as slowly, ever so slowly, flowers bloom. Small petals bud across my skin like freckles. Chlorophylls unfurl and my hair grows green, vibrant, and glowing in the dull bathroom light. "Not in a matter such as this."

(24)

AFTER: NATALYA

I slam my feet down into the ground and take off running, a web of fractures spiraling out from the center of the ground where my feet had struck. Until my footprints sear themselves into the ground like a brand. Until the very Underworld is marked by the strength of my hate. Cerberus turns then, some long-buried instinct causing it to turn and watch. A flicker of something primal stirs within the creature's eyes. A calm, almost calculating expression as it sizes me up. It's trying to figure out whether I'm predator or prey.

I watch as the dog pulls three matching snouts into identical snarls. Watch as eyes widen and gums drool, brimstone and Sulphur sizzling through its saliva. Eagerly, ever so eagerly, the creature licks its lips. Dropping down onto one knee, I focus my aim at the creature's center head. Line up the shot. Inhale, and then exhale.

I fire my gun.

Just once.

BANG.

Run closer to the monster, instead of away from it. Squeeze my finger around the trigger and listen as the creature screams. Draw nearer and watch as the hellhound writhes from where it strains against its chains. Gunfire echoes as I fire over and over, bullets slamming into the thickened skin as I squeeze the trigger until he magazine clicks dry. Bullets tear open the thickened skin, and yet it does nothing more than rile the creature up even further.

It's not enough.

"Figures." I curse, ducking behind a nearby boulder. Swear under my breath as I slam another magazine into the chamber. My ears are ringing from the previous gunshots. My hands are stinging from the recoil.

The monster's fur is far too thick. No matter how many bullets I shoot, they won't cause any significant damage to the creature's skin. What I need to do is shoot for the soft spots; take out the eyes, and then rush past while the thing is blinded by pain.

To do that, I'll need to get close. Way closer than I am right now. I look at the chain that holds Cerberus's collars in place.

I start running again.

I duck a sweep of the thing's paws as it crushes the boulder into dust. Sharp jagged canines bite down as the left head lunges, teeth ripping into the dust and rubble half a meter from my head. Cerberus's breath burns, drool pooling from its gums as it drips onto the ground with a faint hiss.

Despite all of Cerberus's apparent strength, he's slow. Caught in indecision the creature struggles, heads snapping and biting in all directions. Cerberus is so confused about which direction to move in that he stands there frozen. Paralyzed. When he does move, it is in a stumble. Clumsy.

I weave between the creature's legs, using the dust kicked up by its legs as sufficient coverage. Weave around his paws, ignore the way each stomp leaves craters from the force of the thing's footsteps. No matter how hard I try, I cannot get past him and through the gate.

I can't find an opening.

Cerberus is covered in too many directions. Every step I take is met with a pair of jaws biting down: forwards and backwards, left and right. Teeth swipe down like spinning blades, each mouth snapping in a different direction. Even the tail

Frantically, I lunge to the right. Jaws snap down, fangs whistling through the air as they pass. Duck to the left and have to throw myself backwards to avoid a swiping paw. It's playing with me.

No matter which way I turn, there's a head snapping down. The teeth and legs are enough of a threat as it is – but with the tail acting as a brace to stabilize its movements, as well as cover its back and rear, there's no way I'm going to be able to move past it.

There's no way I can possibly win this.

Not unless I grab the chain.

The remnants of a boulder half my height- outstretched bricks jutting out of the wall in easy stepping range- shattering under my momentum as I leap and kick and *claw* at the edges of the gate to propel myself up, a final jump throwing my body even higher- I force myself to keep moving even farther until I'm nearly a story up. Pause for a brief second to lock eyes on the band of metal glinting in the moonlight and observe the series of links that bend and twist with each of Cerberus's movements.

I brace my boots against the cracked outcrop, waiting for the chain to swing past as Cerberus turns.

And then I jump, outstretched hands reaching to grab the links of curving metal. Use the momentum of the chain itself to swing under before kicking up and almost finishing the loop. Muscles screaming, I reach up, fingers clawing at the twisting chain links as I try to force one more lunge – the swing of the line pulling slack enough to give me one final push forward. I land on my feet on the surface of the chain.

Cerberus shudders, and I force myself to stay balanced as the chain wobbles. I look down and see Clytemnestra fighting there on the ground level, her axe screeching as it swings through the air. She slashes at the dog's legs without abandon, until small cuts begin to appear up and down the dog's legs. There's a certain confidence to each of her swings. A certain recklessness, left behind in each strike. I suppose anyone would be reckless in her situation, though. After all, it's hard to fear death when you're already dead.

Using my off hand, I reach into my bag and pull out a cord of rope. Tie it around the side of the chain and connect it to a carabiner on my belt. Standing up again, I begin to run.

There's a certain danger in staying still. In pausing to catch a breath or think of anything more than moving forward. Cerberus roars and twists, slamming its back against the gates as it tries to shake me off. Its heads tear and bite at the air as they rush past, minds torn between attacking the corpse flailing on the ground or the leech clinging to their leash. I take that distraction and run with it, rolling and ducking to avoid getting crushed by the impact. The chain shivers under the series of collisions. I move with the chain, rushing and swaying until I find myself near the loops connected to each of the collars. Bracing myself against the edges of the metal for support, I reach back for my bag and pull out my gun.

The closer I get, the more accurate the shot. I move until I'm breathing down the creature's necks. Until I'm sixty yards away. Fifty. I can see the whites of its eyes – glistening, bulbous, six bloated moons all swollen with rage.

My finger unlocks the safety catch. I sink into a crouch.

The smog is so thick that I can practically feel the grime settling on my neck and arms, as ash and dust particles swirl through the air, making my eyes sting and my vision blur. Cerberus bucks and roils beneath me, his snarls increasing as he jerks over and over at his chain. I can hear my heartbeat pounding in my ears. It sounds like a funeral drum, all high-pitched and frantic. Sounds like a funeral drum- that's silly. I don't think anything can really "die" if we're already in the land of the dead. I pull myself together with a swallow. Slow my breathing.

For a moment, Helen's face flashes through my mind. Her eyes – all wide and scared from where she had been surrounded by the beeping heart monitors.

The world fades out of focus until it's just me. The gun. That eye.

BOOM.

The middle head screams, head snapping back as thick yellow pus drips from its weeping. Shreds of shrapnel splinter and break apart from where the bullet lodges itself into the eye socket, slivers of what once was a retina breaking apart and flying out in chunks.

I slam a fresh magazine into the casing with twitching hands. The chain jolts violently. The barrel coughs, and then bullets pour out in a haze of thunder. My fingers are slick with blood, but I don't stop firing. I can't stop.

Not when Helen is waiting for me. My baby is waiting for me.

I reload my gun. Lock eyes with the remaining heads and get ready to run. Fire quickly, as the pairs of teeth bite down.

BOOM.

This time, it's the right one, whimpering as it wails. Pus and tears leak out as its eyes bulge and tear. I grip onto the chain as the monster shudders, and I feel my grip start to falter as the creature writhes. With a scream, Cerberus slams itself against the walls of Erebus. Pulls itself to its feet and then charges at the wall again. Stars fill my vision as my head slams back, ears ringing as I try to cling to the chain. My hands begin to blister and tear open as Cerberus tries to shake me off, rearing back as he throws himself over and over against the obsidian walls.

I'm going to die here, I realize with a start, hands scrabbling desperately to find their hold. The chain is slippery beneath my bloodied fingertips. Cerberus jerks itself, and my gun goes flying, vanishing over the side of the creature's back as it falls.

No, no, no. I start panicking, try to unhook myself from the rope as my muscles scream. Cerberus's left head turns, eyes bloodshot as it scans the area for whatever threat took out its other heads. It slams itself against the wall again with a pained cry, before diving back down to lunge for Clytemnestra once more. The momentum sends my hands spasming, nails ripping off my right pointer and middle finger from where they get jammed between the moving chain links.

I'm not- I'm not allowed to die here. Not when I'm so close to the end of the journey. Not when I've survived everything else. I need to get to Helen. Need to let her know that I'm still coming, that I've fought so hard just to bring her back. Shakily, I breathe in. And then out. Try to ignore how mangled my fingers are; how crushed they feel as I struggle to unbend them. Try not to look at the ends of my hands, nausea swirling up so strongly that part of me worries about throwing up.

I'm not going to die here. I swear to myself, fingers pulling out of the chain links with a bloodied squelch. Pain sears up, sharp and electric. *I'm not allowed to die here, not now. Not yet. I still… I still need to get things done. I need to get my daughter back. I'm not —*

I fall.

They say that when a person is dying, their entire life plays before their eyes in some sort of frozen sequence. When I fall, I can only sense the world in flashes. The wind whistles through my ears as I fall. The broken moon spins. Cerberus howls while the stars splinter overhead. Clytemnestra screams. Tiredly, I feel my lips pull themselves into a smile.

The sky is so damn beautiful.

On the ground, Clytemnestra raises her axe as high as she can and swings. The weapon arcs through the air, blade shining as it twists under the broken moonlight. I watch as the weapon warps, metal thickening as it changes into a netting as thick as tar and as dark as pitch. It feels soft when it catches me. Soft, and vaguely itchy. Like the woolen sweaters my mother used to make me wear as a child.

Clytemnestra hoists me onto her back once I grow close enough to grab and then takes off running, muttering curses under her breath as Cerberus howls. I let my gaze unfocus as I slump over her shoulders, stare at the dirt that flies up from my guide's footsteps as she sprints.

"I told you we should have just ran…" Clytemnestra mutters as fangs lunge through the air with a loud snap. "But no, you just *had* to be a hero and antagonize the hound, didn't you. What is with you heroes and your impulse control…."

My head slumps against her shoulder as Clytemnestra starts running. The sky spins. The wind howls. *I'm not going to die here.* I repeat to myself faintly. *I didn't claw my way through hell only to fail at the gate.*

(25)

BEFORE: HELEN

It's cold on the day of the attack. Cold and dark. The moon is blanketed by a thick grey cloud, and the wind freezes the world around the cottage. When I inhale, the smog that blocks the stars trickles into my airway. When I exhale, frost billows from my lungs.

I throw on my coat, wrapping layers of warmth around myself until I no longer risk getting frostbite. Mother loads up the back of her car, muscles straining as she buries guns under a thick dark tarp. Marek whistles from where he helps her, laughter bubbling out in occasional, short bursts. After a while, I open the car door and slide into the back seat.

A trail of flowers has begun to bloom amongst the woods. Petals pink as pomegranates and soft as snowfall. Wishes cling to the undersides of their stems and whisper under the roaring wind.

Mother joins me and starts the engine. Turns the radio on with a flick of her fingers. Tires spin and push off salted gravel. I stare out the window as, gradually, the flowers along the roadside begin to increase.

"There is a legend rising, among the streets of Durnon." The radio croons, static crackling in the background as the voice buzzes. *"It creeps from the runes of yellowed pages and tongues of wizened seers, and even the very wind itself can be found constantly whispering a name.*

Proserpine.

Flowers have begun to bloom, lining the sides of buildings and growing in the cracks of nearby streets.

They rise in an explosion of color from nearby skeletons and settle ever so quietly in paths that branch off winding roads. They seem to form a pathway that guides from the Capitol somewhere far away and unknown.

Helheim.

It is said that the superstitious have begun hanging flowers upside down above their doorways. That they have stitched the plants into woolen pockets and braided others into intricate crowns. They say a girl is coming, a princess. One who will bring spring in the darkest depths of winter. A child who will forever end the need for child soldiers. They say that the mysterious plants form a path, but the capital is not its starting point. Rather, it is the end. The destination. The place where Durnon will be reformed into a new land.

Helheim.

Others say that this is foolishness. Hysteria. There is a danger in jumping to conclusions. There is a danger in moving against the status quo of the present system. And yet, no one can deny the fact that flowers are blooming in winter. That corpses have begun to vanish from nearby roadsides under a sea of petals, and that the arenas of freshly built stadiums have already started to decay. No one can deny the fact that the temples to the gods are now constantly aflame. And let us not forget, dear listeners, the existence of the girl who brings forth life from her fingertips. Who stood alone among sands soaked in violence and offered peace instead. Let us not forget, dear audience, the strength of that girl and her moniker.

Let us not forget Proserpine.

When I had first declared that I was going to change my country, Mom had looked me in the face and laughed. In a voice doubtful and disbelieving, she had asked, *"You and what army?"* As we cross the border into Durnon, I show her my army.

Because there are people now, standing along the sides of the road. Flowers bloom from where they're woven around arms and legs and heads. They carry blades as cold as frost and lanterns lit by the warmth of the captured sun. Floating above their heads flutter a swarm of banners, the edges of their fabric twisting and curling so much that they almost appear alive. I lean closer, press my face against the car window, and squint through the foggy glass to try to make out what the signs read.

Memento Mori, one poster proclaims. *Remember you are mortal. That you are nothing but a man. That one day, death will come, and you will be powerless to stop it.*

Momento Ver, another whispers. *Remember spring, and the promise that comes with it. Remember the flowers that grow from the corpses of rotting autumn. Remember the healing that comes from moving on.*

Momento. The signs all repeat, over and over again, until the word burns itself into the back of my eyelids. *Remember. Remember, Remember, Remember…*

All too soon, the signs start burning. I watch them shrivel up in the smoke and die under a rain of gunfire. Something is screaming. Something is shrieking. And I can't tell if it's the wailing of the wind or the hailstorm of the bullets or the voices of the people or the scrape of bodies collapsing onto cobblestones or the weep, weep, *weeping* of the earth as it chokes beneath the bloodshed, but I can hear something screaming.

The sky is dark, shrouded by clouds of moving metal as destruction falls in the place of rain. Hellfire pours down in fizzing lightning and feathered arrows and swooping vultures that float with bloated bellies above the scene of the massacre. I look around and I see Thanatos hiding in every creeping shadow, his scythe flashing as he fells souls left and right.

"Sometimes, I think I want to burn all you humans to the ground." Thanatos hisses in my ear then, his voice quiet as venom drips from his tongue. *"The other gods don't really understand this, you know. After all, they don't really have to see the suffering that comes each time a person dies. Do you understand now, Helen?* He leans in even closer, and I hear another scream as one of my followers has their throat ripped out.

After all, you know how it feels to have your ears grow deaf from the constant shrieking.

His voice is soft as he murmurs to me. The tone is gentle, almost soothing. I watch as a man struggles to keep his intestines from spilling out of a split-open stomach. Tries to crawl as he clutches his guts in his arms. *To cry so hard that you exhaust your tear ducts.*

None of my men are running; I realize with a start. Though my people are massacred, they refuse to abandon their resolve. No matter how badly they are injured, these people still believe that I will save them. *To have the skin around your eyes crack and bleed because your body is physically unable to keep up with the force of your weeping.*

It is a mercy to kill them." Thanatos croons, all sickened sympathy and smiling eyes. Retribution has been delayed so long that now all that remains is decay. "*These monsters that mock the very ideal of meaning in mortality. This way, they can be spared judgment from the abominations they would have committed at a different date.*"

He wants me to kill them, I realize then. Wants me to wipe the enemy off the corners of the map, blot them out, and kill over and over again until I can't tell the color of my skin from where it is stained so deeply by the red. Death wants these men who oppose me to die. These *foolish mortals,* Thanatos wants me to rend and tear until I become his angel, a collector of souls who can purge the earth of their wickedness.

I let out a sigh, drink in a mixture of ash and grit when I inhale. Look once more at the lumps of moving gore that flop as they writhe around my feet. Smell the stench of rotting carcasses as vultures tear off chunks of bulging flesh. Hear the earth beg and scream as it chokes under the bloodshed.

At what point does revenge become justice? When does killing become a kindness? How much innocent blood does it have to take for pacifism to turn into cowardice? What does it mean when even the god of gentleness begs for execution?

I clutch my sword in shaking hands. The car slows to a stop. I feel so small as I stand there in the shrieking chaos. And yet I raise my hands. Lift my blade of polished bone up into the air and watch how it blinds the eyes of those around me.

I step out of the car, and the ground *crumbles* under the impact. Cement shatters and cobblestones buckle, and all around me, the earth starts to rise and shift as it bubbles underneath my feet. I hold my hands out, feel a mixture of blood and snow and sleet rain down onto my skin from the darkened heavens.

Gunfire slams into my side almost immediately, knocking me off balance as I stumble to the side. I look around and notice a man crouched up above in the trees. His hands are shaking as he fires over and over again. He seems to think that if he hits me enough times, I'll eventually fall down.

I right myself and start moving. Lock eyes with the gunman and wave, walk towards the tree he hides in just a little faster than before. I watch as he starts to panic, flailing and squirming when he realizes I'm still standing. Incompetent, really. He should have known better. Should have listened to the stories. Should have learned that they already tried bullets when they faced me in the arenas.

He should have realized that they already tried to kill me, over and over in suffocating sands and linoleum tiles; that they cut me up and spat me back out in a variety of ways. No matter what they tried, I still stayed standing. I feel my lips pull into a grin, move even faster as he starts to panic.

I close my eyes and sense tiny little heartbeats, flickering in and out of focus as they dance around the edges of my vision. I try to grab them, but they slip between my fingers.

There are so many of them, I realize with a start. So many small, fragile heartbeats. Thanatos wants me to smash them. Wants me to rend and tear and break them into a million tiny pieces. That way, they won't feel any pain. That way, they'll die quickly.

Is it a mercy to kill them?

I can't tell the difference anymore between the millions of twitching heartbeats. Can't tell which people I'm supposed to kill and which I'm supposed to save. People are screaming my name, over and over again, until it builds up a shrieking din. I'm tired. I'm so very tired. Tired of failing the people who love me.

"Kill them." Thanatos hisses. *"Rend them, tear them, break them, smash them, kill them, and kill them quickly. Do you not see how our people die with your name on their lips? They're calling for you, Helen. Calling for you to save them from these heretics who doubt our might. Won't you save them, Helen? The more you hesitate, the more that the slaughter draws out."*

A sharp pain lances through my shoulder, slicing down my arm with a sickening hiss. I look up. A soldier is standing there, panting from where he grips the handle of his axe. Its blade is buried in my side. I grab onto the metal. Tug the man closer gently, reach out for him with fingers sticky from my own blood.

The earth is screaming. Choking from where it drowns in the sea of gore, gasping from where it's suffocated by the corruption. The earth is screaming, bubbles of pus rising on this man's skin as he chokes and flails under my grasp.

It's all I can see, really, is the rot. Rot clinging to nearby trees in fungus spores and spilling out from split-open stomachs and bubbling under the flesh of this man's arms that I now hold inside my hands.

My touch is gentle when I cradle him. I make sure to hold him softly in my blood-soaked hands and stabilize him as he collapses. His breaths are painless as he dies. Although killed, the action is kind. He falls to the ground gently, flowers blooming across his skin. I raise my eyes back to the gunman, watch him watch me from the trees. I make sure he sees me grin as I look back at him, make sure he notices the blood staining the edges of my fingers as I wave.

I begin to walk closer.

I trip over an outstretched hand, feel fingers wrap around my ankle, and latch on with desperation. There is a woman, flopped on the ground at my feet. Flowers writhe around her hair like twitching snakes, and she watches me with eyes wide in devotion.

"Help me." She sobs, reverence ringing out from the sound of the endless shrieking. Dried blood sticks to her skin like flaking rust, and even in her dying breath, she begs me to save her.

I watch the flowers consume her whole. Watch as her skin gets swallowed up by the sea of plants. Gently, ever so gently, I take her hands and hold them in mine. Allow the sword stabbed through her stomach to prick my skin in return.

Light of my light, blood of my blood. I hold the woman's blood-soaked hands in mine. Watch as reddened droplets pass from my skin into her open wound. Feel a sudden rush of static as my blood travels through her arteries, sense it shudder as it passes through her veins. I close my eyes and lean forward, hold the woman up as flowers bloom up and down our collective limbs.

The woman starts screaming then. Starts wailing as the change begins, as flesh begins to mend and bone reforms with a snap. I hug her tighter as she struggles to stand. Rub circles up and down the sides of her back and shush her softly as she wails in pain.

"It hurts. Oh, how I know it hurts." I murmur softly. Phantom pains travel up and down the sides of my skin, memories of studying in the greenhouse flooding through my brain as I try to keep this woman from collapsing. "If it's any consolation, I've gone through this pain before," I tell her soothingly. "It hurts in the beginning, but by the end it's better." I allow my voice to become firmer. "You *will* become better."

Textbooks say that when a person suffers from life-threatening injuries, a last-ditch effort to save them can be found in a blood transfusion. Normally, it's administered through a needle, a tube, or another type of injection.

I don't have any of those tools on me right now. Right now, the only thing I have with me to help is my hands. And so, I bring them up to hold the woman tightly. Give her a hug as she screams and flails. Show her comfort in those final moments before she is reborn.

Since the very first time I received my magic, the core focus of Death's blessing has been the power of understanding. By using knowledge of recorded findings in the natural sciences, I could rewrite and manipulate cell patterns. Most of the time, this means that I have to learn from my own mistakes. Feel firsthand each change, turn, and impact. It means that every time I use my gift, I must tie it into how I personally perceived it. The only reason that I could melt steel, after all, was when I related it to the red blood cells in my hemoglobin.

When I stare at the woman in front of me, I realize that our lungs breathe with the same airways. Our hearts beat to the same marching drumbeat. She is the light of my light, blood of my blood. Slowly, ever so slowly, I allow her to borrow my gift of magic.

I pull away from the woman once she is able to stand on her two feet. Smile at her softly and watch as she stares at me in devotion. Tears of joy drip from her eyes then, liquid pooling in a mixture of blood and water. She holds her hands out, uncaring of the noise and chaos of the battle raging around our feet. She holds out her hands and stares at them, looks up at me with wonder in her eyes, and remarks –

"I never knew that I could feel so alive."

I vanish back into the sea of shrieking gunshots. Listen to the wind cry and reach out with bloodied hands to touch nearby fighters.

Every handprint stains the skin of each new person, the red oozing through their pores until it coats the outsides of their hearts. For my enemies – all choked with rage and greed and hate – this means death. For my followers - the ones with flowers in their pockets and worship in their eyes – this means resurrection.

I keep walking until the blood loss makes me dizzy. Keep giving until I have nothing left to give. Each transformation causes a loss of energy, a gradual loss that inevitably begins to pile up. *Bone growth, organ repair, blood amplification,* I repeat the process over and over until I nearly collapse on my feet. Until I resemble a living corpse more than a man.

A hand touches my shoulder. Drags me down behind the protection of a nearby tree and fires off several warning shots. I look up at Mom then, notice how viciously my brothers fight.

"It's all right, Helen." She murmurs then, eyes so full of love that it almost makes me sick. Why does she care about me so much? What have I done to deserve her kindness? "I'm here, I've got your back."

I close my eyes. Tip my head back against a nearby tree trunk. Imagine that my fingers are roots tangled deep beneath the forest floor. Anchor myself down into the dirt of this spinning planet. Reach for the thousands upon thousands of spinning heartbeats, those tiny little organs that beat with my blood running through their systems. Carefully, I gather them between my fingertips. I dig in.

Pinpricks of light swell and burst behind the corners of my vision, colored stars rising and falling behind the back of my eyelids. I clutch the hearts tighter as they strain and wiggle from where they flop in my hands, hold them tighter as they drag me out of my physical body. I look down at where I clutch the links like bloodied reins, feel myself tugged in so many directions that I get yanked out of my flesh.

I open my eyes and blink hazily as I stare down at the shifting battleground. My eyes are fogged by drifting clouds. My ears are muffled, as if something similar to cotton is clogging them, leaving the violence distorted. I try to open my mouth, try to plead or call for help. All that comes out is static, an endless droning that blends in with the shrieking of the wind.

My body is lying there, all crumpled and broken from where it flops on the ground. There's something almost morbid about staring at it, seeing myself sprawled out with limp limbs and whitened eyes. Is that what my corpse will look like when I'm dead? I move past it with a shudder and focus back on the reddened heartbeats. Focus on the scarlet chains that wrap around my distorted limbs and tie me to the ground.

I should - I should be afraid, I think. I should be scared of the way my mind is both there but *isn't*. I should be worried about the way the shell of my body isn't really breathing. Part of me feels dead, as I float there with the watching vultures. Like I'm somewhere in limbo, caught between life and something else.

And yet – I haven't feared death in a long time, now. I haven't feared it enough to let it scare me from my mission or drive me away from my goal. If anything, I think I'm a little curious. Curious about what this new evolution of my gift means. What the possible drawbacks are, for drifting in the sky with nothing but the hazy recollection of a body.

Experimentally, I reach for the branching heartbeats. Tug on them a little, wiggle them back and forth, and see what happens as a result. Steadily, ever so steadily, my people begin to march forward. When they fall down, I yank on their string and they rise back up.

If I were to describe it, I would say it's something like a hivemind, or a conductor guiding an orchestra along a sheet of music. A spider, perhaps, making its flies move by twisting certain strands of its web. I guide my followers forward and heal them when they should break. Give them the strength to keep moving, no matter what harm befalls them.

It doesn't matter in the end how experienced my people are at fighting. It doesn't matter how strong or fast or smart they are, or how well they can wield a weapon. No, experience doesn't matter in this fight. Endurance does. The ability to keep pushing when all else fails around you, the choice to crawl when you can no longer walk, that is what makes my men strong as they approach the sea of unending bullets. That is what makes my men press on and break through the enemy forces.

The fire sputters out when it has finally run out of fuel to feed its destruction. Ashes are left to tangle in the wind, spinning and sifting as they float through the air. Gradually, they begin to spell out a word in the resulting stillness. A word that has been repeated thousands upon thousands of times across sheets of yellowed paper. A word formed as a whisper from a god that has now given way to a shout.

Momento. *Remember.*

Remember all that you foolish mortals have forgotten in your hubris.

I watch as my people walk forward. Watch as the ground shivers, winter defrosting as it melts into spring. I watch as the walls crumble. As the metal on the weapons rusts. I watch as the world ends, and then begins anew.

Sometime later, I feel myself pulled back into my body. I pick myself up, legs shaky like a newborn fawn. Mother looks over and catches me when I stumble. Slowly, ever so slowly, we begin to head towards the city.

Up above me, the sky burns, stars scattered across the sky in a series of coordinates, a path laid by poets that in the end leads nowhere. I follow them nonetheless. Follow them as they chill my skin with their own cold caress. Eventually, I begin to pass familiar road signs.

I was never the best at reading constellations. Never really remembered those stories so often sung by the muses. But I draw lines through the obsidian sky with my fingers, connecting. One, Two, Three. Over and over again, as the towns give way to a city. Following behind me in a trail of tears bloom weeping roses.

There is blood on the floor of the Senate. Blood on the grave of the government. It lies there, staining the grounds of the ruling and high offices, rusting under the metallic moonlight. Some of it is mine, liquid gathered from my veins. Part of me lies dead there, dead alongside all those false dreams that kept my country afloat.

There is an iron crown, left cracked and broken in the center of the Senate floor. I force myself to grab it, muscles straining as I climb the crumbling steps. Hold the thing in my shaking hands and watch as it cracks down the middle.

There is a crowd of men waiting in the courtyard below me. They snake between the streets with hands lifted to the heavens while they chant, flowers curling around their throats as they sing to the stars and the sea and everything in between. They laugh, and they cry, and they cheer over and over about the glory of their girl. Their angel. Their messiah. They sing of a muse and a symbol, spinning stories as easily as they breathe, and kicking their shoes off, they begin to dance in the streets.

I go outside. Step out onto a balcony and hold the crown in my trembling hands. My body is shaking from exhaustion. I have burned myself out so thoroughly that a part of me is confused by how I'm still standing.

And yet I make myself stand firm. Make myself stand firm and watch as my people look up. Stand there while the mobs on the streets gaze up, an angel clothed in white whose face ripples under the burning torchlight.

I hold the crown up and *crush* it under my fists. Open my fingers and let the iron shavings drift down like ash on the wind. Pull out my sword, all pearly bone and wrapped in green. I hold my sword in my hands and mold it until it forms a new coronet, only perfected. Completed. Whole. Out with the old and in with the new, and I hold the new crown out and slide it onto my head, an angel glowing under the light of the stars and flickering torchlight.

I stand there before the hunger of a thousand, face their devotion and adoration with hands gripping the balcony railings, and force myself to hold firm. Tonight, I am not merely a girl. Not merely Helen. I am Proserpine. Death's beloved. An angel, glowing in the brooding darkness.

(26)

AFTER: NATALYA

The first thing I notice when I pass the gates of Cerberus is the sunshine. Pure, unfiltered sunshine. Light spills out into the air around me, and it causes my eyes to burn as I stare, makes me shield my eyes, and for a moment, pause because –

I had forgotten, for a moment, just what it was like for everything to be this bright. Warm. *Safe*, even.

"Where are we?" I ask quietly, staring up into the burning light. I close my eyes and look between my fingers, stare at the sky with shock and awe as the very world explodes into a million colors. Millions of clouds float in the air above my head, their colors twinkling and iridescent like a sea of soap bubbles.

I close my eyes, and when I look up again, I'm staring at the Northern lights. There's soft snow crunching under my feet and the scent of softened pine wafts through the air. I can hear a faint crackling in the distance, somewhere there is a hearth with a fire merrily burning. Almost unconsciously, my hands go to my backpack and move to pull out my lighter. It's been a long time since I was last able to feel warm.

Hypnos recreated places from my childhood as well, there in his cave among the putrid smoke and lavender mist. And yet his visions were different from this place, in the same way that the day is opposite from night and the dead from life. His depictions were cold, suffocating, and still. Shrinking corners wrapped around shadowed figures while weeping babies cried from their cradles. Here it is warm, light, and airy. It is easy, here, to forget that those who dwell in this place are no longer alive.

The snow tastes like sugar when I open my mouth and taste it. Spun sugar, the type my grandmother would make on Friday nights when waiting for my parents to come home.

On autopilot, I move to wipe a tear from my eye. I can't exactly recall when I first started crying.

"Where are we?" I ask my guide in a hoarse voice. Her face is dull, eyes lifeless as she stares up at the glittering heavens.

"Elysium." She murmurs in response, tone dead as she looks around. "We're... We're in Elysium. The world of eternal paradise."

Shimmering pomegranates drip from emerald trees as they float and sway in the wind. Sapphire waves rock up against an ever-glistening ice. Fjords stretch up to the sky in towers and glisten in the light of an ever-dancing sun.

"They take your memories." Clytemnestra starts awkwardly, staring off into the distance as she talks. "Once you cross that gate. They take your memories, your wishes, and your dreams. Every object in which you found beauty, every possibility that you once believed in. They put it here, in exchange for your sorrow."

"What do you see?" I ask my guide then, voice breathless as I take everything in. "Clytemnestra, do you see how *beautiful* everything is? How incredible?"

"I don't see anything." She replies. A certain frustration wraps its way through her tone, ripping through her words as she answers. "I–I can't anymore. I'm dead, remember? I don't belong here, where everything is soft and safe and precious. I don't belong here, Natalya. I'm beside the Acheron in Tartarus."

"Now don't get me wrong," She hurries to add, frantic to defend herself and her viewpoints and her own prison sentence. "I probably could reincarnate if I wanted to. I could repent for my sins, and enter the river Lethe, and be reborn as a new person with a fresh new chance. And the thing is, I don't really want to do any of that. You see these thorns winding up and down the sides of my throat?" She wrenches onto the roses and holds them until they choke her, until she gasps and chokes from where the barbs dig into her skin. "See how they strangle my airways and cut off my circulation? I could kill them if I wanted to badly enough.

A rose is a symbol of passion, you must understand. Love. Typically romantic, the rose serves as a symbol for the fact that I harmed the one whom I was supposed to love the most. Agamemnon. My husband. Once I repent and feel grief over the fact that I killed him, the plant will disintegrate. Shrivel up and turn to dust. And yet, I can't find it within myself to regret killing him. Because if I hadn't killed him, I don't know how many more children I would have lost.

And even if I did regret killing Agamemnon, even if I shed enough tears that I drowned these horrid roses, I don't think that I would move on. Because if I were to become free, I would have to rid myself of the shackles that I consider most dear to me: the memories of my children's faces. My new life would cost me my old one."

"I know the sayings that you mortals whisper to each other there on earth. Memento *Mori,* in the land of the setting sun. *Omoide nanka iran,* in the world where the sun once again rises. *Remember that you are mortal. We have no need for memories.* I find those to be such trivial sayings. Of course, we need memories, but not because one day we may die. We need memories because at least for now we are *alive.* It is the memories we cherish that separate ghosts from the shades of Asphodel, that give a certain meaning to the things we choose to die for.

Natalya, my children are dead. They're *dead,* and no matter how hard I try, no matter how hard I fight to go back and fix things, that's something that is never going to change. They're gone.

But sometimes, late at night when I close my eyes, I can still see them smiling. I can still hear them laughing. And that knowledge, the knowledge that even if they aren't there in person, they're still there beside me, is what makes me keep standing. It's what lets me keep taking my punishment, no matter how bitter the waves of the Acheron sting.

Because if I were to repent, if I were to give up and let myself be reborn, then I would forget all knowledge that they had existed in the first place. Even now, standing here in a place where all I can see is emptiness, I don't regret my decision. Because no matter how beautiful Elysium is, no matter how perfect or gentle or deliciously soft, it's inevitably empty. Paradise isn't paradise without my people beside me."

It hits me then how quiet everything is here in Elysium. How empty. Even though there must be thousands, no *millions* of heroes who must be hidden here, I can't see any of them.

"I miss my daughter," I admit, quietly. Cast one glance at the sparkling landscape, and then turn once more to my guide. "I mean, I really miss my daughter," I repeat, voice thick with tears.

There's something broken about the land of Elysium. Something lacking. It's missing the worlds my husband loves studying and the laughter in his voice whenever he reads our children stories. It's missing my daughter's garden, those flowers she bloomed from scraps of seeds, and her sunshine smile as she raced around my house. It's missing the stars Marek broke his leg one night trying to reach when he jumped out of an old oak tree, missing the shock of red you always catch when you spy the back of Pietyr's hair running towards something exciting.

"Paradise isn't Paradise without my people beside me," Clytemnestra said. I wipe the tears

from my eyes. Clear my throat, and then force myself to steady.

Clytemnestra smiles. Grabs me by the hand and then pulls me along a nearby path. Tufts of dandelion fluff rise up under our footsteps.

"Let's go find your daughter then." She replies softly. Hand in hand, we exit the gates of Paradise.

THE HERO AND THE HOUND

Once upon a time, there was a man with hands strong enough to pull apart mountains and a heart like shattered glass.

His name was Hercules.

He had battled monsters, tricked Titans, and lifted the very sky upon his shoulders. People called him a hero, carved his story into the stars, and whispered his name as if it were scripture.

But Hercules did not feel like a hero.

Because one time, long ago, insanity seeped into his mind like powder slipped into a stranger's drink. When it faded, he was left staring at his hands in horror; grief and shock wrestling on his face, the blood of his wife and children stained across his palms like a brand.

No badge, no medal, no pointless *battle he fought after could silence the sound of their screams.*

And so when the Augurs spoke of a chance, a final labor that might wash his soul clean, he accepted without a second of hesitation. "Journey into the Land of the Dead and bring back Cerberus, the hound of Hades. Seize him not by sword nor scheme, but with nothing more than the strength of your sorrow."

The path to the Underworld was not through a cave, like Orpheus, or a crack in the earth, like Theseus, but through a dream he followed into waking. He walked beyond the lands of the living until the sun shattered into a splintered moon, holding neither his club nor his arrows but a small, shivering lantern that gasped like a dying star. There, the River Styx flowed, putrid and tar-like, and Charon ferried him across with eyes as dark as coal dust.

In the Underworld, everything whispered. The sand, the shadows, even the bones in the rivers rattled as he walked past. They offered to guide the hero in exchange for stories; his wife's favorite flower, the first time his son lost a tooth. Hercules ignored them. Not because he believed he was great enough to journey without a guide, but because he feared what answering those questions might do to him.

Eventually, Hercules came upon the gates of Erebus. Instead of a door, the entrance was formed from a whale's ribcage, the bones glowing ivory from where they towered in the moonlight. There awaited Cerberus, the three-headed hellhound, with fur the color of burnt brindle and jaws that snarled as soon as the hero approached.

"I do not wish to fight you." Hercules sighed wearily, setting the lantern down as he sank onto his knees. "The augurs did not specify that I needed you dead, and there is already far too much blood on my hands.

Cerberus eyed the hero in silence. Slowly, ever so slowly, the snarling ceased. In a voice that rasped from centuries of growling, the right head said:

"No man passes through the realm of the dead without giving something up, Tell me a story, and I will let you pass unscathed."

"What type of story?" Hercules asked in confusion. He was a man known for his brawn instead of his brains, a brute that was more beast than man. Hercules didn't tell stories. He was the man about whom stories were told.

"A story about the sun, I suppose." The right head mused after a pause. *"It's been too long since I've felt its warmth against my fur. As a matter of fact, I don't think I can remember the last time I saw a sunrise."*

So Hercules spoke to Cerberus about the sun, how it shone so brightly in the sky that you couldn't bear to pull your gaze away, even when it burned your eyes. That it glowed so bewitchingly, flowers turned their heads to follow it, and the warmth seeped into your skin anytime you stepped outside. That he imagined it smelled like citrus, and bonfires, and dripped from the sky the same way your wife's runny eggs would slip down the sides of your plate.

The right head sighed, jaw relaxing as it stared at Hercules with bright, wide eyes. It's gaze seemed to burn almost, as he nodded at the hero. *"Very* well," He growled out "I will go with you to see this wonderful sun."

Hercules relaxed, and for the first time since that dreadful night, a smile stretched across his face. He turned around to leave when a second voice barked, all sharp and pointed.

"Are you really going to give one of us a story and go on your merry way? The Left Head snapped, glaring at the hero as he bared his teeth. "You rude, insolent man. I demand a tale as well, as a sign of respect." Hercules sighed.

"Very well. What story do you want?" He called out wearily. Cerberus puffed up his chest.

"I want a story about the rain." The Left Head demanded. "Tell me a story about the rain, and how it trickles down into the earth. We don't have rain in the Underworld after all. We only have our rivers, and you already know what those are full of."

Hercules did indeed know what the rivers of the Underworld were full of. Corpses, and Gelatin. Flames and hatred and tears and oblivion, and how was Hercules supposed to explain water, let alone rain, to a creature that only knew rivers made of anguish?

"Rain," Hercules began after a pause, "is sharp at first. It tastes cool, clean, and pure like melted snow, and when I was a child, I used to unhinge my jaw and try to see how many raindrops I could catch in my mouth. It sounds like music, almost. Dozens upon dozens of clear crystal bells or swinging windchimes that ring out every time a droplet hits the ground. It's a song only the living can hear, all soft and hopeful and carrying the promise of change. It smells like growing things, soil greedily drinking in the water as it spills onto the ground. You need rain in order for things to properly grow, you have to understand. Nothing can survive without water, that liquid that pours from the sky in the form of rain and swims throughout the blood in our veins.

The left head closed its eyes and whined, as if the thought of rain healed a deep-seated ache. It was a mournful sound, that whine. Pitiful in that it longed for something so easily accessible in the realm of the living, a world that normally they could never touch.

"How beautiful," The Left Head rasped at last, "How beautiful this thing that you call rain sounds. I would like to see it, if you were willing to show me."

Hercules once more began to leave but stopped and paused. Turning, he faced the head in the middle. Unlike its brothers, the Middle did not growl or bark. Its eyes were dull, and the head drooped dejectedly as it stared at the ground in silence.

"Would you like a story as well?" Hercules asked. It was hard to keep his voice soft, as the man was far too used to shouting. And yet he tried in spite of that, for the sad, tired head that drooped in the middle.

"Could I have a story about laughter?" The Middle Head asked. "I want a story about the sound of laughter, wild and unrestrained. Loud. I want to hear about something known for its loudness. Here in the Underworld, all sounds are muffled to a dull whisper."

So Hercules spoke of laughter, the wild kind. The type of humor that tore itself from your chest and left you doubled over, gasping for breath. He explained to Cerberus the difference between guffaws and giggles, between muffled snorts and dramatic cackles.

"Laughter," Hercules explained, "is an expression of unrestrained emotion. It can be high-

pitched and nervous or loud and boisterous, but perhaps my favorite type of laughter is the type that is contagious, that spreads between friends and family when someone finds something funny. I'm not sure how to describe what finding something funny is- deciding something is amusing, I suppose. Looking around a group of your loved ones and waggling your eyebrows to see if anyone else noticed what you did. You smile a lot, with laughter. Smile because it's fun to find things funny (perhaps that's why fun is in the name), and a part of you feels happier when you hear a friend snicker under their breath. Laughter means that, for a moment, the world is brighter than the gloom it rests on. It means that, even if you don't understand why something is so funny, you feel a smile stretch across your face."

"How wonderful," Cerberus murmured, as his tail slowly began to wag. "It sounds strange, and kind of painful, but above all else, very exciting. Do you think that if I were to go to the world above with you, you could teach me how to do this laugh?"

"Perhaps the pair of us could learn together." Hercules offered with a tired smile. "It's been a while since I've had a proper laugh. Come with me to the

world of the living, and we can teach each other how to live again."

Cerberus agreed, and so Hercules returned to the Land of the Living with the hound at his side and shadows in his eyes. He did not boast. He did not parade.

Instead, he began to rebuild his life on a series of winding roads, defending villages from men and monsters alike. And there, with Cerberus following at his heels, he learned to live. Not as a hero, but as a man who had faced his demons and emerged stronger because of it.

Legends say that even now, when a person mourns for what they've done and is convinced that they are beyond redemption, a giant three-headed hound will stalk their shadow.

Not as a hunter.

But a guard.

Because even the most ferocious of beasts and the most monstrous of men can learn to rest.

(27)

BEFORE: HELEN

I don't know why I was stupid enough to believe that the screaming would stop once the senate fell. That the blood would stop pouring from gouged gouged-open skin. That the bodies would stop falling once I reached a certain point. Maybe it's stupid, but I really did think that once I won, I could at least fix *some* things.

"HELP, SOMEONE HELP THE HEARTBEAT'S FAILING, I'M LOSING

PRESSURE!" The doctors are screaming, over and over, until their voices grow hoarse.

"GAUZE, I NEED FRESH GAUZE I CAN'T STOP THE BLEEDING!"

"ANTISEPTIC! DOES ANYONE HAVE ANTISEPTIC!"

I try to remain focused as I stare down at the teenager on the nearby gurney. There's a chunk of metal stuck through his sternum; some sort of roughened spear cobbled together from metal rebar. My job is to remove it before he bleeds out.

"Repeat after me," I tell the teen. "Slow, deep breaths, ok? Inhale, then exhale. Inhale…"

I sink my hands inside the skin and try to fight back the urge to vomit. Grit my teeth and ignore the way the blood spurts out and stains my skin as I burrow through his gaping chest. Swallowing, I grab the pole with both hands and yank. "Exhale."

"Inhale…" something between a sob and a scream chokes out as I toss the metal to the side, tugging the edges of his chest together as I cover the wound with my hands. I can see his heart as he sucks in air. I can see his heart twitching as it beats, and I can feel it shaking under my palms.

"Exhale." I close my hands and focus inward, letting my magic seep in until I jolt back in surprise. The teen spasms, blood spraying from his lips as I swear.

Punctured lungs.

"SOMEONE HELP, I NEED BACKUP OVER HERE!" I scream, panic growing as I stare at the teen while they convulse.

I've never experienced interior bleeding before. Never taught myself how to heal wounds like that, and I ignored it like a fool as I focused on more external injuries. Terrified tears begin to well up in my eyes. My magic is as good as useless right now.

I grab a sterilized needle and dive back in, stabbing through the sternum over and over as I try to drain the lungs. The teen's lips begin to grow blue, asphyxiation begins to creep in, no matter how desperately I try to stop it. Frantically, I look at the doorway. No one is coming. I look back at the boy and try to get him breathing.

Nobody ever comes, in the end.

I find myself breaking down when the teen's heart finally stops.

A teenager with a stab wound through the sternum and blood clogging the lungs, a boy who never woke up despite how desperately I tried to save him.

"Time of death…"

An older woman with a bullet lodged in the back of her head, begging for her children as she bled out on the operating table.

"Time of death…"

A light-haired girl with both of her legs missing —

"Time of death…"

A child not that much younger than I am, crying and screaming as I try to soothe the burns mottled up and down their skin, the wounds so bad that the fabric on their shirt has fused itself into their flesh-

"T – Time of death…"

Gradually, the flood of wounded begins to slow. Doctors collapse to the ground in exhaustion, nurses and medical assistants flitting around as they tend to hundreds of lesser cases. My eyes are bloodshot, and my hands are shaking as I stare at the last person at my table.

It's been forty-eight hours. I've lost thirty-seven patients. My gaze is wild as I stare at the child on the table. There's a lead bullet buried in the edge of her thoracic cavity, the metal shining from where it rests embedded in her flesh.

I've already lost thirty-seven patients. I'm not going to let this girl, the last patient here in the hospital wing, be number thirty-eight.

Thanatos stares from where he sits in the corner of the room. It's strange to wish him anywhere else. To look in the face of someone I love and quietly beg them to leave. He smiles sadly and points at a nearby clock. He winds the hands back as it steadily ticks down. Ten minutes. Thanatos is giving me ten minutes to help the girl, to decide whether she lives or dies.

I swallow and then get back to work.

I ran out of sterile sutures ten hours ago. I used up all my fishing wire twelve minutes ago. In the end, all that I have is my magic.

My hands sink into the edges of the girl's chest and find the shrapnel embedded in her beating heart. I rip it out, ignoring how the edge of my wrist gets sliced in the motion. Reddened droplets ooze from my fingertips into a gooey lining, cushioning the organ in an almost solidified sack while it pulses.

Squeezing on the edges of the skin, I begin to tug the flaps together, close my eyes, and focus inwards as cells begin to bind and gather platelets. Slowly, layer by layer, I begin to build up an epidermis. By the time I finish, not even a scab remains. All that is left is unmarked skin.

With a sigh, I turn away and rub my aching eyelids. The world spins and twists beneath my feet. I try to think about the last time I slept. Or ate. Or drank anything. Cursing and grabbing onto the wall, I force myself to start moving.

I can feel my blood flowing through the arteries that line the inside of the child's veins. Can feel it swimming through her bloodstream, absorbing chemicals, rebuilding cells. A rush of dizziness rises, and I stumble, holding onto a nearby railing with shaking arms. I have no idea how much blood I gave her. I have no idea if it was enough.

I try to clean up in the bathroom, wipe the stains off my hands, and scrape the blood out from under my fingernails. The cracks in the tiles reek with the stench of bleach. I let the water from the faucet drip onto my hands as I wash and crank the handle as hard as I can until it grows hot enough to burn. Hot enough to *feel* it burn. I just want to feel something. I'm so tired of feeling nothing.

My eyes focus on the mirror, then drop back to my hands again. I've scrubbed them so raw that they're nearly bleeding, all red and inflamed and slightly swollen. That's unsanitary. And yet no matter how hard I try, I can't wash the blood off.

Inside the mirror, my face peers back. I sneak a glance briefly, then look back at the sink. *Sick.* I look sick. Pale, ashy skin and sunken eyes, and my hands are burning from where I try to scrub the blood off. It's not coming off.

"Helen," Thanatos calls out quietly from the nearby doorway. His voice echoes as it bounces up and down off the bathroom tiles. I ignore him, rotating between looking at my hands and face. I'm not sure that I want to talk to him. "Helen, I thought I told you already not to let your skin get red like that. You're a human after all, not a lobster."

"Lobsters aren't red, Thanatos," I respond distractedly, trying to remember the last time I drank something. Or ate. Or slept. I can't remember. That's a problem, isn't it? "That's only when they're dead, and more specifically, about to be eaten. Normally, lobsters are a blueish green in order to blend in with their environment."

"They only change colors when they start to get boiled." I continue absentmindedly, wondering half hysterically why I'm so fixated on explaining to Death lobsters. "When their environment changes so drastically that they no longer have the chance to hide. They feel the heat and then they change, turning a vivid red before they're eventually burned from the inside out." Out of the corner of my eye, I turn and look at Thanatos. I can't quite read his expression.

I keep thinking about that day on the battlefield. The limp bodies flopped brokenly across cracking cement, vultures struggling to fly after how bloated they became from gorging on rotted flesh. The sky burned, then. Burned as it cooked my skin from the inside out, and in the shadows of the nearby shade, Thanatos lurked as he whispered. Did I really do the right thing, plunging my country into battle? Or did I just blindly follow the whims of a selfish god?

I can't tell. After all this time, I still can't tell.

"They're riddled with parasites, you know, those lobsters." My hands are starting to burn from where I hold them under the water. "That's why they have to be boiled before they can even be considered being eaten. There's no other way to remove the parasites. Still, doesn't it seem so awful – the idea of burning from the inside out?"

"Humans shouldn't look so much like lobsters, Helen." Thanatos insists softly. I fight the urge to scream as I sit down and stare at the sea green tiles. Above my head, the sink continues to run.

"I can still hear it, you know," I whisper. "The screaming. They won't *stop* screaming, all those men and women. Even after the battle, even after I gave them my magic or saved them here in the hospital, they kept on screaming. Just like the rats in the sanitarium. Did I do the right thing, Thanatos?" I ask him quietly. "Did I actually save these people like I thought I would? Because I thought I was helping the rats before, when I was just causing them more suffering."

And Death- Death is silent. I wait for him to speak, and yet he never does. Eventually, I get up. Pull myself to my feet. Tug on the bathroom door. And then begin walking.

My hands hurt. I look at them in silence, all sore and red and swollen. I think it hits me then that these hands are not the ones my mother held when I was a baby. That this skin is not the same flesh that I was born in.

Logically, this shouldn't be an issue. After all, everyone regrows their skin every seven years. I simply sped up the process. It's natural. Normal. But there's some part of me, some small animalistic corner of my brain, that mourns the fact. I wish that I were still small. I understand that I needed to change, needed to grow, needed to evolve, but there is still a part of me that wishes I were small.

I blink my eyes, and suddenly I'm standing outside. The sun is shining. Somewhere a bird is chirping. There's a statue of a girl in the middle of the sidewalk. She's got flowers in her hair and skulls crushed beneath her feet. It's me. Or, rather, what everyone else sees when they look at me. Only the statue is just a little taller and a little older; any trace of humanity has slowly been stripped from the marble, until all that's left is a shrine to a god.

I am not a god.

There's chanting, up and down the cobblestone streets. Wooden scaffolds stretch to the sky as buildings are slowly rebuilt one by one. They look like scabs, almost. All dark and ugly and a sign of the nation's past injuries. And yet at the same time, it's a symbol of regrowth. Healing. Moving on from all the ugliness of the past and creating a brighter future.

I sit down by the statue and wait for Natalya to come pick me up, close my eyes, and smell the incoming bloom of budding roses. Spring is coming. The world is healing. I open my eyes and observe ragtag tents from where merchants run their local stalls. Even after all the chaos, people are starting to heal.

Good.

I watch them closely, observe the way men strut across the hastily constructed city hall, and watch mothers with their children as they skip along brand-new flowerbeds.

I'm doing my best to create a system that will outlive me. Some sort of *legacy* (and oh, how a part of me laughs at the use of that word) that will stay standing long after my bones have finished decomposing in the dirt. So far, it seems to be working.

And yet -

Even now, spring is coming. The world feels fresh and clean, and slowly, ever so slowly, the sun has begun to peer out from behind its clouds. The war has appeared, and the war has disappeared. The war is over, and now I am dying.

I stop sleeping over the following weeks, dark circles beginning to droop beneath my eyes until my skin sags. I try to force myself to bed on the good nights, inhale chamomile and melatonin, and curl up under thick fuzzy blankets. No matter how hard I try, though, I can't block out the sound of the voices praying. Screams arise from where bones crumple with a series of sharp snaps, and people continue to chant my name as they fall to their knees, and I am so *sick* of seeing that sickly devotion rotting behind the backs of their eyes. If I were just a touch more violent, I think I would claw it out with my fingernails.

One day Mother finds me, arms crossed and eyes far too sad. She looks me up and down, observes the way my hands shake as they struggle to hold a hairbrush, and remarks firmly,

"That's it, we're leaving."

It's an order, not a suggestion. She's not asking, she's telling me.

"I can't just leave Mom." I spit feebly. "This isn't something that you can just walk away from." I show her my hands then. Make her stare at the drying blood caked under my fingernails. We match now, in our propensity for violence. "Look what I did, Mom. Look outside and see my country. I destroyed it. I ruined it."

"They have taken enough from you." Mother answers simply. "And I have stood by and let them, because I knew that you would stop for nothing until your country was free.

They have taken enough from you, please, let me at least have this," she begs. "Don't make me bury my only daughter."

"And what is it that you want?" My tone is tired. Defeated. Whatever trace of venom I once possessed has now run dry. I am too tired to bite.

"A vacation." She answers simply. "A break. Somewhere you can *rest*, Helen. Don't you want to rest?"

"It would be selfish." I protest weakly.

"Then let me be selfish for you." She states softly. "Let me be selfish now, and the next time, and the time after that. Let me be selfish for you until you are strong enough to be selfish for yourself."

I start struggling to get out of bed in the mornings. My joints stiffen, and pop, and my bones grow so brittle I can barely walk. A faint fuzziness begins to thicken like a fog as my vision turns hazy, and a small static grows when my hearing fades out. I lie there in the bed like a living corpse and watch as my body decays from the inside out.

On the days that I can actually drag myself out of my room, Mother makes me pancakes. She watches me from the other side of the table, and I try to keep myself from trembling too much as I try to shovel food into my mouth. Once, I cut myself with a butter knife when the shaking got too bad. After that, Mother cuts up my food for me, like a bird does for her hatchlings.

It's strange, really. How gentle Mom is as I lie there trembling. Blood crusts the bottom of her nails just as brightly as jam, and yet her hands are so soft as she prepares me food.

I don't deserve this, this *kindness* that she shows me. Don't deserve the hearts drawn in syrup along the side of my plate or the dandelions that she places beside my bedside.

I try to tell her this when she sits beside my bed at night and reads me stories. I try to tell her this when she braids flowers through my hair and pushes me outside in a wheelbarrow so that I can still look at the gardens.

Mom always looks sad when I talk that way, though. After a while I stop asking. It seems to make her uncomfortable, almost. Like, she doesn't understand what it is I'm so confused about.

"I'm going to die in the spring," I tell her one day when the pair of us are sitting on the front porch. I stare at the sea, try to ignore the look of sadness that crosses Mother's face. "Death told me so, and he ought to be an expert on those things."

For a moment, there's silence. Mother sits perfectly still, knuckles whitening from where she clenches her hands. Her shoulders are tense.

"No, you're not." She states eventually. Decisively, as if she had any control in the situation.

"Yes, I will," I respond. "Don't tell me you haven't already started seeing the signs. I can't even cut my own food anymore Mom. It won't be much longer now."

"It makes sense, you know, when you think about it." I continue, voice shaking. "From a scientific standpoint, that is. After all, cells can only be reproduced forty to sixty times before they start to break down. I may not know how many times I've used my gift, but I know that it's been a fair amount." I smile bitterly then.

A lot of the time, I think that there's this misconception that it's always planned. A date circled in bright red on a torn-up calendar, rooms carefully prepared for when they'll become covered in dust.

Perhaps that's true for a great many.

Sometimes, though, it's not. Sometimes you just pick a random direction and start walking, half knowing and yet at the same time *not*. Sometimes, you just get up and walk away, unaware of the fact that the path you're going down is your own funeral march.

Sometimes, it's planned.

Just as often, it's not.

"I don't understand," Mom protests, voice rising. "How… how could you be so careless? How can you sit there and act so calm, knowing that for the past year you have been killing yourself?"

"Because my life doesn't matter much," I answer shortly. I could continue with that, make myself a martyr, and say that compared to all the innocent lives I've saved, it would only make sense for my own to pay the price. I could make myself a hero, a sacrificial lamb content with its own slaughter. I could – I could invent a noble cause, some honorable reason that would leave me with a dazzling legacy. And yet, while not a lie, that answer wouldn't be the full truth.

"It didn't matter before I received my gift, and it mattered even less before then," I add haltingly. "Can you imagine, Mom, how it would feel to know that nobody would care if you just died? That your life is worthless because you were so weak? People only started loving me when I began bleeding."

"I loved you." Mom spits then, voice breaking. "I would have loved you even if you didn't have a gift, or known how to wield a sword, or…" she cuts off with a sob, "I would have loved you," she repeats hoarsely, "simply because you were Helen. I wouldn't need any other reason."

"Yeah," I agree, "you did. I've never doubted you love me. But you keep *hurting me,* Mom. And I just… I just wanted someone to love me the way people do in sitcoms, those types of families that you learn about in magazines or on TV. I didn't expect things to be perfect, of course, but I just wanted there to be more love than hurt. I'm so tired of being hurt."

"I thought… I thought we were getting better." Mom protests, voice breaking.

"After the sanitarium. I thought we were fixing… whatever this thing was between us."

"We were." I agree. "That's what…
makes this so hard. I think we
really *were* mending, even if it was only in
pieces."

(28)

AFTER: NATALYA

"You know, sometimes I want to take all of your so-called gods and tear them into tiny pieces." Clytemnestra frowns almost imperceptibly as I talk. "I want to pull them apart and claw them with my nails and I want to rip their immortality off them limb by limb.

I want to shove them into suits of sagging flesh and burn them in their own damned hellfire. I think I really hate your gods. Like really, genuinely, hate them. As a matter of fact, I wouldn't even consider them to be supposed gods. Because gods are pure beings that are meant to be worshipped. And those *creatures* sitting there with their drawn-on halos are anything but holy."

"What else is there that you would wish for in a god?" The woman beside me wonders. "Purity – you seem to use that word as if it's something that the gods lack, something that they could possibly be without. Purity – an untainted presence – something so completely itself that nothing else can defile it. Look at Venus, for instance. Aphrodite. The goddess of a love so consuming that it has begun to devour her from the inside out. Is love beautiful? Certainly. Is it passionate? Absolutely. Breathtaking, overwhelming, sacrificial, a tidal wave that makes you delight in drowning, love is all of these and more. Can it be kind? Why of course. Most people prefer when it is kind. But does it have to be – can there be times when it is cruel, or jealous, or toxic? Sometimes. The thing about the gods Natalya, is that the gods are not required to be good. It is a privilege to receive their grace, not an expectation."

"What is it about them that makes you think that they must be gentle, or sweet, or kind?" She asks with a snort. "They are beings of nature, creatures of chaos lit up by human ideals and flying stars. What about the stars would make you think that they are kind?" My guide asks back, her pace never faltering as she continues walking.

"When people say that there is evil in the world, or that something isn't fair, or wrong, the only logical assumption is that there must be some certain standard or law that people once believed to be right." I shoot back. "Injustice, after all, is nothing more than the lack of justice. When someone proclaims that there's too much evil in the world they assume that there is supposed to be good. If the world isn't supposed to be fair like you claim then why does everyone so desperately believe it should be? If this is the most complete that our world is going to be, then why do people constantly long for more?

"In order for the gods to truly understand us, they must feel what we feel." Clytemnestra continues calmly. "When mortals are angry, they shake their fists and raise their voice. When the gods are angry, thunders roar and volcanoes erupt. It is a matter of exchange if you think about it one way. The gods gave us their power, and we gave them our vices."

"The gods are supposed to be made up of more than just human ideals." I counter, matching her stride. "They are supposed to be better than us, something greater than the mere mortals that created them. Otherwise, what's the point in worshipping them?"

"Those beings tricked my daughter into selling away her soul for nothing more than a new name and a chance at love." I spit. "They took a scared little girl, and they tricked her into giving up her life. How could I not hate them?"

"Would you blame a spider for sitting there and watching as a fly flew into its web?" Clytemnestra responds, her face still as she speaks. "Would you hate a Venus flytrap for doing nothing more than sitting there with its mouth open wide?"

"But Helen didn't understand what was fully going on," I protest, voice breaking. "She was hurting, and tired, and desperate. She was *fourteen,* Clytemnestra. *Fourteen.* That's too young to drink or enlist in the military or even drive a car. How can she be old enough to sell her soul when she wasn't old enough to drive?"

"She was old enough, Natalya." My guide stated defeatedly. "In the end that's all that matters, not her age or maturity. In the end, she was old enough."

There's a garden, on the other side of the gates of Elysium. A metallic garden, all dripping in rubies and diamonds and gold. Moonstones hang from the sky in a series of iridescent clouds and sapphires pool so vividly along the ground that they almost appear made of liquid.

It looks like my garden. The one Helen made at my house. Pomegranate trees line pathways in roads and Emerald firs hang drooping over golden dandelions. It feels like my garden; somewhere frozen in time, safe from all the rot and decay that plagues the rest of the Underworld.

Perhaps that's the thing that makes it worse, in the end. The fact that it looks so similar even though it's not. That no matter how realistic it may seem it still is *fake,* a cheap copy of the world I used to have. It would be easier, I think, if this place didn't look so much like home.

"What a pity." My guide states softly, shaking her head as she stares at the bejeweled flowers. "Such a poor, poor being Thanatos must be. Despite knowing how completely futile the idea was, he still tried to save her."

"What are you talking about?" I ask her, blinking back tears as I stare at the flickering jewels. It hurts, almost. Seeing how richly the gemstones shine.

"He tried to give Helen a world she could live in." Clytemnestra explains softly. "One where she could grow, somewhere safe that she could rest her bones. Look around- see that greenhouse there between the pomegranate trees? He took all her favorite things that reminded her of home and tried to preserve them here down below. And yet even gods it seems have their own sets of limitations. Thanatos tried to create life down here, even though the action goes against his very nature."

"*I* gave her that life." I force out from between clenched teeth. "All of this: the trees, the flowers, this *cheap imitation* of a home and a greenhouse, I gave all of it to her for free."

"I know you did." Clytemnestra soothes, voice placating as she looks at me. "Still, isn't that even more heartbreaking? A mere mortal can help more than a god."

"It means that your gods aren't enough." I spit, throwing my hands in the air as I stare at the sky. I don't think I can look at the ground.

Can't stare at the golden dandelions, can't handle the fact that the paradise my daughter so desperately desired was simply my house. "That your deities are *worthless*, in the grand scheme of things. I mean look at how pathetic this all is Clytemnestra. Weren't you the one who told me that money can't fix grief?"

"You shouldn't talk about him like that Natalya." Clytemnestra whispers, eyes darting nervously around the darkened shadows that line the garden. "Not when *he* can hear you. Travelling through a god's domain is one thing but insulting them is another."

Thanatos, she means. Hades. Pluto, Donn, Letum, a million names to describe one single entity: Death.

"I want him to hear me." I state quietly. Quietly, because my anger is so thick that it chokes my voice box. "Want him to face me, instead of hiding away in the shadows like a sniveling coward. CAN YOU HEAR ME DEATH?" I scream then. "AM I CLOSE

ENOUGH THAT YOU CAN HEAR ME NOW?"

"I've drowned myself in your Styx," I begin, voice shaking with barely restrained fury. "Burned myself on the bank of the Acheron, let my skin be cut open from the salt of the Cocytus. Journeyed between lands of fear and desire, walked without ceasing upon sands made from a host of dying stars. Tell me, WILL YOU FACE ME NOW? HOW MUCH MORE DO I HAVE TO BLEED BEFORE YOU NOTICE ME?"

"Thanatos." I rasp out lowly, because while I may not worship these deities I know they're summoned to their name like a moth to a flame. "Hades. Pluto, Letum. Here my cry and answer it with your own."

Softly, a faint sound of stirring arises. The noise of an unseen wind, shadows creeping until they begin to writhe and twist like snakes. Slowly, they begin to swallow the stars. And then the planets. Trees, flowers, cobblestones, the shadows grow larger and larger until they eat away at the edges of the world. Until they consume every light including the moon. I squint my eyes in the darkness, spinning around desperately as I try to peer through the hungry shadows.

Eventually, a voice cuts through the ensuing silence.

"yOu sUmMoNeD mE?" The void asks. An eye opens, and suddenly I find myself staring at the face of Thanatos.

(29)

BEFORE: HELEN

Mom moves us to the top of a mountain one morning. Packs up all our belongings in the back of her car and moves us up North, to a land filled with moonshine and fuzzy pine trees. The world seems softer here, almost, with lights from the aurora borealis streaking across the sky in a series of dazzling pigments. I lick my lips, and the very air tastes crisper, powdered snow falling sweet as sugar from where it lands and dusts the corners of my lashes.

We're so high up on the mountain that we seem to live in the very sky itself, clouds bubbling under my feet that explode into color as soon as the sky rises. In the night, stars sway and dance from where they float among the heavens. I like watching them twirl at night. Have Mom remove the shutters and open my eyes up wide as I sit in bed and stay up late watching the stars dance.

THE LANDS OF ETERNAL WINTER. A sign by the house proclaims. Mom smiles when she sees it, lifts me into a wheelchair, and takes us racing across the tundra.

"You can't die if spring never comes." She declares brightly, her smile wide and her hands trembling. She tries to push me forward, and my chair tips on its side, wheels spinning uselessly as I fall and land on my face.

"I'm not quite sure you can push me here, Mom," I reply absentmindedly, staring up in awe at where the stars spin in circles as the sun rises. "My chair keeps getting caught in the snow.

"I can fix it." Mom insists. Her face crumples, and her voice begins to shake. "Just hold on, ok, Helen? I can fix this. I'll make sure things are ok again."I keep hearing her cry at night when I stay up watching the stars. She goes outside and she wails over and over as she sobs until her tears run dry. I can hear her curse, hear her yell repeatedly as she screams at every god whose name she can think of and then begs them for help in the same breath. There's something guttural about her wails as she breaks down. Something heartbreaking, about how much she folds in on herself.

"I can fix this." She tells me, face haggard as she wheels me across the ice. I let her hold me tighter, try to ignore just how much her shoulders shake as she does. Instead, I look at the stars, and then the snow. The soft, fuzzy pines and the frozen fjords that stretch up to the sky with an almost angelic grace. Everything is so breathtaking here. Ethereal. The ice is beautiful in the same way that pearls from the ocean are, elegant and refined, an image of ethereal regality.

It's almost too beautiful to die here, really.

Flowers start creeping in and blooming again in the cracks of my room. Snowdrops. Violets. Sweet, elegant primroses that lack the barbs I normally associate with such a flower. Jasmine. Witches' Hazel, heath, and pansies, and over and over the flowers bloom until they grow so dense that they begin to smother up my walls. Until they cluster so tightly that you can barely breathe under their cloying scent.

I start hacking up flower petals when I get up in the morning. Sneeze and watch as leaves trickle out of my nose in the place of snot. My skin begins to discolor, blueish veins taking on a greenish tint as my muscles weaken. Natalya burns the flowers whenever she sees them. Gathers them in bushels and burns them out in the backyard, screams and curses when they grow back each night. The ice begins to melt as the days on the mountain pass, each patch of frosted snow revealing a budding, rosy slush. Spring is coming, and it makes Natalya go insane. Gradually, ever so quietly, I begin to grow quiet.

I don't feel any pain anymore.

I used to. I can still remember it vaguely, the way my skin screamed before it grew numb, and now…. Now I feel nothing. Soft, perhaps. A little spacy. Like swimming through molasses, my movements slurred, and a little sleepy. I've run empty. Given everything I had, bruised and bled and let myself be torn open for the sake of some greater good. I've run empty. And instead of being scary, there's something comforting about the thought.

There's something reassuring about the fact that I have given all I possibly can. That I did my *very best,* and sometimes that's all that can be done. It doesn't matter now if it was enough or not. I gave my all, worked as hard as I could. Now I'm allowed to rest.

My brothers come back at some point or another. I don't remember when, exactly.

My brain's been feeling a little sluggish as it decomposes, memories twisting and scattering as they struggle to slot together. What I do remember is the soft brush of Marek's fingers through my hair, the subtle shake in Pietyr's voice as he reads me stories.

I sit there quietly when Mom wraps me up in furs for the last time and takes me out once more along the ice. Lie my palm flat against my chest and memorize the way my heartbeat sounds as it pitter-patters inside my ribcage. Feel my lungs as they inhale and exhale, swallow puffs of air that seem to infuse my chest with stardust. Look up at the sky with tired eyes and let the reflection of spinning comets dance within my gaze.

"Do you ever wish you could become a star, and dance forever embraced in the arms of gentle pines?" a nearby radio asks. Its voice crackles through the portable speaker, crisp and clear. *"That you could let your body rest in the forest beneath a sea of spinning snowflakes as you sleep, and have your body sheltered for all eternity? Do you ever wish that your last battleground could be somewhere you*

432

loved?" Mom's hands shake as she tries to start her lighter. Her fingers tremble as she struggles to make a flame. *"Next to someone who loved you?"*

When the pair of us finally stumble home, I am already half dead. Fingers numb as they clutch onto Mother's skin, discolored from the mess of bruises and greenish veins. Roses grow until they bloom out of my mouth, until they crawl up my throat in softened pinks. My limbs are stiff and heavy, and it is so hard to move when I can feel gravity laughing as it pins down my bones.

Mom clutches onto me like a lifeline, voice frantic as she calls healer after healer to check on me, eyes rimmed in red as her fingers dig into my skin. For three days, she doesn't leave my side. I think a part of her is scared that the second she looks away I will leave.

Death is silent from where he watches in the corner of my room, the flowers blooming up and down his robes doing little to hide the sadness hidden within his eyes.

"I am sorry, Helen, that I do not know how to be kind," Thanatos whispers as he hugs me. I look around the room one last time. Take in how soft the bed feels, how warm Mother is from where she holds my hand. I look outside at where the sun has started to rise.

I will never see it again.

Yesterday was the last day that I would ever see a bright blue sky. It's strange how you never realize what things you'll miss until they are already gone. "Kind in the way that you deserve, all sweet and soft and complete with a long, perfect life. I am sorry that you bore the consequence of being my child." A bitter laugh wracks his spindly frame. "None of my children are ever known to have an easy life."

"That's okay," I respond to the being that shivers in their guilt. "It's not your fault. In another world, I would have liked to teach you how to love someone without them breaking."

(There is a reason that Death's children never really seem to live long, you know. That's not to say that it's his fault, of course. After all, Thanatos can be kind in his own way. He can be the final warmth of Hyperthermia, or the comforting haze of closing your eyes. And yet, Death is so fundamentally opposed to Life that his children seem to suffer when in the other's realm.)

"Thank you," I whisper to Mom, this woman with blood under her nails who still chooses to sit by my side. Who did not understand how to be kind yet had tried to give it to me anyway. Perhaps not everyone would consider it a mercy. And yet I do not know a better word to use.

A second of brief consciousness, the last note of my own small melody, the glimpse of a fading star, the final gasp of air before I fade—

How wonderful, I think faintly, looking at my parents from where they stand on either side of my bed. *How wonderful everything is.*

Belonging is the last gift.

It is the greatest for me. The most precious. To realize that I died in a place where I was *treasured. Wanted.*

When I come back, I am soft. Delicate. My skin is as cold and pale as snow without the presence of blood to warm it. I blink my eyes and watch how frost clings to the edges of my lashes. Stretch out a hand and see how even now warmth still blooms at my fingertips.

Winter winds its way around my bones. Enshrines me in its fondness. I look down at the sea of white that veils me in its silken folds. My funeral shroud has morphed into a veil. I bring the fabric closer and run my fingers through it, marveling. Look on with eyes all pale and hollow from where the irises have been eaten away.

It would be a lie to say that I haven't changed. Frost swirls around the hollows of my lungs where oxygen used to be, and snowflakes crystallize as they tangle themselves inside my hair. Sap as sweet as evergreens replaces the blood that used to flow through my veins, and my heart is silent where it used to hum like a radio inside my chest. And yet when I look up at Death's eyes and grin, I find myself feeling the exact same.

Because it's true to say that I'm… different. But at the same time, I'm still *me*.

"What would you like to do now, my child?" Thanatos asks quietly. He stands on the opposite side of a void, the two of us floating in the darkness among a sea of whirling stars.

"What do you mean?" I ask curiously, staring down at the way snowdrops wrap their way around my legs like anklets.

"I mean, what would you like to do with your afterlife?" He explains, voice soft as he stares. "Helen, you are now in the unique position where, down on earth, you are considered to be practically a god. If you wish, I could grant you the role of a small deity, allowing you to truly embody the name of my angel. I could give you power. Power over anything you wish for, any facet of death that you so desire. Helen," Thanatos asks me softly, "What would you like to do now?"

I pause and think. Stare into the distance where moons waltz with whirling planets. Gradually, I grow silent.

"I would like to have a garden," I say at last. "A special garden, filled to the brim with all sorts of incredibly enchanting sights. And I would like the children." I add. "Those children caught in the limbo of too young and too old, the ones who find themselves wishing to die more than they ever wanted to live."

"Don't you ever wish that you could become a star, and dance forever embraced among the arms of gentle pines? An old, battered radio once asked. *"That you could let yourself rest there in the forest beneath a sea of spinning snowflakes, and as you sleep, have your body be sheltered for all eternity? Do you ever wish that your last battlefield could be somewhere you loved? Next to someone who loved you?"*

"I want – maybe it's foolish, but I want to be the one who loves those children." I continue. "I want those children to know that they have someone who loves them, just like I knew that you loved me. I want to own a garden and make it a place where people feel calm, safe, and serene. I want to make a world where people feel cherished. Where they can rest."

"You understand, don't you, my child, that this role you ask for is no easy task," Thanatos warns. "The lives of those souls are some of the hardest ones to deal with. You will encounter sorrow that you could never dare imagine."

"Let me take that sorrow," I insist, "and make it into something loving. Let me take that anguish and give them peace instead. I know what it is like to suffer Thanatos. Let me make sure that no other child has to suffer that way again."

"Very well." Thanatos agrees. With a wave of his hand, a cluster of stars nestles across my skin like freckles. "So be it then. I pronounce you Helen, ruler of Helheim. Goddess of Life in Death and Death in Life."

The people on earth call me Death's angel. His precious, his darling, his sweet little blessing. The only part of the cold that knows how to be warm. To be kind. I walk between the lands of the dead and the living with a sea of snowdrops trailing in my wake, eyes constantly searching for plants and souls to add to my garden.

Evergreens. Poplars. Sweet, softened ferns nestle into the nooks between neighboring tree trunks. Roses. Dandelions. Weeping cherries that trail rosy tears as they drip down over a lake made of moonshine. I guard my garden carefully, plant pomegranates and hang Wisteria, and make my forest something beautiful. Something breathtaking.

The forest only unlocks itself to those who need it. To those who need a home, somewhere safe and calm where they can rest their bones away from the dead and living. After a while, the local patrols and tired knights stop finding the bodies. Not for any lack of trying, of course. Just that any time they stumble in they find themselves spit out around the same area from where they started, left with nothing more than the faint memories of steps passing and the scent of prickly pines.

Eventually, the public begins to take notice. Parents begin to warn their children not to play between the tree trunks, spin stories of gruesome monsters and faces stitched into leathery bark. They keep going, stories growing more and more horrific until the children begin to shake whenever they go to sleep underneath their covers, until they shiver whenever they see a dancing leaf.

It's better, the adults think, to let them avoid the woods this way. Better to let them think that it's some wicked monster that's making all the lonely disappear. Better that they don't understand why it's earned the name Wood of the Suicides.

And yet, even though parents spin nightmare after nightmare, a new legend begins to spawn about the sleepy forest. A story that paints the woods as gentle instead of vicious, a forest that is loving instead of cruel.

A story that finds its origins in the laughter of a babbling brook and the footsteps of a young girl dancing. A tale that's lesser known, and yet more true than the assumptions presented by scholars and professors.

If you are lonely, the forest will shelter you. If you are lost, the Woods will become your new home. There's an angel that dwells there, dancing eternally among the sea of unending snowdrops. She sings songs of starshine, sweet and soft, and as you listen, you'll grow hazy. Like falling asleep. And she'll adore you. She always does.

Always has.

Always will.

(30)

AFTER: NATALYA

He looks different than I thought he would. Thanatos, that is. Different in the way that I would have expected him to look like *something*, vaguely humanoid or not. I can make out folded wings; long, softened feathers that sweep through the darkness in shades of plutonium, indigo, and violet. He's got eyes, I think. Large, bright holes cut into the darkness that look like rotted bone. When he inhales, stars get swallowed up into his gaping maw. When he exhales, shadows pour from his lungs in the form of shifting smoke.

He's got a hooked nose that you could mistake for a beak and a cloak so dark it verges on obsidian. Long, pointed horns twist and spiral into the heavens. A large silver sword stretches along the width of his hip, forged from the metal of fallen comets and long-gone dreams. It's a misericorde if I can name it correctly. The type of sword used on the sick as a form of fatal mercy.

"WeLl?" Thanatos asks, lips curling up in amusement to reveal his bright sharp teeth. "wHy HaVe yOu sUmMoNeD mE?"

"There are stories, you know. That if you miss someone badly enough, you can travel down into the underworld and bring them back." Death is quiet as he stares at me. I make sure to square my shoulders; and widen my stance. Plant my feet so deeply into the earth that nothing could possibly move me, neither fire nor frost nor wind nor hail. "They say that if you love someone enough, you can go down into the land of the dead and bring them back." Death watches on in silence.

I make sure to raise my voice then. Force his eyes to meet mine as I look at him. "Orpheus, Theseus, and Hercules. Each of them journeyed past the Styx for the sake of those they loved." Orpheus, Theseus, and Hercules. Love, pride, and guilt. The names ring out against the resulting stillness. I bear them close like a trio of worn-down talismans.

"They all failed." Death's words are monotone, his face still as he watches me. There's something mocking, hidden in this god's tone. Something bitter, resentful. "What, did they not tell you that in your little stories? They were the mightiest men of their time, weren't they? Each of them swore that they loved the people they came for. And yet, when the time came for them to prove their claims, they faltered. It is nothing to be ashamed of."

His speech is calm. Matter of fact. As if this is merely just another one of life's certainties. The sun rises, and then it sets. People try, and then they fail. "Tell me, why do you think that this time would be any different?"

"Because I love her. "I answer simply. "I love her, more than anything. More than *everything*. And if that means that I have to fight even Death himself, then so be it. There is nothing I wouldn't do for her." I add desperately.

"The others said the same." Thanatos merely responds. He lounges on his throne, waves his fingers as he counts. "Hercules claimed his strength could best even Cerberus. Orpheus declared his music so skilled he could make the very stones weep. Theseus boasted he could outsmart the gods. They proclaimed that their love stretched to the very heavens, sunk them down to the darkest sea and all other such poetic nonsense that you mortals so love to go on about. And yet this love that they so gallantly spoke of failed. Every single time. Tell me, why do you think that you are special?"

"Because blood is thicker than water." I tell him. "And if you dare to question how far I would go for my child it is obvious Thanatos that you have never been a mother. The men you speak of were fueled by romance. And while romantic love is passionate it is volatile. My love is the love between a family. It is comfort. Stability. It is the knowledge that no matter how far you try to run, there will always be someone waiting that you can return to. My love is an anchor. And it may not be as flashy as all the love that stories so often speak of, but the truth of the matter is that I will always be there for my children when they need me. And if that means that I have to make Death himself die, then so be it". For a moment, Death is silent. I watch him as he thinks, my fingers itching for my sword as I wait.

"I will have my daughter back." I call out through gritted teeth. "That is a statement, and not a question."

"Your daughter, that you so bravely fight for," Thanatos asks "What was her name?" A flicker of amusement dances in his hollow eyes, and I swallow up the sob that is trying to tear itself from my throat.

"Her name was Helen." I answer. "Helen, but you would know her by the name of Proserpine."

Thanatos freezes, smile dropping off his face. Goes rigid, turns so still that you would have thought he was carved of stone.

"Impossible." Thanatos whispers. "Take anyone else. Anyone you want, any wish or dream or object that has long since passed. Take anything but her. That one is mine."

"She's *my* daughter." I spit. "Not yours, not anyone else's. She's *my* daughter, and I'll be damned if I leave this place without her."

"Wrong." He hisses then. There is something frantic about his tone. Something twitchy about his movements. "She was my child long before she was yours."

"And look at how well that turned out." I call out scornfully, waving a hand through the darkness at where the gemstone garden lies. "Considering all the poor souls in your domain I thought that you of all people would understand wealth is useless at fixing grief. Your greatest riches are but poor imitations of the scraps I have given Helen."

"And who, pray tell, does she deserve to be with?" Thanatos laughs scornfully. "You? You're the reason she went running to me in the first place. Maybe, if you could have been a better parent, none of this would have happened."

"I know that." I protest, voice cracking. "I... I fucked up, ok? I'm an awful, despicable being who instead of handling my own issues took it out on my children. I'm selfish, and bitter, and failed my baby. But I... I can *change*, Death. I can... I can be better. Because you're right, Helen deserves better. She deserves better than either of us. I would do anything, *I will do everything,* to make sure that she's safe and happy and healthy again."

"My child is happy here." Thanatos offendedly insists. "She's happy, and content, and has her own garden filled with people who love her. I have made her a god, given her all that she could possibly want. Her wish is my command. I owe it to her after how cruelly you among the living have treated her."

"But she didn't want to be a god." I reply confused. "She never did. All she wanted was to be Helen. To exist as herself and be loved because of it. She absolutely *hated* being your Proserpine." Death flinches, curling inwards on himself as he sulks.

"Let's cut to the chase Natalya." Thanatos declares tiredly. "Enough of the bickering. I think the pair of us both know what must be done now."

"The trial of Orpheus." I agree hoarsely. Grudgingly, Death nods.

"I'll go fetch Helen." He states. "And then we can begin. I hope you know that everyone fails this challenge, you have to understand. No one before you has ever succeeded."

"Then I shall be the first." I call back. As Thanatos vanishes from view, I feel my hands start to shake. I have to be the first. Have to win. Otherwise, I'm not sure *what* I will do.

(31)

AFTER: HELEN

The forest begins in the same way that most of these tales often do, in the aftermath of a horrific tragedy. Because by the time the first child comes into my woods, they're already half dead.

She comes in stumbling, footsteps sluggish. Her hands are battered, skin bruised like overripened fruit. I don't know her name, and yet I can tell that she's been hurting for too long.

"Have you ever- wished, for a moment, that someone could hear you?" She asks the woods. Her voice rasps out as rough as tree bark. Children only sound like that is from utter silence or prolonged screaming. "There's this saying I've always heard, about if a tree really falls in the woods if no one is around to hear it. I think it would, even if no one notices. Trees still fall regardless of if the Woods is silent."

She's so young. Small as well, her eyes far too dull as she curls up in a ball and simply *crumples* at the silence the wood gives her in response.

"My name is Kalli, short for Kaliope." She croaks out, pulling herself together as she shakily tries again. "Last name Finch, like the bird. Did you know that my name means beautiful voice?" Something gurgles in the back of her throat as she laughs wetly.

She certainly looks like a finch, even if her voice resembles a frog more then something with wings. She's got bird bones, all thin and skinny to the point that she struggles to stand on her two feet.

"I was meant to tell stories." Kalli continues, eyes blank as she sways listlessly.

"I think- I think I want to try telling them again, if you don't mind." She declares shakily, sitting down as she pulls out a worn-down notebook. "All the stories I've come up with, just for a little while. You won't mind, will you? It will only take a little while. And I- I've heard stories, you know. About the one who haunts these woods. They say that you collect children, squirrel them away under drifting snowfall and stitch their stories into nearby bark. They say that you'll take anyone, that you want everyone. They try to make you some sort of warning, but all I can think of is the possibility that you might want me. Do you want me?"

I try to tell the child that of course I love her of course I want her how could anyone not want her? But no matter how much I yell my voice is silent. Ever since I died I've became intangible, a being caught between life and death.

Hours pass. Eventually, the girl tries to get up. Her legs buckle and she sits down with a thump. Listlessly, she stares into the forest.

It's starting to get dark out now, stars poking through the dusk. Desperately, I close my eyes and listen for the sounds that throng the edges of my forest. No one has come close since Kalli first entered the woods this morning.

"Kalli?" I ask hesitantly when the stars begin to poke through the dark. It feels wrong to see her splayed out on the ground like that. No matter how old they are, children shouldn't be in that much pain. "Kalli can you hear me?"

The child swings her head and looks at me in silence. Takes in my white eyes and frozen skin and the stars that glow across my arms like constellations.

"Am I…. dead?" She asks curiously. There is no fear in her voice. Only worn-down acceptance.

"No." I answer determinedly, coming closer as I hold out my hand. "Not yet. Right now you're between. My name's Proserpine, and I inhabit the world of death in life and life in death. I've been trying to reach you for a while now, I'm so sorry."

"It's alright." Kalli says, and a part of me breaks at the words. But she still wraps an arm around my shoulder and lets me help her up, the pair of us limping together as I lead her out of the woods. "I'm happy you were trying to find me." She confesses gratefully.

"A lot more people should be." I answer darkly. "But it's alright, I'm here now. And so is this garden, whenever you want to visit. Just know that I'm here for you whenever you want okay Kalli? Your story isn't over yet."

Kalli goes home. The lights are off, and the house is quiet. She creeps into bed unheard, and wonders when she started haunting her own house.

"If a tree falls in the woods…" she whispers in the dark. The wind laughs back, the trees creak, and Kalli goes outside and screams until her voice goes hoarse.

No one hears.

The ache starts slowly, an itch growing from her voice box and hollowing out her bones. She misses Proserpine. Misses someone caring. Misses sitting in the garden, having someone watch her as if she's made up of stardust.

"I want to go home." Kalli whispers quietly. Nothing responds save for a tree tapping against her bedroom window.

On the ninth day, Kate drags her half dead body to the grove in silence. Sloppily written letters clutched desperately in her frozen hands. Her voice is barely above a whisper now.

"I don't quite know who will read them." She admits when she finds me, voice rough from disuse. "But I still thought I should write them just in case. I always wanted to tell stories. Maybe one day someone stronger can read them for me.

"I'm sure someone would love to tell your stories." I respond, hugging her close. "You could wait, you know. I'll listen. Your story isn't over yet."

"I know." Kalli responds. "But I'm so tired Proserpine. I've tried so hard, is it okay if I rest now? Please don't be mad."

"Oh, sweetheart, never." I smooth her hair. "I wish you could live, but I understand that life is hard, and sometimes all you can do is sleep. I love you too much to ever hate you. For what it's worth," I add, "I thought your stories were *beautiful.*"

"Do you think you could stay with me until the end?" She begs.

"Of course." I assure her. "Here in these woods, you will never be lonely again." I hold the child in my arms and nestle against the roots of a nearby oak. Comb my fingers through her hair and hold her softly as she begins to die. Softly, ever so softly, I begin to sing.

"When the moon finally burns, and the sun fades into blue…. Above all else, I will always look for you."

Kalli has no mouth now, only branches that creak when the wind passes through. Nobody listens to her, but then again nobody did before.

There's no hesitation, when the second child comes. He's all steady footsteps and a calm heartbeat and there's no wavering when this one comes.

There's a certain confidence, in his footsteps. A type of stubbornness, some determination that lets him keep trudging even when the very world screams for him to give up. I look in the boy's eyes and I see erosion. The type that eats away at moving metal until it finally slows to a stop. I stare at the boy in silence, notice how even now he still has his shoulders straight and his head held high.

"I've been looking for you." He says quietly. Smiles just enough that I can see his teeth. "Gosh, you wouldn't believe how long I've been looking for you Proserpine." A pause, as he tries to deepen his voice. Widen his stance. Tries to seem older, taller, *stronger* as he talks to me. "Can you take me home now?" He asks.

I take his hand in mine. Lead him gently around the woods, point out flowers and ferns and drink tea inside a cluttered greenhouse. He squeezes my hand when we stop in front of a gnarled hickory tree. Stops and reaching out with a finger begins to trace his name into the knotted bark. Over and over until you could read it with your eyes closed. Until you could see it from the sky just as easily as from the ground. *Callum.* Still gripping my hand, he sits down between the nearby roots. I sit down with him, watch as he traces his name along the back of my hand while he tips his head back and looks up.

Curled up together beneath the night sky, the pair of us watch the dancing constellations. Callum tells me stories about them, describes planets and meteorites as easily as breathing. Callum gives me his dreams with the trust that I will keep them safe. Will let them sleep in peace here under the stars where they belong, safe and sheltered among the rest of the forest.

"Can I tell you a secret?" Callum asks. "I always wanted to be a bird. Or maybe a bat. Something that could stretch its wings and fly away at night, able to shed the ground and drift wild and free among the cosmos. The stars would have loved me."

"They already do." I answer in response, my words sure and steady. It's hard to believe me, I think. Hard for him to believe in anything, out here in the woods with a ghost who dances to rock and roll. And yet for some strange reason, he inexplicably does.

"Have you ever felt that type of love?" He asks me suddenly. "Loved like the stars do, all bright and warm and all-encompassing?"

"Of course I have." I reply with a smile. "I love the springtime and the raindrops and crackling radios and burning candles and the sun and the moon and the living and the dead and everything that chooses to be kind in spite of this cruel thing that we call a world and most importantly of all I know that I love you."

"Is everything going to be okay?" He wonders sleepily. "Are things going to get better, after all of this?"

"Of course, Callum." I whisper, eyes shiny as I lie. "Of course they will be. You can rest here now; you don't have to be so strong." Callum smiles then, eyes tired but trusting. Even though he knows I'm unsure he still trusts me to make sure things will become ok. That I'll let him rest because he's tired.

"They will be." He echoes, pressure dropping off him as slowly his eyelids droop. "I've never felt so safe before." He admits with a small laugh.

My voice is shaking, eyes too bright as I hug the child tighter.

"I love you." I declare fiercely, holding Callum close. "I love you, so much." I treat the words like they're sacred, precious. An unchanging truth, a special vow.

"You really mean that don't you." Callum asks, almost disbelievingly. A wild grin spreads across his face, as bright as the sun and sweet as starlight. "Can you sing for me?" He asks then, half disbelievingly. I smile and holding him close slowly begin.

"Dust is my skin and ash is my bones… let my mind be set arrest and make the stars my home…"

The next child stumbles into my woods legs shaking under a hazy summer sky. They wonder if they're really alive anymore. If they ever were. I barely have time to react before they throw themselves into my arms, body going limp as they sag beneath my hold. We're strangers. And yet they are such an utterly *empty* human being.

"Do you know who I am, my child?" I ask hesitantly. Tremors run up and down the scrawny thing's frame.

"You just called me *your child.*" They repeat disbelievingly. "Please, can I please be yours?"

At least this way it's a hug. At least they can die in a hug and pretend that they were loved, even for a little bit. I watch them shatter as I cradle them between my arms, their heart spilling out into a million pieces like broken glass.

"I don't think I know you." I whisper softly into the child's hair. "But I know I love you."

"You don't even know my name." A muffled sob, some heartbreaking wretched gasp as the child breaks down within my hold.

"I don't need to, to know I love you." I protest firmly. "To know that there is a place here for you to rest for as long as you need."

"I want to believe you." The child mourns, voice hoarse from how hard they have been crying. "I want to believe you, I promise. I just can't."

"Let me show you then." I soothe quietly, interlocking our fingers as I hold them tighter. Nuzzle our foreheads together and let my eyes fall shut. The child gasps, clutches on tighter as the world begins to spin. As love begins to bloom behind the back of our eyelids bright enough to dim the stars, warm enough to melt the moon. A gentle scent of evergreens, a smell of flowers that remain the same through rain or snow or shine. A promise of devotion. A whisper of eternity.

"Is it really that simple for you?" The child wonders awestruck. "To love me so much, just because that's how you are? Because you can?"

"Of course it is.". Once more, the child shudders. I let them fall apart in my arms. Let them break down from where I hold them. I will be there, after all, to help them pull themselves back together.

"There is a legend," I whisper softly "that in a land far, far away from here there is a form of pottery making where people take broken scraps and mend them together with gold. Until its very imperfections become precious. Until the things that made it broken are now pure."

"Proserpine," The child timidly asks. "What happens when you die?"

"Let me show you." I answer, and letting the child grab me by the hand pull them up to their feet. I lead the child past a sea of hickory trees and rigid oaks. Eventually, the child points out a small pine tree."

"This one," They state quietly.

It doesn't matter that I never asked them to pick a tree. A part of them already understands, can see the names written on bark and hear the whispers from shifting leaves."

"An evergreen." I remark approvingly. "That's a good choice."

"Is this the end?" The child wonders. "Does everything stop after this?"

"Depends on what you consider to be an ending." I reply. "After all, I personally don't believe that anything that goes is ever truly gone. Life is much more circular than that, it ebbs and flows in a cycle of rebirth. When we are born, the atoms used to create our bodies are recycled particles left over from fallen stars. When we die those same atoms feed the earth, bringing life back in yet another form.

"Vi är gjorda av damm, och som sådana återvänder vi till damm." I murmur softly, wrapping a pine needle around my finger until it forms a tiny ring. *We are made of dust, and as such to dust we return.* Do not be so foolish to believe that my story ends this way. Not when saplings grow between the hollows of my bones and my dreams live on within the gaze of another starry-eyed child."

"This evergreen is small." I state after a pause. "It can grow bigger if you give it the chance."

"What are you saying, Proserpine?" There's something frantic about the child's voice.

"I'm saying that this woods, this garden, this tree of yours, it can wait. We can all wait if you so choose." I explain. "I'll always be here, whenever you need me. You don't have to go to sleep now."

466

The child pauses. Stares at the tree in silence, watches the way its branches sway and move in the wind.

"Are things going to be better, after all of this?" The child asks.

"I'm not sure." I'm honest when I answer this time. "But I hope they do. I really, *really* hope they do."

"I'm so tired, Proserpine." The child protests then, pouting as they cross their arms. "I'm so of living in a world where everything hurts."

"I know, trust me I know." I respond hurriedly. "And if you really want to, you can stay here with me and sleep. But Sweetheart you can join me at any time. Don't you want to know what it's like to *live* first? And I mean really live, not just exist like a walking corpse."

"Do you think it's possible?" The child begs wistfully. "I didn't think it was possible to experience life like that."

"I'm sure it is." I declare confidently. "And if not, well. I'm not going anywhere."

The child pauses. Thinks some more. Eventually, they nod and stand up.

"Thank you." They whisper softly. I smile and lead them out of the woods.

"Of course." I answer. "And remember, I'm always here if you need to talk. I'm not going anywhere, and neither is the forest."

The road to recovery is never easy, my child ends up coming back, over and over again. But every time they fall down, they get back up. Gradually, the visits become easier. My child tells me that they feel happier now, that they no longer feel so alone. And maybe the world isn't always perfect. But it's gotten easier for them to get up in the mornings.

They grow. I don't think it's possible for me to be any prouder. I watch my child as they smile on their birthday, candles spelling out a year that they never dreamed they would touch. *They grow.* I watch their eyes shine with tears under the flickering candlelight, wrap my arms around them tightly and dance around the walls of my greenhouse.

"They're incredible." I gush to Thanatos breathlessly, running all the way to the Styx to reveal the good news. "Look at them, Death. Can't you see how strong they are, how brave? Look how much taller they are now since I saw them last. That's *my child.*"

Thanatos simply laughs in response. Ruffles the top of my hair, shakes his head, and says teasingly "Sweetheart you believe every one of your children is incredible."

"Are you saying they're not?" I gasp offendedly, mind flitting through the sea of faces, all those children who dwell in my garden or the land of the living. My special, *precious* children. Wryly, Thanatos shakes his head.

"Why of course they are." He concedes with a chuckle. "You remind them of their value."

"You bloom so brightly too my flowerchild," Thanatos adds somberly. Bittersweet, with a certain guilt mixed into the confession. "There is nowhere I would rather be than with you."

I laugh, spinning beneath the caring eyes of falling constellations, tears streaming down my face as Thanatos whispers over and over *I love you.* There's a chipped teacup clutched in my right hand, reddened liquid sloshing over the sides as the porcelain cracks.

"Helen," Thanatos hesitantly starts "would you like to be like that child whose birthday was today?"

"What do you mean?" I ask confused.

"Would you like to live again." Thanatos clarifies, tone stiff.

I freeze, feel my smile drop as I stare at Death in silence. "I thought – I thought that wasn't possible."

"It normally isn't." Thanatos agrees awkwardly. "It's just- well. There's this mortal woman- she's come to take you home. If you want of course."

…Mom?

…Mom came after me?

(32)

AFTER: NATALYA

"Pick a game." Thanatos intones, appearing once more in a puff of smoke. There's something forced, about his tone. Something agitated, about the shadows crackling out from under his hood.

"What are you talking about?" I ask voice rising. "You said that you'd let me see Helen."

"You will." Thanatos agrees. "You just have to prove yourself first. Orpheus had his music, and Hercules his strength. Pick a game, a skill, anything you wish to compete against me with. Pick a game and show me that you are worthy."

"You're stalling." I hiss, glaring at Thanatos from where his eyes shine in the dark. "Stalling for time because you know that I will win. Where is my daughter? You said that you'd bring her."

"If you're so certain that you'll win, then pick a game." Death is smirking now, arrogance curling around his brow as he straightens. Slowly, the shadows begin to ease, revealing hands dripping in a sea of rubies and sapphires and emeralds. Elongated rings formed in the shape of skeletal bone, clinking, and clanking as he shifts his fingers. "A game of cards, wits, speed, pick a game Natalya."

"You're taunting me." I choke out. Thanatos merely grins in response. His smile is wide: wide enough to eat the moon, sharp enough to swallow the stars.

"Maybe." He giggles. He starts to grow then, until he's as big as a horse. And then an elephant. A two-story house, and then a castle with large turrets. A tall, sweeping mountain with cold snowy peaks. A shadow tall enough to block out the sky or suck the warmth from your bones. "But then again there's nothing you can really do about that now can you?" He smiles even wider. "You're in my domain now, Natalya. And here *I* make the rules."

I wrack my brain then, trying desperately to think. There has to be a way for me to win. Otherwise, he wouldn't be trying so hard to stall me in the first place. He can laugh all he wants but it doesn't change the fact that I have survived all of the Underworld's other challenges. I have crossed the Styx. Survived the Acheron. Walked through the lands of Hypnos, let my skin become cut open by the salt of the Cocytus. I passed the gates of Erebus, went before his monsters, and *won*. No matter what madness I've had to endure in this world of the dead, I always emerged victorious. And it drives him insane.

"Swear then, that after this game you will do nothing more to stop me from bringing my daughter home." I respond at last. "Swear that when this trial is done it's all done, this endless charade of games and tricks. No more hiding, Thanatos. Let's face each other and settle this once and for all."

"What should I swear it on?" Death mocks, leaning forward to stare at me with hungry eyes.

"Swear it on Proserpine." I answer. "Swear it on Persephone, and Kore, and all those thousands of names that you gave Helen at the beginning of this."

"I swear on Proserpine and all her thousands of names that once this game is done it shall decide her fate, with no more dawdling on either side." Thanatos rattles off, looking at me expectantly. "Now, you insolent mortal, what game have you chosen for us to play?"

What trial could you possibly pick that would beat a god? Hercules chose strength, but there's no way I could win an arm wrestle against the god of age. I could try a game of wits, but what knowledge could I use against a creature who has existed for all eternity? Still, perhaps I'm thinking about this the wrong way. Instead of thinking of what traits Thanatos has, I should think of what he lacks. What is the opposite of death?

I think back then to Death's Garden. The one he had made for Helen, filled to the brim with gems of all different shades and colors. No matter how hard Thanatos had tried, he couldn't recreate the plants that grew in my backyard. Not even the weeds that grew in between the cracks of my driveway.

"Gardening." I answer at last. "I challenge you to a test of gardening."

Death stares at me in silence. "I'm sorry, come again?" He asks confused. "Did you say gardening?"

"Whoever can keep a flower alive the longest wins." I continue, and now I'm the one grinning. "After all, my daughter was so fond of flowers that it only makes sense for her trial to deal with horticulture."

Thanatos goes silent. Stares around the garden in silence, understands the knowledge that I have left unspoken. *No matter how hard he tries, Death cannot be anything other than death. To claim otherwise would go against his very nature.*

"Do you suppose to taunt me, choosing such a game here in this garden?" He wonders, waving his hand as two roses appear. Their petals bleed as I clutch them, thorns tearing open my skin while I hold them within my grasp. He barely has to touch his before it starts to wither, stem curling inwards with a defeated whimper.

To his credit, Thanatos does try to win. He puts on gloves and cradles it in his fingers, fixes bruised petals as he puts the plant in water. Even though the action goes against everything he stands for, he still tries for my daughter's sake. If I was only a slightly nicer person, I suppose I would feel sorry for him. And yet, I don't.

He gets up then, wiping the tears from his eyes. Walks off into the dust and returns leading someone by the hand.

Oh.

Oh.

I see her then. My sweet, darling girl. She looks different than I remember, eyes now a milky white from where the iris and sclera have rotted away. Starshine dusts the edges of her skin like powdered sugar, constellations spelled out across her skin where once there were freckles. She looks different, and yet I can tell it's her as soon as I look. I think I could recognize my daughter by touch alone, could reach my hands out and feel the way her palms warm from where I cradle them in mine.

I could recognize her by her smile, the way her lips curl up and her eyes widen in some expression of shock. Could tell her by the sound of her gasp, that sharp inhale that she lets out whenever she's shocked. I would know her blind, by nothing more than the way her footsteps ring out against the earth.

"Hi sweetheart." I whisper, voice choked as I take her in. My precious, *precious* little flowerchild. My darling girl. Helen.

"What are you doing here?" She asks dumbly, confusion and wonder coloring her words as she stares. As if I'm some miracle, standing here before her in the flesh. As if our positions are reversed and I am the one who was dead standing before her. She drinks me in the way that men returning from the desert look at water, eyes wide and disbelieving. She looks at me as if I'm some mere figment of an illusion.

Like if she blinks or closes her eyes I might disappear. "The living normally can't travel this far into the Underworld. Are you dead?" She asks worriedly, frantically checking me for a pulse.

"No, I'm not dead or planning on staying here long." I reply, laughing quietly. "And as for why I'm here, I've came to see you, of course. I'm here to take you home Helen."

"But why?" She presses, still staring at me with her wide, wide eyes.

And I – I could tell her so many things. I could tell her that I love her, that having her as my child has slowly become one of my main reasons for living. That she's so kind, and strong, and brave, and so much better than I could have ever been at her age. That she makes me want to be a better person. That I'm so incredibly proud of her, and all her achievements she's left behind that still ring out on the world. That being able to have her as my kid has made me one of the luckiest people alive. I could tell her; I could tell her so many things.

"I came here because you're Helen." I answer eventually, my smile wobbling as I stare into her eyes. "I don't need any reason besides that. I came here because you are you, and I am me, and I would follow you to the farthest stretches of this universe if I could. Because Helen," She's started crying now, tears freezing as they drip from her eyes "I would follow you to hell and back. I would tear the stars out of the sky if it would make you smile, I would set fire to the entire world if you told me you were cold. You are Helen, and I am Natalya. And that means that I will do anything I possibly can to keep you happy, and healthy, and safe."

I watch as Helen breaks in front of my eyes. Watch as she wails, hear her shudder and gasp as she sobs until she exhausts her tear ducts. Behind her, Thanatos is silent. He watches her with an unreadable look in his eyes, and cradling her close he tells me,

"Start walking." Eyes still stuck on the child in his arms he continues "You heard me, start walking. Retrace your steps until you find your way out of the underworld, and as you walk Helen will follow you. No more tricks, and no more pretenses. There is only one rule, one chance for failure. Don't turn around until you find yourself back in the realm of the living, and then you can have your child again. On this I swear my very divinity: all my power, all my names. No more treachery, and no more deceit. All you have to do is not look at her until you are once more standing in the sunshine."

I take one final look at Helen, one last glance at my sobbing child as she curls up in Death's arms. One last look, and I burn her gaze into my memory. My precious, darling Helen. My lovely, *lovely* flowerchild.

And then I turn around and begin to walk. Place one foot in front of the other and try to ignore how I can't hear any footsteps behind me. Gradually, I begin to think of the overgrown greenhouse settled at the foot of the entrance to the damned. Remember an old, battered radio, babbling merrily amidst the rain and thunder.

"…For I would walk five hundred miles, And I would walk five hundred more,

Just to be the man who walked a thousand miles to show up at your door…."

(33)

AFTER: HELEN

"You don't have to follow her, you know." Thanatos says at last, after Natalya starts walking. I sit there in silence, thoughts racing. "I make sure to tell this to every soul who has a mortal travel down after them. It's your life, not theirs. No matter what anyone says or does, ultimately it's your decision what you do with it."

"But she travelled all this way for me…" I protest guiltily. Thanatos cuts me off with a shake of his head.

"You don't owe anyone your life, Helen. If you stay or if you go, that's your choice and yours alone."

"Is it worth it, Thanatos?" I ask eventually. He turns to look at me in surprise. "Is living worth it? I had so many children ask me that when they visited my garden. And I never knew how to answer them, I was always scared of making a mistake or giving the wrong answer. I never experienced life or death enough to give a confident answer. But Thanatos, you've existed in tandem with life for eternity. Surely, of all people you would have an answer. Is it worth it, to go back? Does life get better?"

"It will be very hard." Thanatos answers after a pause. "So hard it's almost not worth it. The road of recovery is one that is long and fraught with setbacks. Weeks, years, decades down the line, you will still be hurting. Life is cruel little one. It is rarely easy."

"I'm not asking if it is easy, I'm asking if it is worth it." I insist then. "If I go back, Thanatos, and give life a try again. Does it get better than it was before? I don't care if it's hard, you know I can handle hardship. But I would like to know that it gets a little easier to live, than it was before. Is the good that I will experience able to outweigh the bad?"

"Yes." Thanatos answers at last. "It will take time, and love, and patience. Months, years, *decades* down the line, you will still be hurting. But it will eventually get easier to breathe. To not only exist, but also *live*. In the end it's up to how tired you are little one. Would you like to stay here in dreamland, where nothing can hurt you, at the cost of staying forever asleep? Or would you rather wake up, wake, and stand among the sunshine, wince and squint because while your eyes may burn you've never seen a light so bright? The choice is yours Helen, and only yours. No one, no matter how hard they insist, is allowed to make the choice for you."

And so I stop and think. Sit down and watch as Natalya continues walking, now a brief speck in the horizon. My bones are tired. And yet my head feels light, almost like I'm floating.

I stare down at the chipped teacup clutched in my hands; its cracks made whole by delicate swirls of gold. I look at it in silence, watch the way light sparkles and dances from its edges under the sleepy moonlight. I don't look at Natalya. I don't look at Thanatos. Instead, I look at the cup, and I remember my garden. I remember my children, all those pure little souls who chose to either stay or go.

Eventually I stand up. Turn to face Thanatos and look at him in silence. I don't need to give an answer for him to know my decision. Wordlessly, he pulls me into a hug. Holds me for a couple seconds. When he pulls away, he smiles. I try to ignore the tears in his eyes.

"Thank you." I start, unsure of what to say. Death laughs and gives me one more quick squeeze before shooing me away.

"I'm always here if you need me sweetheart." He responds wetly. "Whether you want to stay forever or have a quick chat. Don't be a stranger, now, I think I'd miss you too much. Run along little one, have fun exploring life. I'll be waiting eagerly for you to tell me how it goes."

I turn around and race after Mother, my feet flying so fast they hardly touch the ground.

"Mom wait!" I scream, chasing after her shadow as I sprint. "Slow down, I'm having trouble keeping up with you." Mom speeds up in response, hands covering her ears as she starts to mutter to herself.

I trip over a rock and go sprawling, my ankle flaring up in pain from where I sprain it. Head over heels I tumble into a ditch, the walls of the hole swallowing me whole. Desperately I try to climb out, Hands scrabbling at the walls of packed dirt as I struggle to find a foothold.

I can't get out. Can't pull myself up, anytime I try the dirt crumbles under my grasp, and I go tumbling back down. When I jump, I can see Mom walking, her back getting smaller and smaller as she vanishes into the horizon. Gradually I begin to panic.

"MOM WAIT!" I scream again, terror rising as I throw myself against the dirt packed walls. What if I lose Natalya, and stay trapped here forever? What if I made my decision, but it was too late?

"Don't turn around don't turn around don't turn around…" Natalya chants, over and over as she keeps on walking. She shoves her fingers into her ears hard enough to make them bleed, as if that'll stop my screaming. She's not

– she's not stopping. She's not waiting, and I am going to be stuck here trapped and forgotten, rotting down here in the dirt with all the worms and maggots.

"MOM." I choke out, sobbing as I lunge once more at the edge of the hole. "MOM PLEASE WAIT, PLEASE DON'T LEAVE ME AGAIN." Mother stops. Freezes.

"I'm not…I'm not leaving you baby." She calls out, voice catching. "Ok." She decides, still keeping her back to me. "Ok, Helen can you hear me right now? I don't think I can turn around, but I'm going to stand very still and stay right here alright? When I'm able to move forward you can tell me. I'm not leaving you sweetheart."

"Mom I'm scared." I choke out, scrabbling at the dirt as I claw at the walls. "I'm-I'm stuck in this hole, and I don't really know how to pull myself out."

"You will." She assures me. "Don't worry I know you will. And I'm going to be waiting right here when you get out, and then we're going to go home and everything will be okay again. I'll – I'll help you build a greenhouse, would you like that Helen? Your own very greenhouse, where you won't have to worry about the winter because your plants will continue growing. You won't have to worry about your garden dying anymore, because I'll help you build a greenhouse and we can plant anything you want in there, I promise. Just take your time okay Helen? I'm not going anywhere."

Eventually, I pull myself out of the ditch. Heave my body out of the ground and scramble desperately towards where Mom stands waiting. Grasping her fingers, I give them a squeeze.

"Can I hold your hand?" I ask nervously, holding on with desperation. "I know you can't really turn around and look at me or anything, but at least this way we can both know where the other is. I don't want to lose you again."

And Mom doesn't look at me. Because it's not allowed, and after everything that happened she won't risk losing me with just a simple look. But she squeezes my fingers, and hesitantly nods.

Slowly, hand in hand, we walk out of the Underworld. We get back to growing. We get back to living.

EPILOGUE

The moss is soft, from where it wraps its way around the marble columns in the gemstone garden. I reach out and brush a hand against it from where I sit, take in golden branches weeping emerald leaves and admire how the starlight turns iridescent when it touches the roses carved from Labradorite. A part of me is shocked, to see the moss grow along the columns. To see anything living flourish so deep in the heart of the Underworld. Thanatos isn't exactly known for his skill in creating, after all. Most of the time he simply finds things that already exist and takes them home with him, like the stars and the souls and the glittering gemstones.

Taking. I've never really liked viewing Death as an act of taking, you know. Violence takes. Greed takes. Death just *is*. It is more of a response, a result, a *symptom* of mortality, as opposed to a cause. Maybe it's an ending, a closing of a story and a final rest. And yet at the same time maybe it *isn't*, all the ferries, roads, and stop posts creating another endless journey. When we die our bodies turn to dirt, and from that dirt grows life in an even brighter bloom. When we die our minds fade away, off to find a resting place among the stars where souls can dance for all eternity. I don't quite know what exactly Death is, and none of the beings I meet down here will tell me. In the end, I think I'll find out just like all the other people do.

I think I'm okay with that.

The garden is in bloom now, foliage sprouting up and blossoming every time I visit. Daffodils, and Daisies. Moss and roses that climb around marble columns and great big cherry trees that weep tears of joy instead of sadness. Perhaps the funniest thing about them is that no matter how many different plants sprout out of the soil they all inevitably end up sharing the same message: rebirth. Healing. The power to claw through the soil and keep growing, regardless of how toxic or unlivable an environment may seem. Carefully, I reach out a finger and loop it around a looping dandelion. The flowers is soft as I hold it, it's petals staining my skin butter-yellow from where I cup it in my hands.

Hugging my legs a little closer, I lie down and watch the comets as they buzz around the void. Nebulas burst and bloom above my head and I watch as entire universes rise and fall before my gaze. They look like fireworks, almost. The type that my family lights every winter around my birthday.

I can feel the presence approaching more than I can see or hear them. The hairs on the backs of my arms raise and faint static begins to charge up and down my skin. Behind me the soil crackles, darkened electricity pulsing as a familiar set of footsteps begin to walk along the beach.

It feels different than Charon, and different than Hypnos. There's some sort of distinction, something to do with the difference between a chthonic deity and an eldritch god. I don't particularly mind either way. The Gemstone Garden is a place that only the beings of the Underworld feel comfortable beside, and I am beloved by most of them.

A smiling face leans down and blocks out the site of the dancing galaxies. I grin back in return, take his outstretched hand and let them help me to my feet. Thanatos's hand is warm from where it holds mine.

"Hello Helen." He murmurs softly. I swing our arms back and forth, smile wide enough it nearly hurts and lean in for a hug.

"Hello to you too, Thanatos." Thanatos chuckles from where he holds me. He tugs me down to the ground, pulls small asphodel petals from his pockets and begins to braid them into my hair. I close my eyes and tip my head back. Close my eyes and ignore the sights of the spinning galaxies, all the buzzing planets and fizzling stars. For now, all I want to focus on is the warmth that can be found in Thanatos's fingers carding through my curls.

"What are you doing down here again, my little polliwog?" He asks curiously. "It's been a while." He adds in a hollow voice. Slowly, my smile begins to drop. "Years in fact."

"Not so long." I argue uncomfortably. "I visited you three months ago. And I mean look around you Thanatos – every growing thing in here sprouted each time I visited. Isn't that enough to show you how often I visit?"

"Not like you used to." Thanatos mourns. "But then again I suppose that is a blessing. It is a natural state of growing, or so the other gods have told me. Birds fly the nest; polliwogs form their own legs; eventually every living thing has to find their own way to grow up. You can't stay a baby forever, Helen, though heavens know how much I wish you would sometimes."

"A – a polliwog?" I ask curiously, staring up at him in bewilderment. "Are you trying to call me a tadpole?" He chuckles sadly and I roll my eyes. Thanatos has taken to calling me a series of nicknames, each one stranger than the last. "What is up with all your silly nicknames?" I whine exaggeratedly, crossing my arms with a pout. "I'm not a polliwog. If you are going to call me something, at least make it cute."

"Sure, you are." Thanatos assures me gently. He brushes a hand through my mossy curls.

"After all, you're green like one. You like swimming like one. And most importantly, you survive like one. Polliwogs are known, after all, for switching to lungs from gills as a way to breathe outside of their small pond. They are a creature that will change the very structure of their anatomy so that they may survive."

Thanatos has smile lines etched into the surface of his skin. Distinct little crow lines, that crinkle around his eyes whenever he grins. Despite his eternal youth, Death has a series of wrinkles around his face from smiling too much. A part of me loves him for that. Loves that not even the coldness of immortality can hide the joy he feels at seeing me.

"Why are you here little one?" He asks again. I pause, and then let out a sigh.

"I turned eighteen today." I confess quietly. The phrase feels so simple when it comes from my mouth. It's just four words. But those four words mean everything.

"A momentous occasion." Death replies encouragingly. "Happy birthday my child."

"No, you don't get it." I retort sharply. Get up on my feet and begin to pace along the starlit sand. "I turned *eighteen* today, Thanatos. I'm all grown up now. Officially an adult. I can, I can go off into the sunset and not worry about turning back. I can have a job, create my own company or study at a university. I can stay here and buy a house or move to the other side of the world and spontaneously create a new identity. I can live for the first time all by myself or fall in love and decide to get married. Thanatos, there are so many things that I can do at eighteen." My breath catches. My voice stutters. I start to sob then, tears welling up as I look at Death with watery eyes. "Thanatos I didn't think that I was going to make it this far. I didn't – none of my plans prepared me to live this long."

He stands up and hugs me then. Hugs me close and holds me tightly and I feel myself break down in his arms.

"I have no idea what I'm going to do tomorrow." I admit quietly. The confession makes me uncomfortable, fear and exhilaration thrumming through my heartbeat and knocking against my ribcage.

"How exciting." Death remarks in response.

Touch, sitting here by the river Styx, has never been anything other than soothing. Thanatos, here with his bright smiles and warm hugs, has never been anything other than gentle.

"Oh, *sweetheart*." Thanatos murmurs. I hug him tighter, grab onto him in desperation and cry even harder. "Sweetheart I'm so proud of you." It's not natural, for Death to be soft. That's not to say that Death is cruel, of course. It just simply is. A rite of passage, a simple game of back and forth played between him and Life. Death is not necessarily nice. But he tries so hard to be nice for me. To be soft, and delicate, and able to handle me whether I'm strong or weak.

"Why did you choose this, this decision to continue to live?" He asks at last, watching me desperately. I suppose it must be strange to Death, this idea of anyone picking life. It must be confusing to an immortal god, this process of surviving for longer than you thought you would.

"Because I have hope." I answer after a pause. "I have hope that something is waiting out there for me. It means that no matter how terrible life becomes, I have faith that things will get better. Hope means that I have went through too much hardship to not receive a happy ending. That I owe it to my younger self, that little girl who worked and begged and fought to do more than just survive. I owe it to myself to *try*. To get that second chance and *live*. I want to have fallen in love with living before I come to rest with you."

"Little Polliwog you are a marvel." Death sighs at last. Thanatos is a *god*. He can't quite comprehend the concept of mortality in relation to life, no matter how hard he tries. But he sees the light sparkle in my eyes and the fire in my tone and a certain passion that did not exist before I actively began to pursue life. "You are different, my child." He announces decisively, as if he's a researcher who has just discovered an important finding. "You seem more… bright. Loud. Joyful. Can you explain to me please, what this thing is that you call hope?"

"I read a poem once," I explain, "that hope is like a thing with feathers, some cheerfully optimistic bird that flutters within your ribcage and sings of dreams that you will one day see come true. After looking back on everything, I would say that that poem is wrong. Hope is not a chirping songbird. It is a sewer rat. It's this ugly thing with matted fur and gnarled claws and it makes a home for itself amongst the discards of other people's everyday lives."

"Hope is this tenacious rodent that finds itself buried in the bottom of the most repulsive parts of our world and finds the ability to climb up out of it when no one else can bear to give it a second glance. It is something that is often treated with disgust. *Disgust,* because here is this ugly little rat climbing out of a sewer drain because it refuses to lie down and roll around in other people's filth. Hope is something that is wretched, and matted, and only really seen in the worst of places because that is often where it is needed the most."

"Living isn't always easy. Sometimes it never is. It can be painful, and cruel, and unfair. And yet despite all that, we continue to press on. Because when we do gain joy, it is made even more precious. Our victories are made more valuable by the contrast of our losses. And when we do lose, when we try and fail and grieve and love and all we feel is pain, aren't we blessed to have ever loved at all? Sometimes, I take it all for granted. Sometimes I simply forget how… rare it is to be alive. How fortunate we are. We move though life regardless of Fate's challenges, in tribute to it." I murmur. "Regardless of its terrors but with the eternal help of hope. I believe my magic is a gift, in some ways. And as for knowing you, how could that be anything but a gift?"

How fortunate we are that enough things went right for us to be sitting here today.

Thanatos sets down his flowers then. Ties off the edges of my finished braids. Inhales, and then exhales. "Darling, you wouldn't believe how proud you make me every day. Although we haven't talked as much since you fell in love with life again, I want you to know that seeing you grow has brought me more joy than I could possibly imagine." Thanatos hiccups and tries to wipe the tears away from his eyes. "I don't – I don't want you to think that I'm not excited for you, or amazed with how well your recovery has been going. You truly are an exceptionally wonderful person, and I'm so, so *grateful* to have the honor of calling you my child." Death chokes out a sob. "I just – maybe it's selfish Helen, but a part of me hates how the process of you getting better means I have to see less and less of you. I'm fine with it because I know it's what you need in order to truly blossom. But little polliwog – *I miss you.*"

Thanatos holds me tighter, then. I try to ignore how desperately he hides his tear-stained face. Listen to the sound of his pounding heartbeat. Lower my head against his chest and hear his pulse repeat a phrase over and over and over again. *IloveyouIloveyouIdoIdo.*

"I – I can feel how sad you are still, little polliwog." Thanatos whispers then. "I can feel your *pain,* Darling it hurts so much. And yes you may have grown but you're still so little. So *tired.*" The words hurt as they tear themselves from his throat. "I want you to be happy, Helen. I want to respect your choice. But little ones shouldn't be so *tired* all the time."

I start crying again, let Death hold me in his arms as we sit there by the Styx. "That's the thing, Thanatos. I've decided to live regardless. Can I tell you something? Leaving you was one of the hardest things that I have ever done. It's something that I've had to struggle with each and every day, knowing that if I just stopped and lay down everything would end. But slowly, ever so slowly, I've found it easier to get up out of my bed each morning. I've found myself starting to love the sunrise, even though sometimes it burns my eyes. I want – I want to see what happens if I stick around a little longer. I want to see if life is truly as beautiful as fairytales always make it out to be. I want to see what happens if I choose to stay."

I feel my tone soften then. Hug Thanatos as he shudders and rub gentle circles along his hands. Hold Death up as he breaks, marvel at the fact that something immortal like Death would care so much for the life of a human child.

"These years will pass quickly." I say gently. "After all, what is a few short decades compared to the scope of eternity? You'll have *forever* with me by your side. You just have to be patient for a little bit. I'll come home eventually."

"I love you my child." Thanatos rasps out, voice hoarse from crying. His hug grows tighter before softening. "I think I always will. When the last speck of the sand of time drips from its hourglass. When the last star fizzles into the fading darkness. Even then will I treasure you. I love you my darling. I'll have the rest of eternity to tell you that."

I feel my lips curve into a smile, something hopeful. Wistful. "You will." *So let me live first.*

Afterwards, I walk back up into the light of the living. Thanatos watches me go. Watches me go with a smile on his face and tears in his eyes because he loves me like how moths love light. To the farthest stretches of this thing we call a universe. To the coldest parts of the wintry moon, and the searing heat of the rising sun.

How fortunate we are, that enough things went right for us to be here today.

ACKNOWLEDGMENTS

If I'm honest, acknowledgements are probably one of the hardest parts of a novel for me to write. There are so many people that I have had help me not just in the process of creating the story, but also in my everyday life while the book is drafted. First off, I would like to thank my friends: Kellyn Boyd, Audrey Coons, Sophia Bryant, Keely Haner, Paisley Smith, and Eva Thibodeau. From listening to my unhinged rants to designing book covers and fanart to reading my book before anyone else ever dared, you are all so incredibly important to me and I am so blessed to have your friendship. My life would not be nearly as worth living without having you guys in it.

Secondly, I would like to thank my squash coach Dave Morris. Since coming to college, you have helped me not only on the court, but off it as well with your connections to fellow writers, unwavering enthusiasm, and constant support. You are the type of coach who gives everything for his athletes, and I may be an author but I don't think words can describe just how much that means to me.

To my mom and dad, thanks for your constant love and support. My stories would never have made their way onto paper without your constant enthusiasm and support. When I was little my favorite thing in the world was hearing you make up stories before I went to bed each night, and seeing the pair of you read my stories now fills me to the brim with a mixture of flustered pride. I love you guys.

To my creative writing professor and editor Pedro Ponce, thanks for having the patience to sit down and edit this thing in such a short time on top of your normal work load. Your care and passion that you give your students is amazing. To my therapist Danielle Ludlum, thanks for teaching me to fall in love with life again. To my sister Ulla, thanks for always humoring my madness, you're the best little sister I could ever ask for.

ABOUT THE AUTHOR

Raised on a steady diet of folklore and fairytales, Mariam Dodd has been spinning stories almost before she could speak. A passionate lover of all things enchanted and whimsical, she writes books about brave protagonists, tender monsters, and the strength to keep fighting even when the very universe seems determined to go against you. Currently a sophomore at St. Lawrence University, Mariam studies Creative Writing and Political Science in an effort to understand the stories that shape the world around her. Since publishing her debut novel, Where the Monster's Grew, Mariam's works have been read by readers spanning across North America, Europe, Africa, and Asia- and she's only just getting started.

513

www.ingramcontent.com/pod-product-compliance
Lightning Source LLC
Chambersburg PA
CBHW051253130726
47987CB00004B/1504